Bound by Betrayal

Sins of the Underworld, Volume 3

Amara Holt

Published by Amara Holt, 2024.

Copyright © 2024 by Amara Holt

All rights reserved.

No part of this book may be reproduced, distributed, or transmitted in any form or by any means, including photocopying, recording, or other electronic or mechanical methods, without the prior written permission of the author, except in the case of brief quotations in book reviews.

This is a work of fiction. Names, characters, places, and incidents are the product of the author's imagination or are used fictitiously. Any resemblance to actual events, organizations, locales, or persons, living or dead is coincidental and is not intended by the authors.

PROLOGUE

Alessio

Surrounded by temptations. That's how I felt when I opened my eyes that morning, hearing my phone ringing incessantly.

The room smelled of sex and good tequila. A bit of lime too, of course. If salt had any aroma, it would certainly be in the mix.

Sin hovered around me all the time, like a gentle, chivalrous friend, pulling out a chair and inviting me to stay. My limits were different from those of other people because I was unaware of prudishness, morals, and chastity. I was a son of the Cosa Nostra, for God's sake. Killing and torturing were almost delicacies on the menu... so why should sex be a taboo?

I woke up smiling, but it didn't take long for me to gulp and realize that this easy, enviable life wouldn't last. Despite being the second son, not having responsibilities as pressing as my brother's...

Look at this shit, I would need to get married!

I rubbed my eyes, trying to clear the fog. Once I managed to open them, I saw the three girls who had spent the night with me. One on each side of the bed, and another a bit lower, lying on my legs. I smiled as I remembered why she was there. My cock got hard just recalling her wonderful little mouth and the things she made me feel.

I loved that life. But starting that day, everything was going to change. Especially when I heard my cellphone, which had stopped ringing, start up again, with that annoying tune that made my head throb once more.

I urgently needed an aspirin.

I got out of bed, stepping over one of the girls who was stirring and mumbling, which made me smile.

I loved women. I loved their bodies, the sounds they made, their scents, their hair—especially when it was long, straight, or curly, it didn't matter—the curves, the softness. I liked looking at them naked, dressed, kissing them.

I really loved to kiss.

So it was always a torment to pull away, even when I didn't even remember the names of my companions.

I tapped the screen of my iPhone to take the call and heard my brother-in-law's voice on the other end.

"Go fuck yourself for making me wait, asshole!"

Yeah, Dominic was a real gentleman.

"Good morning to you too, sorello."

"I'm not your brother."

"You married my sorellina, I brought you into my family, you'll have to accept that now you're like a brother to me. Even if you don't make any effort at all for that. I'll make the effort for both of us, I promise." I knew how to make the almighty Dominic a bundle of nerves.

It was way better dealing with him than my brother, who seemed like a door without feelings.

Don't get me wrong, Enrico was my hero; I always loved him since he was a little diaper-wearing kid, but the world changed him. The Cosa Nostra transformed him, and I adapted to his way because I loved him. I had to change too before my brother and I ended up clashing. With him, I was constantly walking on eggshells.

"We agreed you'd be here by nine."

BOUND BY BETRAYAL

"No. You agreed. I think nine o'clock, on a Sunday, is an affront. And, if I may ask: what time is it?"

"It's ten-thirty, Alessio! Ten-thirty!" he shouted from the other end of the line.

"But the flight is at noon, right?"

"Fuck it, man. You need to be more responsible. This mission of ours is crucial to protect your sister. It seems like you don't care about her."

Of course I cared about Deanna. The problem wasn't that, but everything that involved that trip.

I was going to pick up my future wife. The girl I barely knew, whom I hadn't even noticed the one time I met her, and the poor thing still lived in a convent.

I never imagined myself getting married, not in a million years, but to the most inexperienced, innocent, and scared girl in the Cosa Nostra? That shit wouldn't work. How would I deal with her?

"Dom, calm down. I'm leaving here now, running over, and we'll make it on time."

"We need to go over the plan. That's why I asked you to arrive earlier."

"Our flight is long. I'll easily get tired of you"—I tried to say with a smile, ignoring the fact that I was still naked, talking on the phone with my sister's husband.

"Oh, and I won't get tired of you?"

"Impossible. I'm adorable."

I could hear Dominic cursing on the other end, spewing countless swear words in Italian, and I could only laugh. Maybe I was a little bit of a pain...

We hung up, and I busied myself saying goodbye to the girls, giving each of them a nice kiss, promising that one day we would meet again.

Little did they know that this would be impossible, since in a little while I would be a married man and I intended to be loyal to my wife, come what may.

Thinking about it gave me a chill.

I grabbed my bags, which were already packed—especially since I was in a hotel in New York, Dominic's turf—and headed out to meet the beast.

Or better... I was leaving to meet my destiny. From that point on, my life would be completely different, and I didn't know if I was ready for that.

CHAPTER ONE

Luna

Touching my chest, I made the sign of the cross, intertwining one hand with the other, resting them on the bench in front of me. The long skirt I wore was lifted so I could kneel on the kneeler. The position wasn't comfortable, but praying was something that calmed me. And I needed a bit of serenity at that moment.

I had just received the news that my fiancé, Alessio Preterotti, had arrived at the Abbey, ready to pick me up at my father's request. I was informed and told to wait while the abbess confirmed the information.

I couldn't believe it was true. My intuition had always been very good. Perhaps because I spent so much time talking to God, He had filled my mind with some kind of supernatural wisdom, giving me a clarity of thought that helped me understand things that didn't need to be said.

When I was younger, I liked to imagine myself as a future Joan of Arc; the French heroine and saint who saved her country amid war, blessed by God with the gift of clairvoyance.

I was a daughter of the mafia. My world lived in war.

One day, I still hoped to save something or someone amid the bloody chaos into which I was born.

Many liked to consider me innocent. My father had thrown me into a convent because he believed it was the best way to keep me chaste and ignorant of evil, so I would become a more placid and submissive wife. Without knowing anything about the world, what would I have left but to obey my husband?

In a way, he had managed to fulfill his intent. But I didn't want to remain ignorant about everything.

So, when I was told that Alessio had come to get me, I soon imagined that something was happening.

Something that would turn me into a pawn in that war.

"Lu?" A voice interrupted me in the middle of the Our Father. It wasn't the first time she had done that.

I gestured and finished the prayer a bit more quickly than usual. I turned my body, looking over my shoulder just to see my fifteen-year-old sister approaching.

She knelt beside me, also making the sign of the cross.

Tizziana had the awful habit of wanting to gossip when we should be in the chapel praying.

"What's this story about you leaving and me staying?"

There was that detail: how was I going to leave the convent and leave my sister there, all alone? Not that she wouldn't be well cared for, especially with Conccetta around, my best friend, who was like a sister to us. The problem was that Tizzi was too rebellious, and I always had the impression that if she wasn't under my supervision, she'd end up setting the entire convent on fire.

But more than that, living without my little sister would be unthinkable. Tizziana had been my companion all those years, ever since we were locked away in there. For a while, I had to practically raise her because my father took her there when she was very small. He didn't know how to deal with girls, and when our mother died, he preferred to hand his two daughters over to the nuns, swearing it would be good for them.

Our age difference was only four years, but I felt a bit like a mother to my little sister.

"It seems that's what's going to happen. Dad sent my fiancé to get me." I wouldn't share my suspicions about that story with her.

"But that's not typical of Dad. He has so many men, so many soldiers, why send your fiancé?"

"Maybe because he's an important man. Because he wants us to get to know each other..."

"He came with Dominic Ungaretti!"

I fell silent, looking at Tizziana, trying to find a way to respond that could convince her of something I didn't even believe myself. I didn't like lies; it wasn't in my nature to deceive someone, especially my sister, but it was something for her own good. I couldn't allow her to worry.

"I imagine it's an arrangement between them, reinforcing my safety. I wouldn't be in better hands than my fiancé's."

"You know his reputation, don't you? And, for Dio, sorella. He's so, so beautiful."

"Don't say those things like that. Not where we are."

"Okay!" Tizziana looked at the image of Jesus Christ on the cross right in front of her and made the sign of the cross again.

She didn't have time to say anything else because one of the sisters appeared with the information that my father had confirmed he had sent Alessio, so I would need to leave.

I didn't have much time to pack my bag, but I also didn't have many things with me. A few clothes, personal items, documents, and some treasures I considered part of myself. Things from my mother, mainly.

When I finished packing everything in a small suitcase, I turned to Tizziana and realized she was crying. I took a deep breath because I wouldn't break down in front of her. I needed to show strength, show security, because her time would come, and I wanted my little sister to face everything with the head held high that a Cipriano needed to have.

I hugged her. Despite the age difference, she was a bit taller. In fact, I looked younger, being smaller and more girl-like. Tizziana was a beauty; she would be a lovely woman one day. I just hoped that papà would choose a good husband for her.

Just as I hoped Alessio would be good for me too.

I kissed her on the top of her head and pulled away, promising that we would see each other again soon.

Then I was guided to the abbess's office—who was like a Mother Superior—where I was placed in front of the man designated to be my husband.

My destiny.

My owner. As was to be expected within the mafia.

I lifted my eyes, and the fallen angel beauty of Alessio Preterotti nearly blinded me. I already knew him, but it was the first time I saw him so close, looking directly at me.

His eyes were so blue they could be mistaken for the sky. The curls falling across his face gave him an innocent yet rebellious air, which could easily become an illusion. An innocent and inexperienced girl like me didn't know how to handle such handsome men, let alone one who exuded sins from every part of his body.

He also couldn't look away. Some kind of connection formed between us in that moment.

It was then that my heart changed the course of its beats, and I understood it was yet another premonition. Those that accompanied me in a way I couldn't explain.

Those that made me feel a little crazy.

Somehow I knew, the moment I saw him, that this man would be my ruin. For better or for worse.

CHAPTER TWO

Luna

I remembered the first time I understood that there was something very peculiar about my family.

Besides being sent to a convent while still very young—which definitely didn't happen to my friends, who were mostly sent to boarding schools—I always had some suspicion about how things unfolded under my own roof, almost right under my nose.

Men in suits would come and go from my father's house, and I would watch them when I was little, hidden, as they discussed in Italian, moving with their silver suitcases and the shine at their waists, which I always knew was from revolvers.

At school, I could never tell my classmates what Dad did, nor could I write about his profession in essays, because I honestly didn't know. Although he almost never paid me any attention, when he had the opportunity and I asked, the answer was always the same: you're still too young to understand.

Certainty only came when I was nine years old. I was a cute little girl with long dark brown hair, and I was chosen to be the flower girl at my older brother Mattia's wedding. Not that I liked him much, but I suspected it wasn't something I had a say in, even if I were a bit older and had some right to an opinion.

Mattia was quite young when he got married, and his bride was even younger. She had just turned eighteen and, like me, had lived in a convent for a long time. I was already at the abbey by then, and I knew it had been a recommendation from her father.

I didn't dislike my life; even though there were many rules, I had to wake up very early, and the schedules for everything were very strict. The sisters were caring, the classes were interesting, and I enjoyed studying the Bible. My faith did me good.

The only thing I missed was my family. Less so Mattia.

I was still finishing getting ready when the bride herself appeared in the room where I had been placed, at her parents' house, which was a true mansion, where the wedding would take place.

She was beautiful. Her hair was almost the same color as mine, and she had very blue eyes that made her look like a doll. Her face was delicate but very young, and I knew she was scared.

"Oh, you're here. And you look so beautiful..." We had almost never spoken, so I found it a bit strange that she approached me, already dressed as a bride, holding her bouquet.

Shyly, I tried to smile since she would be my sister-in-law. We needed to get along, right? Almost like sisters.

"Are you nervous? Because I am very," she said, pacing back and forth without sitting down.

"I'm not the bride."

That seemed to surprise her, as she looked at me with wide eyes but ended up laughing gently.

"You're right." The girl, whose name was Olena, paused, stopping her pacing for a moment. "I tried talking to my mother, but she's more excited than I am. She seems like the bride herself, all thrilled, believing that I'm so lucky, that it's the wedding of my dreams." She laughed sarcastically. "As if... But anyway, I just came to see if you were okay."

"Yes, I am..."

"That's good!" Olena didn't know what to do with her hands, and I felt she didn't want to leave. If I could, I would hide her and take her with me to the abbey. I imagined it would be a better fate than marrying my conservative, cold, and violent brother.

She cautiously approached the door, hand on the doorknob. When she turned back one last time to give me a fleeting look, what I saw were the red flowers in her bouquet, contrasting with her very white dress.

They looked like blood.

For a moment, that's what I saw. It was the impression I had, and it was strong enough to torment me as I walked down the red carpet of the church, needing to concentrate doubly hard not to trip as the flower girl, while I heard people whispering, looking at Olena, who was right behind, accompanied by her father, that she was a perfect mafia bride.

It was at nine years old that I understood what my father did.

He was a mafioso. A killer. A criminal.

Knowing all this, I began studying the mafia in the convent, hidden from the nuns, reading books in the huge library that I visited regularly, under the pretense of wanting to study a bit more geography or literature. As I learned about the nuances of the world I belonged to, I wasn't surprised when, years later, my beautiful sister-in-law was shot in the belly, pregnant with my first nephew.

It was with this image that I woke from my tormented dream, in one breath, finding myself lying on the benches of what seemed like an airplane, covered by a blanket, all curled up.

For a few moments, I didn't remember where I was, but then the last moments returned to my memory. I squirmed in the seats that would be uncomfortable for anyone else, but I was very small and used to the hard mattresses of the convent. At my father's house, my bed was huge, soft, and had good quality sheets, but I spent very little time there to indulge in that kind of frivolity.

The dream still haunted me when I got up, even coughing when I breathed deeply to try to catch my breath.

In two seconds, the large and imposing figure of Alessio Preterotti was in front of me, with a glass of water, attentive.

"*Grazie*" I replied softly.

I had hardly spoken to him until that moment, although he seemed a bit friendlier than Dominic. I adjusted myself, sitting, leaving one bench of distance between us, and fixed my hair, because it must have been all messy.

Many of the things I was taught in the convent contradicted what I learned from my mother. To be a girl within the standards of the world I lived in, I needed to always be presentable, well-groomed, well-dressed, and composed. In the convent, I had to wear modest clothing, could never wear makeup, and my hair was usually kept in severe buns.

I was a contradiction because of the two worlds surrounding me.

Faith and violence.

Sins and holiness.

"Are you okay? You look a little pale," he asked.

"Just a nightmare, that's all."

A broad smile curved his lips, which I saw from the corner of my eye since it wasn't easy to look at him, given my upbringing and the fact that he was so handsome it almost hurt to look at him.

"Oh, so she speaks," he joked. "Are you hungry? Want something?"

"No, thank you. I'm still sleepy. How long did I sleep?"

"Almost nothing. About an hour or so. You can sleep more if you want."

"How much longer is the flight?" This wasn't the question I should be asking. They had taken me from the abbey and were taking me somewhere I didn't even know where it was. They claimed it was my father's wish, but they didn't confirm whether they were taking me home.

It felt much more like a kidnapping than a courtesy from my fiancé to protect me.

Fiancé.

Alessio Preterotti was my fiancé.

It was inevitable to remember Olena, her beautiful dress, and the impression I had when I saw the red flowers and compared them to blood. I couldn't help but associate her desperate face and the fear she conveyed to me that night, just before walking down the aisle, with myself and how scared I was at the thought of marrying a guy I didn't even know.

"The flight is sixteen hours long. We still have at least eight left."

Sixteen hours?

Of course, we weren't heading to the United States. I was used to traveling on my father's jet when I needed to return to Texas for holidays or someone's birthday, and it never took this long to fly, without a doubt.

I should rebel, demand to be told what was happening, but I was scared. If they were indeed taking me somewhere without my family's knowledge, they must have had some plan in mind.

"I'll try to stay awake a bit longer. I wake up very early in the convent, and I'm used to sleeping before nine."

"I can't remember the last time I went to bed that early. Maybe only when I was a kid."

"It's just that there's not much to do..." I managed to smile, still a bit shy, without looking him in the eye. I shouldn't be being nice without knowing what was happening first, but he was still my fiancé.

Or at least I thought so.

When I finally lifted my eyes to him, I saw the smile again that made him look like a boy.

The smile that could deceive me. Because all I knew about Alessio was that he had the seductive power of a sinful devil while enchanting with the gaze of an angel.

That was what I heard some of the women in the Cosa Nostra commenting, especially after our engagement was made official. During Deanna and Dominic's wedding, they looked at me and said he would never be faithful; that I would have to deal with his flings, but at the same time, I was very lucky because he would warm my bed every night.

An experienced lover—those were the words used. But I didn't understand anything about that. I could never compare.

"Would you mind leaving me alone?" I asked, again looking away because I didn't want to fall into temptation.

Not until I understood what his role was.

"Of course..." He seemed a bit disappointed, but hurried to get up and move away, running a hand through his tousled curls, which gave him an even more nonchalant air.

Sin personified.

And I was in his hands.

What a contradiction.

CHAPTER THREE

Alessio

I had never, in the slightest, had any trouble approaching women. Girls usually liked me, I liked them, and it all ended up, typically, in bed. If there was one thing in life I was good at, it was what to do with them.

At that moment, looking at the young woman who might one day become my wife, I had no idea how to act.

Minutes ago, she had simply asked me to step away, which was new for me as well.

The girl wouldn't look me in the eye. She didn't know *how*. She was just a scared girl, terrified in my presence.

Another novelty concerning her. No woman had ever been afraid of me. I had experienced that feeling from others when I needed to carry out some tasks for my family, and I could swear it wasn't exactly the kind of thing I enjoyed doing. Inflicting pain, terrorizing, and killing were not pastimes. I took each of those lives seriously. But causing harm to an innocent girl? That was a different feeling.

It embarrassed me.

The problem was that there was a lot at stake. One of them was the safety of my family. Pietro Cipriano was a good player; a cruel adversary. Why wouldn't he be capable of hurting someone to accomplish his plans? How many people could die for him to rise to power, as he so desired?

Luna would not be harmed. I firmly believed it was not Dominic's intent, but even if it were, I would never allow it.

Shortly after I left her, at her request, I sat away, but I couldn't stop watching her from a distance, because there were a million possibilities: mainly that she might freak out and put herself in danger upon discovering we weren't taking her home to Texas.

I saw her begin to move, reaching into the pocket of her heavy gray skirt that covered her legs completely, and I almost feared that, in a twist, she would pull out a weapon and threaten us both, catching us by surprise and unprepared.

But what she had in her hands was a rosary.

I was somewhat lost, watching her, but I ended up dozing off, napping for a while. When I woke up, she was once again lying across the three seats, unconscious.

I approached cautiously, glancing at her and adjusting the blanket she hadn't used. She looked beautiful and very young, seeming more innocent, all curled up—which made her look even smaller—one arm under her head, yet her expression was not serene. It was as if her dreams were tormenting her. And she had indeed woken up very startled.

Which wasn't surprising. Perhaps she was already beginning to understand what had happened.

Bored, I moved away from Luna and went to find Dominic, who was comfortably seated with his legs crossed near the window, working on his laptop.

"Aren't you sleeping?" I asked, sitting next to him.

"Someone needs to keep an eye on things. The plan was for us to talk while we were on board, but the girl seems to entertain you more than anything."

"Being grumpy doesn't suit you, *fratello*.

"It's a quality I reserve just for you, Preterotti."

"You don't seem like a lamb when it comes to my sister."

Ah, I managed to throw him off.

Dominic shot a look my way, eyebrow raised, but in a totally disgruntled way, as if I had hit exactly his weak spot.

Entertaining, I would say.

"You seem very relaxed, Alessio, to the point of not even appearing to be the precursor of a war. What we're doing here will cause chaos in the Cosa Nostra. There will be fucked-up consequences we'll have to deal with."

"I know that. This is how I deal with pressure. If I took things as seriously as you or Enrico, for example, I wouldn't react so well."

He raised a finger at me, almost as if he was going to give me a lesson.

"Then you'll have to learn, kid. We're not playing around. This is serious."

"Once again, I *know* that," I replied as seriously as I could. "The difference is that I care about people. More so about a girl who was ripped from the only life she knows and is with two men with our reputation. She needs someone to take care of her."

"And the fact that she's so beautiful undoubtedly shouldn't make the mission a sacrifice for you, should it?"

I fell silent because it would be pointless to respond that I would act the same way in any circumstance. Of course, I had noticed that Luna was beautiful. With her clean face, those modest, old-fashioned clothes, with little signs of vanity, she was much prettier than many I had met. Still, that wasn't the reason.

Or was it? Was I that frivolous to let my cock think for me even when it came to a serious situation like this?

"It doesn't matter what you think, Dominic," I tried to assert with conviction. "If you need to talk to me, I'm here. We still have enough time."

He grumbled again but eventually relented, and we discussed the plan. I had no idea how long it would take to resolve things with

Pietro, but I would be the girl's babysitter in Scotland. I needed to stay with her, ensuring she was protected.

More than that, preventing her father from finding her.

Dominic's idea was to talk to her as soon as we landed and fill her in on everything. According to reliable sources, and considering she was a woman of faith, she might be an ally, although neither of us believed Luna had much power within her family, much less many opinions about the Cosa Nostra. Despite all this, we wanted to be fair.

Which was ironic, considering who we were.

The conversation was long, but as soon as we finished, the landing was already approaching.

I knew we needed to fasten our seatbelts and that I should wake Luna so she would be in a safer position, but all I did was sit close to her and place her feet in my lap, leaving my arm available in case I needed to hold her.

Even with all the movement, she didn't wake up, and I was sure it was a result of the stress from what she'd said about sleeping too early. It was the middle of the night when we landed in Glasgow.

I decided to carry her off the private plane in my arms, thinking it would be nice for her to wake up in a more comfortable place, ready for the conversation. I imagined it would be another stressful moment and that it would be better to have her more rested and calm.

The déjà vu didn't escape me. When had I become an expert at carrying sleeping girls off planes to take them to destinations different from what they initially imagined? It had been the same with my sister when I literally had to kidnap her in Brazil, at my father's orders, to marry Dominic.

Luna remained asleep the entire way to the house we rented for the two of us, and I carried her to the room that would be hers. During the last stretch, she stirred a bit, as dawn was approaching, but still, I placed her on the bed, covering her and watching her in her deep sleep, almost worried, but knowing it was just a matter of time before she woke up and we revealed our intentions to use her.

I hated that things had to be this way, but it was how everything was done within the mafia. She would understand that our intentions were noble, as much as possible.

Before leaving, I returned to Luna, placing my hand inside her pocket and pulling out the rosary, just as I had seen her doing earlier. I opened her delicate little hand and placed it between her fingers, hoping it would be a source of comfort for her. If she could cling to her faith, perhaps she would fear us less.

With that in mind, I left the room, closing the curtains, turning off the light, and slowly pulling the door shut, planning to take a shower and prepare for the conversation and the girl's reaction, which I had no idea what it might be.

CHAPTER FOUR

Luna

I opened my eyes, feeling strangely comfortable, unlike the last times. The place was dark, and I could barely see anything, but it was clear we were no longer on the plane. It was easy to tell I had been placed in a bed, and we were no longer moving. We weren't gliding anymore.

I got up carefully, thinking it was completely disorienting not to have the slightest idea of where I was.

At least I didn't take long to find a lamp and turn it on, hoping to see something.

When I did, something fell from my hand, and I bent down to pick it up, finding my rosary.

Even with my memories a bit hazy, I could remember using it and putting it back in my pocket before snuggling up in the plane's seats to sleep a little more.

Someone had placed it in my hand, returned to me. It was a very significant gesture, and I almost suspected it was Alessio. After all, he had a sweet way about him, and I could see in his eyes a compassion that could convince me, which was even dangerous.

Taking a deep breath, I looked around. The room was large, and the bed had high posts that looked like parts of Greek ornamentation. There were several pillows, a deep green quilt, and tasteful rugs. The entire decor of the room resembled a medieval castle, but with some modern touches, which could have allowed me to feel at home since I was used to that kind of oppressive room in the abbey.

I walked, feeling my feet on the cold floor, and approached the window. I opened it and received the dawn light on my face, forcing me to close my eyes before I burned them with the blinding brightness.

Once I managed to adjust to the light, I tried to investigate what was around me, and I came across a large area, filled with greenery, trees with aged leaves, shrubs, and surrounded by a tall stone wall, which reminded me so much of a prison. Birds flew in an overcast sky, and one landed for a few moments on a branch of one of the trees.

The animal's eyes turned toward mine, as if it were a sentinel and not just a random creature that had appeared and approached by chance.

I recognized the species. The brown feathers, the imposing body, the yellow eyes. The courage to approach so closely to an unknown person. It was a golden eagle.

I liked birds. I liked animals in general.

To be honest, I enjoyed studying everything, without much criteria. My memory was excellent, retaining information for a long time. It wasn't photographic, but some of the sisters used to say they didn't consult encyclopedias for almost anything, just me, if it was a topic they believed I knew.

How was it possible that I already missed them? Perhaps it was the impression that I would be away from them for a very, very long time.

The eagle took off into the sky, and I recognized the fog, beginning to form my own theories.

As I tried to orient myself regarding what I could see around me, I heard a knock at the door. The creaking of it opening just a little startled me, making me place a hand on my chest.

Not that I expected to be alone in that place, but I didn't know if I was prepared for company while I hadn't even composed myself from sleep.

"Excuse me, are you okay?"

There was Alessio. He hadn't entered the room but was waiting at the threshold, wanting permission.

"I am, as well as can be expected."

I never thought I would find myself in that situation, not knowing exactly how to act, because I didn't know my position with respect to that man. He was my fiancé, but I no longer had much certainty about anything. Everything that had happened up to that moment was very strange.

Alessio put his hands in his pockets and began to approach me.

I wasn't used to having men around me, and when it happened, they were priests. At Cosa Nostra parties, my father and brothers always made sure I stayed as far away from everyone as possible, talking only with the women. To the bosses, I owed obedience, kissing their rings, but exchanged few words.

I imagined Alessio knew my life and probably expected me to be innocent. Which was true. I just didn't know what game to play.

I wasn't naive. I wasn't stupid; on the contrary. They wouldn't be able to manipulate me so easily. I just needed to stay alert.

"I know you've already asked this, but I need to tell you that we brought you here to..."

"Scotland?" I interrupted him, giving him the answer, which seemed to surprise him.

"How did you guess?"

"I saw a typical eagle land in a tree. The climate, the sky... it was a hunch."

Great, I had surprised him in some way. It was good that we started off that way so he wouldn't treat me like a child.

"Um... well... I guess I don't have any news to share then," he stated, scratching his eyebrow with his thumb.

He wore a checkered flannel shirt, almost like a farmer, and I could see another one underneath with a round collar. All his movements were very charming and didn't seem calculated at all. It was something natural.

I lowered my eyes as soon as I started thinking about those things, gripping the rosary in my hand.

He was not only an unwanted temptation, but he could also be an enemy. I still couldn't judge.

"It's not like that. Why did you bring me here?"

Alessio began to move and leaned his large body against one of the bed's posts, crossing his arms. It felt a bit too intimate to see him so close to the place where I had just slept.

"It's complicated. I think it's better if Dominic explains it to you."

"You don't know?" I looked into his eyes once more.

"I do, but I've never been very good with words. Except when... well... when they were used to win over a *bella ragazza*," he said sweetly, a mischievous smile on his face, but not in a wicked way. It was, once again, something charming.

"I don't even remember leaving the plane."

"You were sleeping. I carried you here."

I felt a shiver at the thought of being so vulnerable in his arms, but it was also a bit disconcerting, for a girl, to imagine such a handsome man holding her like a character from a romance novel.

I hadn't read many, but Tizziana always smuggled some when we returned to Texas, hiding them under the mattress. It was fun to read them together, and we even passed them on to other girls and novices, creating a chain of rebellion.

"Thank you, I guess."

"You're welcome. I know it's still early, but I wanted to let you know that Dominic and I are downstairs and breakfast is already served. Take a shower, get dressed, and come down if you want. He wants to talk to you. He might have your answers."

I nodded once more, watching Alessio leave the room, close the door, and leave me alone.

I needed to move because I had no choice. I had to know what my fate would be from then on, even if I didn't want to be so close to Dominic because I feared him.

Not that Alessio inspired me with more confidence. In fact, I felt like I was in the lions' den, just like Daniel.

I felt as if I were in the middle of a bonfire, not knowing how to save myself.

CHAPTER FIVE

Alessio

The girl didn't come down for breakfast. Not for lunch either. I knocked on her door later, but it was locked.

Okay, if she wanted it that way, so be it. We had already forced her into enough things that we could wait a bit longer to have the conversation. I imagined Dominic must be eager to return to his wife, but we couldn't rush anything. It was on Luna's time, because it would be much better if she were on our side, although that was difficult since our adversaries were members of her family.

I was willing to be more patient. Dominic, however, was not. Still, I would manage to convince him to accept the situation without blowing up and barging into the girl's room, but the universe wasn't cooperating.

Things turned chaotic in an instant.

Dominic interrupted his meal—dinner—to answer the phone. He had been attentive to his cell lately, because the recent contact with Pietro Cipriano, confirming we had his daughter, would certainly lead to retaliation, but my brother-in-law's reaction worried me.

"*Fabarutto! Diavolo!*" he began to yell, rising from the chair and moving away. I wanted to go after him to understand what had happened, but I thought it wiser to wait. I already imagined the news wouldn't be pleasant, so if I could delay it as long as possible, better.

I couldn't, however, take another bite of my food because my stomach felt knotted.

"If you do anything to her, I swear I..." I managed to hear Dominic saying, but he was interrupted.

Who interrupted Dominic Ungaretti? I definitely wasn't crazy enough to do that.

I grabbed the beer bottle cap we had been drinking from and started tossing it in the air, catching it and throwing it again, trying to use that gesture to blur my thoughts about what could be causing Dominic so much distress.

It was a technique I used to keep my mind occupied, thinking only of the rise and fall of the small object. Anything could become a distraction when we wanted it to. Anything could protect us from pain, which often was a psychological issue. That was what I had learned over the years.

I let my entire attention focus on those rhythmic and constant movements until the sound of all the dishes crashing to the floor brought me back. I didn't even flinch because it took a little more effort to startle me.

"They got Deanna!" my brother-in-law snarled, and I, knowing his temperament well, stood up calmly, trying to absorb the news.

"Who got her?"

"Pietro Cipriano's men. They took your two brothers. Enrico, for some reason, was with her."

"What?"

Yeah... some things could actually scare me.

"How did they get the two of them, Alessio? Why the hell didn't Enrico protect Deanna if she was with him?" Dominic continued speaking as if he were a wild man. He was clearly losing control, and I had no idea what he was capable of in that state.

BOUND BY BETRAYAL 27

"Enrico is very well-trained. Probably more than any of us. He wouldn't let her be taken without a fight. He must have been ambushed."

"HOW?" He moved closer to me, raising his finger toward my face. "You were supposed to be responsible for her in my absence. Your father and your brother. How is it possible you can't keep a woman safe?"

"We don't know what happened and..."

Dominic barely let me finish speaking before he started moving away, kicking one of the chairs that had fallen on the floor, heading toward the stairs, beginning to climb them two at a time.

Realizing what he intended to do—obviously to look for Luna—I hurried to follow him, running and flying up the stairs until I caught up with him.

"Dominic, don't do anything stupid! You'll lose your cool," I warned, placing a hand on the same shoulder as he turned to look at me, twisting his neck.

"I'm apparently already out of it."

Believing I wouldn't be able to dissuade him, I continued to follow him, cursing under my breath as I saw him kick down Luna's door, breaking it open.

"Dominic!" I shouted, passing by him and positioning myself in front of Luna, extending my hand to prevent my brother-in-law from touching her.

"I'm not a madman, Alessio. I won't hurt the girl. I just want her to speak."

I felt one of Luna's hands clutching my shirt, crumpling it, and I didn't even want to look at her because I already imagined she must be terrified.

"Did you know your father is a traitor? What do you know about this?"

I finally needed to glance at her out of the corner of my eye because I wanted to see her expressions too. I had the impression that Luna knew absolutely nothing about her family, but I wouldn't be able to convince Dominic of that.

"I don't know what you're talking about, Mr. Ungaretti," she replied with a tone of subservience she hadn't used with me before.

This surprised me. Not that she had loosened up in my presence or spoken without her usual shyness, or been bold or anything like that. With Dominic, however, I felt a respect—or a fear—that was a bit more palpable.

"Well, you should know. Do you know why you're here with us?"

"I imagine I do, sir."

Dominic stepped forward, positioning himself closer to us. I extended my arm to the side, creating a barrier so he couldn't even sidestep and get close to Luna.

It didn't matter that we both had the same goal, that we had agreed on this mission from the start; I felt responsible for that girl. She would be my ward from then on because she would stay with me. Anything that happened to her, I would feel guilty about.

"Dominic..." I said softly, almost in a whisper, hoping my brother-in-law would hear me and that something in my tone would alert him that he was taking it out on the wrong person.

He took a deep breath, pulling in the air heavily, but let his shoulders drop. I thought he was going to tell Luna more, to explain to her what our intentions were. In fact, that was what we had agreed on from the start. Once we had her in our power, she would know everything. We would tell her about the plans, explaining her father's betrayal, what he had done, and what it meant for the Cosa Nostra. Neither of us doubted that the girl didn't know what was going on and that, being innocent, she could validate our position.

BOUND BY BETRAYAL

That idea seemed to have faded. Dominic straightened up, taking another deep breath. At that moment, he seemed even more powerful; embodying the image of the boss that he truly was.

"Keep your convictions, child. What you know about us and your position with us. Given this scenario, you will have to remain in doubt."

He turned his back on us, leaving through the broken door, slamming it shut with force, probably to create an unwanted and intentionally frightening noise.

I turned to look at the girl, and she quickly lowered her eyes to the floor, avoiding my gaze, but when I looked at her hands, I could see them trembling.

"Are you okay?" I asked, concerned, because I couldn't imagine what her feelings must be in that position.

"He scares me," she replied, sincerely.

"People usually feel that way about Dominic; you're not alone." It wasn't the time for jokes, but I really didn't know how to handle her. Still, I needed to ask a question because it was important for me to have the answer and feel a bit better about the whole situation. I extended my hand, bringing it to Luna's face and lifting it so she would look into my eyes. She did, but still reluctantly. "And me? Do I also make you feel scared?"

Luna didn't answer at first, and I saw again that disconcerting innocence in her eyes, which I wasn't used to.

It wasn't the same impression I had when talking to the virgin girls of the mafia. It wasn't that. It was because that girl seemed pure as an angel.

"I don't know," she finally said after a long pause, and I stopped touching her, withdrawing my hand from her face because I didn't want her to feel cornered or that her space was invaded.

"Don't be afraid of me, *dolce angelo*. Please. I won't hurt you. It's a promise."

She clearly didn't believe me. But there was nothing I could do about that. For her to grant me her trust, I needed to earn it.

I didn't linger near her for long, and when I went to look for Dominic, he was leaving with his bags in hand.

Minutes later, he got into a car, bidding farewell in the least gentle way possible.

And just like that, I was left with that girl.

Just the two of us, mere strangers, in a house. She was afraid of me, and I didn't know how to understand her.

It would be a very peculiar journey, I could swear.

CHAPTER SIX

Luna

The property was immense, almost as I could imagine a castle in Camelot would be. It was imposing, majestic, but not just the house itself. The entire grounds around it.

From the outside, when I looked at it, taking in the whole view, its gray walls didn't let me forget my old home. The appearance wasn't so different, except for the very vibrant greenery around and the countless evening primroses that seemed to spring up in thousands of bushes all around the house's perimeter.

As soon as we stepped through the front door, there was a little stone staircase, surrounded by greenery and white flowers. Some of them were evening primroses too, and I spent a good amount of time caressing the petals just to see them slowly close, alongside the miracle of nature. It made me feel as if there were magic at my fingertips.

Sunny days had been rare since I arrived at that house a few days ago, but I imagined they didn't quite match the atmosphere that had formed inside. I wasn't frightened by the loneliness. To be honest, I managed to settle into it, like someone feeling comfortable in a new home. In the convent, there were always people around me; among novices, nuns, and other girls who had been thrown there like I was, to study and become good wives.

There, in that house with Alessio Preterotti, I was living with silences and my own company.

I knew something had happened since Dominic had burst into my room, breaking down the door in a fit of rage. I had been taught that listening through walls was a grave sin; that gossip was an evil sent by the devil himself, but no one had ever told me that eavesdropping unintentionally could jeopardize my place in heaven.

I knew that Deanna Preterotti, Alessio's sister, had been kidnapped. I didn't know the details exactly, but I hoped she was okay. Every afternoon I sneaked away to what I called the little chapel of the house, at the back of the property, and prayed for her. I wanted to ask if she had been found, if she had been rescued, how she had reacted after such a huge trauma. My prayers always included a request for her to be strong and not succumb, even after the shock had passed.

I understood absolutely nothing about the world we lived in, but I imagined it was cruel to its women. Even to me, who had always lived protected, I had never been consulted about my desires, what I wanted, what I wished for, what my dreams were.

Dreams... what a joke. A woman couldn't dream in the Cosa Nostra.

A woman could accept everything in silence, be a good wife, bear healthy children—preferably boys—and be loyal to her husband and family.

How loyal was I to the Cipriano from the moment I started feeling comfortable in that house, in the presence of the enemy? Eating his good food, enjoying the soft bed, smiling as I felt the wind tousling my hair? I wasn't fighting against it. I wasn't begging to be returned. I didn't rebel.

I just... accepted.

It was probably something in my nature, in fact. I wasn't a fighter. I wasn't a warrior.

I woke up much earlier than Alessio. It was a habit I doubted I would lose, but I was always out of bed before dawn. There was a spot

BOUND BY BETRAYAL

in the house, a wall within the taller ones, where I could climb up and watch the sun rise, staining the sky in various shades of color.

I particularly enjoyed hugging my knees, resting my head on them and admiring, just as I was enchanted by the evening primroses and the evening flowers of the house, as they began to wake. Then I would head to the little chapel and say my prayers.

It wasn't exactly a chapel, to be honest. It was a little house at the back of the property, with an altar, a kneeler, with Jesus on the cross on the wall and a space to light candles. There were a few there, all extinguished, mostly remnants. I tried to imagine how many other people had been there, praying too. Residents, guests, owners of the place, caretakers? What would be the story of that house and that chapel? It probably had never served as a hideout for anyone.

Because that was how I liked to think. That they were hiding me and not imprisoning me.

I knelt before the makeshift altar and said my prayers. I prayed the entire rosary, fasting, and it took me about forty minutes to do so. In a loud voice, but in whispers, because I liked to hear.

Then at the end I would stand, make the sign of the cross, and go back to the house to have the coffee I prepared myself. I left some for Alessio too, because I knew he usually woke up later and worked out. He trained his body with the same devotion I went to the chapel. As early as possible, every day, without fail.

The difference was that he seemed a bit lazier, because he hardly ever got up before ten.

I left the drink in the coffee pot, so he would just have to heat it up, and headed for the garden of the house. Normally I would return to my room to read a bit or to knit—since it was the only activity I could manage, with the little I had brought from the convent. I also had a recipe notebook that I started copying neatly and another for hobbies, which made me feel very old.

There was a chessboard in the closet of my room, and sometimes I played alone, against myself, waiting for time to pass.

That morning, I decided to change my routine a bit.

As soon as I reached the garden, by the pool area, I heard characteristic sounds. For a moment, I swore it was the wind rustling the water, but I ended up coming face to face with arms swimming vigorously, going back and forth, propelling a long body that floated as if it were a professional at it.

I should leave. Looking at someone like that wasn't right, especially since he didn't know I was there, but I couldn't. Something in his movements made them incredibly hypnotic, and I couldn't bring myself to leave.

Not even when Alessio noticed my presence and stopped swimming, slowly climbing out of the pool.

"Good morning. I thought you'd be upstairs... Or in the chapel." He seemed a bit embarrassed. Still, he didn't rush to cover himself.

My eyes immediately turned to his body, droplets of water falling abundantly, soaking the ground as he walked toward the chair where he had left a towel. He wore a black speedo that covered almost nothing of his body, which was full of muscles.

Very toned legs, thick thighs, a narrow waist, a chiseled abdomen, a broad chest, and huge arms. He was even bigger than I had imagined.

Not that I should have imagined at all.

His wet hair hid his curls, especially when he tossed it back with those equally strong and sun-kissed hands he got from exercising like that every day. I didn't even know if he used the pool more times throughout the day, because I tried not to get too close, but I imagined he did.

His very blue eyes always seemed to be smiling and appeared kind. Gentle.

He *always* was very kind. Sweet. A contradiction for a mafia man.

BOUND BY BETRAYAL   35

I realized I took a while to respond, but I didn't notice I was staring at him from head to toe. I heard a mischievous chuckle and lifted my wide eyes to meet his.

"Sorry. I shouldn't have been looking." And I should also have known how to lie or at least pretend, but deceiving someone wasn't my strong suit. Not only because I didn't have that malice, but because I hated lies. Never, in my nineteen years, had I told one.

Alessio's smile grew even bigger. He seemed to glow when that happened.

At the same time, he grabbed the towel and began to dry himself.

How was it possible that this gesture was even more sensual than him coming out of the pool?

"You can look as much as you want. We're engaged, aren't we?"

Yeah, we were. Or at least, I thought so. Which meant that soon he would have permission to touch me with those same hands.

I preferred not to comment, not to respond.

"Your sister? How is she? I imagine she was found."

Alessio shrugged.

"Dominic found her, as was to be expected. He would go to hell for her, no doubt."

So the feared boss of the New York mafia really did love someone. His wife.

What would it be like to have the love of a man like him, who had no feelings for almost anyone? How would he be at home? Would he be different from how he was with others? Could the same hands that caused so much violence touch Deanna with tenderness?

But what did I know about that kind of feeling? Between a man and a woman? I knew nothing.

"I'm glad she's okay. I hope, too, that there's no lasting trauma."

"For Deanna? She probably traumatized the kidnappers."

I managed to smile softly, thinking it would be friendlier. Then the idea was to pull away, with a nod of my head, but I felt Alessio's wet and cold hand grip my wrist, preventing me from leaving.

It was as if an electric shock ran through my body. Something completely new, an unfamiliar sensation.

Like a disease... but a good one to feel.

"Don't isolate yourself. I'm not your enemy. We can coexist."

I turned my eyes back to him, somewhat lost, because I didn't know how to act.

"I'll try. It's not easy for me."

"Not for me either. Let's try together." Then he let me go and extended his hand to me, so I could shake it. "Let's start over: I'm Alessio Preterotti. Nice to meet you."

I hesitated, tucking a strand of hair behind my ear, looking at his hand for a few moments. Then I extended mine too and accepted the handshake.

"I'm Luna Cipriano."

We had known our names from the start, but I understood his strategy. Breaking the ice, that's what they called it, right?

I just had no idea how it would be from then on.

CHAPTER SEVEN

Alessio

Since I was born, I knew my family wasn't conventional. Not just because I was trained to survive all kinds of violence, but because there was a certain excessive concern whenever we went out or were away for too long.

Security would go up and down behind us, and as far as I knew, we weren't celebrities. We weren't movie stars or rock bands.

But something worse than that.

Over time, they taught us to get used to it and to accept that when we went out on any *mission,* there was a great chance we wouldn't come back. For a starry-eyed kid, I often wondered if my father had connections with the FBI or Interpol, since we were foreigners living in the United States.

And yes, over time, the certainty that death would come one day lived within me. Dying young in the Cosa Nostra was no surprise. Many of us had fallen, caught in ambushes, cold-blooded murders—when they were lucky. Others were captured and tortured in the most cruel ways for information.

Still, I was one of the lucky ones who kept my father and brother, both holding important positions within the organization, alive.

I wanted to believe I didn't fear losing them, but upon hearing that Enrico had been kidnapped along with Deanna, I could swear I lost ten years off my lifespan. I was losing another ten trying to call him without success.

AMARA HOLT

Since I was told he had escaped from the hospital, I had been desperately trying to call, but to no avail, waiting for news, but couldn't get in touch.

And it was as if no one else cared. Of course, resolving the situation with Pietro Cipriano was more important, but it was my damn brother who was missing. How could no one care about that? My father only worried about his heir, the future boss he had trained to be a cold and ruthless leader.

"This girl knows something, Alessio. You have everything in your hands; you should be a little tougher with her," my father stated during a conference we held, in the company of Dominic and Giovanni Caccini—the boss of Chicago.

I was using an earpiece so no information would leak and reach Luna's ears. Not because I didn't trust she was innocent regarding all this; but because I didn't want her to know her father had become a traitor.

"We're in contact with Mattia Cipriano. He's on our side. I believe it's just a matter of time before we find him," Dominic began to speak. "When we catch him, he's mine. I don't want any discussion about that."

"He kidnapped my two children."

"Fuck that. We're talking about my wife. He took her from me and allowed them to hurt her. This is my problem," Ungaretti nearly growled, clenching his fist. He was ready for anything. Pietro would undoubtedly regret being born.

"He'll surrender if we use the girl," my father insisted.

"I won't hurt her," I stated firmly.

"Don't get all soft-hearted, Alessio. I need you to be tough. We're about to go to war."

"She's innocent," I spoke softly, almost in a whisper, but feeling like I could explode at any moment.

"We're all innocent until proven otherwise. If it's necessary, whose side do you think she'll take? Her father's or ours? Use your head, Alessio. Don't let the fact that she's a pretty young girl cloud your judgment, if you still have any left."

In a fit of anger, I clenched my jaw and closed the laptop without even saying goodbye or ending the call. I unplugged it, which was its only source of power since I had removed the battery, so it shut down automatically.

I got up from the chair, starting to pace back and forth in the room, completely losing control.

I shouldn't have been bothered anymore, because it had always been like this. I was the black sheep of the family, the one who was good for nothing, even though they always sent me to do dirty work, and I usually succeeded at it. I was the pariah of the Preterotti, but I never refused anything. As capo, I had gotten myself into the worst places to gather information, had scars that were never valued, and learned a million things on my own while my father praised Enrico's efforts.

When I was younger, I felt envy. I once came to hate my brother, wishing he would die so I could be the underboss and prove my worth.

It was the same period when I became a rebellious teenager, choosing the path of drugs and limitless sex. So instead of grabbing the attention of those I wanted, I only further sullied my image.

I wanted and needed my father to respect me. So the same drive that led me to fall from grace was what saved me and brought me back to trying to follow a less disastrous path. I got clean, trained hard, and put myself into the family business with dedication.

Giving up sex wasn't an option I ever considered. And why would I, when it was one of the best things in the world?

Even with all my effort, it wasn't enough. They saw me as the useless, rebellious kid who couldn't handle anything serious, who was only good for beating some punks, torturing insignificant bastards, and attending meetings without giving much input.

So much so that my role at that moment became babysitting a girl, in a dead-end world, cooped up in a house while all the action happened far from me.

"Alessio, are you okay?"

And there she was, that girl.

We had been living together for a few days, even though we weren't particularly close. We talked little, and I wasn't sure what was better or worse in this situation. Given her father's circumstances, I was no longer certain we would even get married.

I wasn't sure of anything. In the midst of my rage, there was nothing I could see in front of me. It was as if a red haze filled my vision from the anger I felt.

"No. It's not okay. I think it's best if you stay away from me today," I almost growled, more irritated than was prudent. It wasn't her fault, not at all. But it didn't matter to me.

"I can help, maybe."

Luna's sweet and generous demeanor only made me angrier. I didn't want that lovely girl near me while I felt my rage beginning to boil over.

All my charm and chivalrous manners were ways to mask that I also had a wild side that I kept secret, tamed under piles and piles of darkness. When it exploded, I needed to be alone. I hated being seen becoming someone I despised.

"Get out of here, Luna," I shouted, turning my back.

She should have left.

"Alessio, please. I'm not going to leave you like this." I felt her delicate hand touch my shoulder, so I turned and grabbed her wrist, witnessing the shock that appeared in her eyes.

Shit! Just when I started to trust myself, I terrified her again.

BOUND BY BETRAYAL

"I've already told you: stay away from me. Right now, your family is one of the reasons I'm like this."

"What? My family?"

"Your father is the one who kidnapped my brothers. Why do you think we came for you? It wasn't his order since he decided to become our enemy. Everything is falling apart over there, Luna. We can't pretend anymore that something isn't wrong, and you can't remain in ignorance. Your family has betrayed us. Your father is a traitor to the Cosa Nostra and will soon be in Dominic's hands. You'll have to be strong to deal with this."

After dropping a bomb like that on the girl, I stepped back, because even though I was still in the heat of anger, I knew I wouldn't take long to regret what I said and that I would hate myself for treating her that way.

I was an asshole, and not just because of what my family thought of me.

I was an asshole because in a ridiculous battle of egos, my first reaction was to succumb and inflict cowardice on a girl who had nothing to do with the story.

Or did she...

Somehow, I should have understood, at that very moment, that Luna and I would be marked forever.

CHAPTER EIGHT

Luna

I always tried to save my tears for less trivial pains. Tears, in my opinion, were too precious; the greatest evidence that emotions were genuine. It was possible to fake a laugh, a smile, even love, but unless you were a trained actor, crying wasn't so simple.

Despite that, I ran out in that moment, nearly tripping over my own feet, wanting to escape Alessio as far as I could.

I pushed open the heavy back door of the house with all my strength and dashed across the vast property, my bare feet touching the grass and feeling the wind toss my hair, which I had finally started to wear down after so long of having it tied back severely in the convent.

I heard Alessio's voice calling me from afar, but it could have been a hallucination. Remembering how pissed he was, it was hard to imagine he would want me nearby.

I knew things weren't easy for him. After his sister's kidnapping, I started paying attention to his behavior and realized he was looking for his brother. I overheard a conversation where he mentioned someone not answering his calls or texts. Enrico Preterotti had escaped from the hospital where he was recovering from his injuries after a torture session, and no one knew his whereabouts.

It wasn't surprising. I always found Enrico to be very strange. Very mysterious; and that was because I hardly knew him.

BOUND BY BETRAYAL 43

But it wasn't my concern. I hoped he was okay, but at that moment, something else pulsed in my head, as if someone had connected an electrode to it, sending electric shocks through my brain.

My father was to blame for everything. He had betrayed the Cosa Nostra and harmed the family of the man I was engaged to.

To whom he had promised me in marriage.

What were his plans? How did he want to use me in all this chaos?

I ran as fast as my legs would allow and entered the chapel, slamming the door behind me, literally throwing myself down in front of the small altar. I grabbed onto it, burying my head in my arms, feeling my shoulders convulse with sobs.

I hadn't cried since I arrived at that house, but it wasn't as if I felt comfortable within the claustrophobic walls that surrounded me.

It wasn't the imprisonment that bothered me, because I lived in one, in a way. The problem was the uncertainty of what was happening outside that place. Not knowing how they were toying with my life and turning me into a manipulable pawn.

My own family...

"Why, Lord? Why?" I whimpered softly, surrendering to my weakness. "I'm not complaining about my family, because I love them. But why did I have to be conceived in the midst of so much evil? Why?"

I buried my head in my arms again, still clutching the kneeler, and let myself cry a little more.

I heard the door open, but I didn't move. Not only because I didn't want to look at him at that moment, but also because I could hardly move.

"Luna?"

Alessio had *that* kind of voice... The one that enters your ear like the whisper of the wind softly hissing in a comforting way. Like a bird singing at dawn.

Or maybe I was trying to find poetry where I shouldn't. Alessio was a seducer. He knew exactly how to act, how to speak, and what to say to make a person—especially a woman—believe in his words.

When I turned to him, feeling his gentle grip on my arm, I knew my eyes were red, and the compassion I saw on his face was the kind of thing even someone very good at deceiving and manipulating couldn't fake.

I was angry—a feeling I had not been prepared for my entire life. I had my moments during my nineteen years; I had been outraged by things, but never to that extent. I had never found myself completely lost in a fog of rage, to the point of wanting to disappear or lash out at someone.

And then I did.

"I'm sorry, Luna... I..."

I twisted my arm, having no experience in hitting any other human being, and slapped Alessio.

Of course, I immediately regretted it, bringing both hands to my mouth, feeling the sting of the other hand I had used for the slap.

"Oh my God, what did I do?"

To my surprise, there was a smirk on Alessio's insanely beautiful face.

"We need to practice that slap if you want to do it again, *dolce angelo*."

"No, no... I don't want to. Please, forgive me."

"I'm the one who needs to apologize. I deserved the slap and much more. I shouldn't have spoken to you that way."

I stayed silent, because I wouldn't deny it. He had indeed been very rude to me, but my reaction was the worst possible. An assault was not justifiable by absolutely anything.

BOUND BY BETRAYAL

I was still looking down when Alessio took a step forward, and I jumped at his closeness. We were confined in that chapel, under the almost romantic glow of the candle flames.

"Under God's eyes, Luna. You need to remember this. It's a holy place."

"I'm a bit scared because my brother has disappeared. As far as we know, he escaped from the hospital on his own, but he wasn't well. We saw it on the security cameras, and that's what worries me. He could be dead out there."

To my surprise, Alessio sat down on one of the few benches in the chapel. There were only four, and they were much shorter than those in a church. I imagined there had never been any grand ceremonies held there, but from what I found in my quiet explorations, the house dated back to the 15th century. I could almost envision women in those enormous dresses walking around, praying for their men to return alive from endless wars, before Scotland became a colony of England; when it was still a country fighting for its independence.

Just as I had done earlier, he rested his arms on the front bench, lowering his head and resting it in his hands, making his broad shoulders rise and fall with deep breaths.

I swallowed hard, imagining that things weren't easy for him either. It still wasn't an excuse for how he had treated me, and I wouldn't gloss over that, but I could be empathetic.

I walked around the bench and sat down next to him. I didn't even consider the possibility of creating a safe distance because I remained firm in my belief that this wasn't a place where I could allow myself to feel anything for a man. No matter how much he was my own fiancé. No matter how much I inevitably believed I would end up affected by him, in some way.

"Alessio," I called, and he didn't move for a few moments. When he did turn to me, his eyes were red, just like mine.

I might have been a bit more surprised. I understood almost nothing about men to realize they surrendered to emotions in that way, but I suspected it wasn't a characteristic of everyone. Especially when it came to a knight of the Cosa Nostra.

The problem was that Alessio went against all the stereotypes I had formed in my mind. He was a Don Juan, no doubt, with that fallen angel appearance, but there was a tender heart amid the rebellious desires I knew he possessed.

I reached into my skirt pocket and pulled out the rosary I always carried with me. I held the object in my palm, observing it with thoughtful eyes. I was about to make an offer that surely didn't match Alessio's personality, but I wanted to help in some way.

"Here. It might help you..."

He also lowered his eyes to my hand, looking surprised.

"You want me to pray?"

I shrugged, feeling silly.

"Prayer doesn't always have to be a demonstration of faith. Many times, when I'm anxious or scared, the repetition of the rosary prayers keeps me focused on something other than the thoughts that sabotage me. The difference is that I truly believe in the words I say and have hope that God will hear me and intervene in my troubles."

"You deserve to be heard by God, Luna. I don't."

"Your request is genuine. You want news about your brother. If God doesn't hear you, He'll hear me. Can I pray for Enrico, Alessio?"

He took a moment to respond. He looked at me with those heavenly blue eyes, which seemed more confused than I had expected.

What had I said wrong? For a moment, I thought Alessio would laugh at me or consider me foolish for that suggestion. He wasn't a man of prayer. He was a man of violence. A prince of the mafia.

To my surprise, however, he took the hand that held the rosary, closed it in his larger fist, turned it, and kissed it, which took me aback.

"Thank you, *dolce angelo*. Your prayers will be most welcome. But I need you to teach me. I've never been a religious man."

I nodded, shaking my head, still a bit dazed from the kiss, which only proved I was a silly girl and highly susceptible. How long would it take until I was seduced by Alessio?

It wasn't the kind of thing I should be thinking about while in a chapel, so I closed my eyes and began to pray, both for Enrico, as I promised Alessio, and for myself, that I would be protected from any feelings that could hurt me.

CHAPTER NINE

Alessio

I wasn't a man to believe in miracles, but when my phone rang at the beginning of that night, I became a bit more suspicious. It could have just been a coincidence, but I preferred to nurture my hopes that the sweet girl living with me truly had such a deep connection with God that He heard her without interference on the line.

I had just taken a shower and was still in a towel when I looked at the phone screen and saw Enrico's name. I rushed to answer because I desperately wanted news of my brother.

When I heard his familiar voice on the other end of the line, I placed one hand on my chest, at heart level, sighing in relief. Enrico was alive. Nothing else mattered.

I swore to myself that I wouldn't ask him questions, that I would simply enjoy the fact that my brother would eventually return to me.

"Alessio? *Fratello?*" Even though he was clearly alive, he didn't sound very strong. His voice faltered a bit, sounding rougher than usual, and perhaps he was tired. Probably in pain.

"Rico? *Grazie a Dio!* Are you okay?"

"Now I am."

"Why did you run away from the hospital? We were terrified."

"Because I had a place to go."

"In your condition?"

BOUND BY BETRAYAL

"There's nowhere I could have gone but here." There was a depth in his voice that I had never heard before. It was as if Enrico was trying to express a feeling he had hidden for a long time.

I wanted to ask where "here" was. Where he was. But knowing my brother as I did, I knew this must be yet another of his secrets. One he had no interest in sharing. In the height of my desperation for his whereabouts, I should have the right to question him. I should be able to yell and complain until he finally told me what was happening with his damn life. Despite my impatience and my desire to understand what was going on, I needed to respect Enrico, especially for knowing his ways and who he was.

I loved him, and that should be enough.

"When are you coming home?"

"As soon as I can. I hope you pass the message that I'm alive to our father and the others." He paused.

"I will."

"How is Deanna?"

"Well. Worried about you."

"Tell her too. I'm being well taken care of."

Maybe that was a hint that my brother was accompanied by someone who cared about him. I always had the impression that Enrico was a very lonely man, that the darkness inside him didn't allow him to get close to others, not even me. I hoped that whoever was with him, especially if it was a woman, would help him in his healing process.

"I'll let her know."

And that was the entirety of our conversation. I decided to grant him the benefit of silence and be satisfied with the certainty that one day I would return home and we would understand everything that was happening, the reasons for his mysteries and absences.

As soon as we hung up, I hurriedly got dressed and went to look for Luna. I found her in the kitchen, stirring something very fragrant in a pot.

Even though she was clearly the better cook of the two of us, I also took my chances at the stove. But this time, it was her turn.

I noticed she was making some sauce, probably to accompany pasta. A Bolognese, perhaps. I wasn't going to oppose it in any way.

I approached, positioning myself behind her, and stretched out my arm, dipping a finger into the pot, not caring that the mixture was quite hot. I brought the same finger to my lips, tasting the food.

"Hummm," I murmured, appreciating Luna's culinary skills.

"Alessio! It's hot. You'll burn your tongue."

"I did burn it, but it was worth it. Where did you learn to cook like this?"

"With the sisters. Each of us had our functions in the abbey. Some cleaned, others sewed, others washed and ironed, and I went for the kitchen team. I learned many things from them."

Stubbornly, I repeated the gesture, but this time, instead of putting my finger in my mouth, I brought it to hers, making her taste the sauce she was preparing.

It was meant to be a simple, innocent gesture. But I needed to keep in mind that this girl wasn't an ordinary girl. She wasn't used to dealing with men; no contact was casual. Everything for her could carry a completely different connotation than it did for me.

At first, she simply accepted the gesture and tasted the sauce from my finger, but when she realized what we were doing, she clearly became uncomfortable, and her lovely innocent face flushed.

We stayed silent for a moment, exchanging glances. The way she jumped made me aware of how erotic my action could be. Especially when I looked at her and saw a drop of sauce on her lower lip.

The urge to lick it was so strong that I had to take a step back before I committed a madness.

BOUND BY BETRAYAL

51

But that alone wouldn't be enough, because the girl was still too close for comfort. Changing the subject would be a safer and smarter move.

"Enrico called me."

Luna seemed a bit dazed for a moment longer, but soon entered the topic.

"Ah, that's great!" she started, tucking a strand of hair behind her ear. I hadn't failed to notice that she had been wearing her hair down for the past few days. Long, dark strands waved at the ends, framing her face. She looked beautiful that way. "How is he?"

"Well. It seems someone is taking care of him."

"A girlfriend?" Luna smiled, trying to appear casual as she returned to her pot, but clearly still nervous.

Well, I was too, and it wasn't like me to be intimidated by women like that.

"I can't imagine my brother dating anyone."

"He's a very handsome man, Alessio."

I hadn't expected that comment. To be honest, my reaction was more passionate than I anticipated.

It could have been a ridiculous sense of possessiveness, because the girl was my fiancée—and it didn't matter that this commitment was on shaky ground, considering the war going on between our families—but I didn't want her commenting on my brother's appearance. Still, I didn't want to show any silly jealousy, so I decided to give a provocative smile, half-smirking, while crossing my arms over my chest and raising an eyebrow.

"You think my brother is handsome?"

"I think any woman would. At the same time, he scares me. That dark demeanor, the secrets he must have. I don't like secrets. Just as much as I don't like lies. People who have a lot to hide can never be trustworthy."

"I trust Enrico. With my life."

No matter the subject, the girl had finally smiled. I wanted to consider it a merit of mine, after almost causing trouble.

"You're brothers. It's important to trust each other."

I thought that was an interesting segue to try to discover some things about Luna's connection with her family, so I leaned against the kitchen counter as she continued cooking, adding a bit more oregano to the mixture, hoping my questions wouldn't sound like an interrogation.

"What's your relationship with your brothers like?" To be honest, she didn't seem very shaken by the news that her father would sooner or later end up in Dominic's hands.

Maybe having spent so many years in a convent, she wasn't attached to her relatives. But being so religious, it was to be expected that she believed in all that story of honoring one's father and mother, along with everything else I imagined should be taught in the Bible.

"Normal," she replied without much emotion, but I didn't miss the fact that she shrugged.

"Are you good friends?"

"I've never had a close relationship with any of them, except for Tizziana."

Her answers were short, to the point, and cold. Since I met her, I had noticed that Luna wasn't exactly the sentimental person she might seem at first glance. Probably her upbringing in a convent had made her a bit more rational about some matters.

Be that as it may, it was still my role to try to explore as much information as I could gather, since she was there with me, under my protection.

"Mattia is on our side. On Dominic's side, I mean. At least that's what he says. Do you think we can trust him?" Perhaps I was saying more than I should. Despite this suspicion, I had already participated

BOUND BY BETRAYAL

in enough interrogations to understand that sometimes it's necessary to share information in order to receive it.

Luna was tasting the sauce again, and immediately, when I mentioned her brother's name, she dropped the wooden spoon on the floor. Her eyes widened for a brief moment.

I crouched down to help her, but she was clearly a bit disturbed.

She picked up the spoon and threw it into the sink, turning on the faucet and letting the water pour over it.

"He's my brother and he's against my father?" she asked without looking into my eyes, as if that spoon was much more important than the conversation we were having.

"Yes. If your father is a traitor, it's the right thing to do."

It was yet another attempt. Luna might get hurt again by the way I spoke, but she needed to understand what was happening. It was only a matter of time before her father was captured and ended up in the hands of people who would hurt him. More than that, he would be killed. Without mercy. The question remained which side *she* would also choose.

Luna focused her attention on washing the damn spoon. I knew she was avoiding the topic or trying to buy time. This made me slightly suspicious, but I had to remind myself that she was very innocent and that all this talk of betrayal was far outside her comfort zone.

"If my father is a traitor, it's the right thing to do."

I couldn't help but notice that she repeated exactly the same phrase I had said. With all the commas, but with a completely different tone. Lifeless. As if she was hiding something.

I just needed to find out what it was.

CHAPTER TEN

Alessio

There was a list of strategies to follow to ensure everything went as planned. And we needed to eat. Dominic and I structured how my stay with Luna in that house would go, and we bought the necessary supplies to last us a month. But that time was starting to run out, and I knew we would soon be out of supplies if I didn't take action.

The property we were staying in was located in a remote area of Barrhead, southwest of Glasgow. The distance was about thirteen kilometers, though we were far from the center. Either way, grocery shopping couldn't be done close to where we were. The further I went for a simple market, the safer we would be.

I didn't consider myself a mama's boy, but to be honest, I wasn't exactly the right person to buy fruits and vegetables. I probably also didn't know the best type of coffee or the most nutritious foods, but I needed to handle the task. I could take Luna, but getting her out of the house would be a terrible idea.

I needed to trust my instincts and, preferably, buy things we could stock up on. It wasn't like I couldn't return there, as the distance wasn't that great. Besides, I had no idea how long we would stay in the house. Soon things would resolve themselves, and we could both return to the United States.

Engaged or not.

BOUND BY BETRAYAL

I knew it was only a matter of time before her father was caught by Dominic, and how that would affect our fates? We would only find out when it actually happened.

It felt strange to think about this kind of thing while pushing a shopping cart. Back home in Los Angeles, we had people to do that, but here it was just me. I needed to treat the situation like an important mission too.

I strolled through the aisles, stopping in front of products we might need. It might even be ridiculous to think that at the moment I was alert, I was picking up a large package of toilet paper.

A man needed to go to the bathroom, right?

It could be nothing. It could just be something in my head, but when you live the kind of life I did, I felt like I was being followed. Watched.

But damn... we were in Scotland, far from everything. Besides, no one knew our whereabouts. It would be impossible for someone to find us and have followed me.

Wouldn't it?

The problem was that the damage was already done. My attention was completely focused on the guy who might—or might not—be following me, and I ended up giving up on the shopping, just trying to disguise my unease.

He was wearing a cap, which only added to my impression that he was trying to hide, to camouflage himself.

I needed to focus harder to try to see his face. Which might not help at all, because I didn't know everyone in the Cosa Nostra. Anyone could know new associates and hire them. Maybe it was someone doing a job on the side... The possibilities were endless.

But our eyes met for a moment, and I saw a glimpse of a face I thought was familiar.

I moved to the other side, trying to pretend nothing had happened, positioning myself far enough away to go unnoticed while still having access to see where he was.

Discreetly, I took my phone and dialed Enrico's number, hoping he would answer. It had been two or three days since he called to let me know he was okay, but since then we hadn't spoken again. Not because I hadn't insisted, but also because he hadn't given any more news.

But one thing was pulsing in my head. A piece of information that we process but set aside because it was part of the past, and we swore we wouldn't need it anymore. Enrico would remind me.

Fortunately, I not only heard his voice on the other end of the line, but he also sounded a bit stronger.

"Are you feeling better?" was the first thing I asked because that was, after all, what mattered most.

"Yes. I am." A man of few words. For a long time that irritated me, but I learned to cope with it. After all, I was a talker, and Enrico listened to me patiently. Perhaps he was the only one with that gift.

"Can you help me then?"

"If it's within my reach..."

"That guy we *talked* about three years ago, in Palermo, on our trip there. The one we took to that papà's house in Brancaccio." Famous for being one of the most dangerous neighborhoods in Sicily, it was the perfect place for the kind of conversation I referred to. A kind of dialogue where the other party was forced to talk, you know? In a rather unorthodox way.

"I remember."

"Great. Didn't he have connections with someone in Glasgow?"

There was a silence on the other end of the line, and I suspected it was one of Enrico's ponderings. Being a man of few words, he also avoided speaking without thinking. Which made him a good advisor.

BOUND BY BETRAYAL

Consequently, I believed he would be a good boss when the time came.

And I really hoped that it would take a long time. My father and I might have our differences, but I loved him. I loved him so much that often I pushed myself harder than necessary to prove he could trust me.

"He was with *The Westies*—the Irish mafia, in this case—which put him pretty close to us." "Nothing is impossible, Alessio. Do you think he might be following you?"

"Maybe it's paranoia, but I don't want to neglect it."

Another silence from Enrico. I could only hear his breathing, and at one point, I heard a woman's voice humming in the background of the call. She interrupted mid-phrase, as if she had been cut off, which made me think that my brother really wasn't alone.

That made me smile. Who knows, he might have found someone, and that could soften his iron heart a bit?

"Can you check more closely? That guy had a tattoo on his neck. A spider, if I'm not mistaken. They all did."

I couldn't exactly remember the guy's face, especially since many had passed through my hands. Not that I was proud of it, but it was my job.

"I will try."

"Okay, keep me updated."

I tucked the phone into my pocket and slowly approached, starting to almost be certain it could only be someone sent to watch us. Enrico was right. If Pietro was planning a hit against the Cosa Nostra, what better way to do it than to gather people from other organizations, with promises of future partnerships?

I left the cart parked in one of the aisles and made sure my gun was secured in its holster. It was a Sig Sauer P365, a pocket pistol that I concealed under my shirt and heavy leather jacket. I hated going into a market armed, in a place where families were strolling, but given my position, I couldn't walk around completely defenseless.

I didn't take it out, though. I preferred to wait and not raise any alarms. I continued pretending to look for something specific.

I watched from a distance until I noticed the bastard wearing a scarf around his neck. That only made me more alert.

Was he trying to hide part of himself that could give him away?

This was something I had always observed, especially because my father taught us well. Tattoos, earrings, piercings, and anything that could easily differentiate us from others were dangerous. I already had the curls and refused to cut them. Enrico also wore his hair longer than he should have. But marking my body was something I didn't allow myself to do. I hadn't yet found anything that was worth the risk.

I took a deep breath and realized that after circling several aisles—coincidentally those that ran parallel to the ones I was walking in—he was heading towards the exit while fiddling with a phone.

As subtly as possible, I grabbed my weapon and placed it in my pocket, closer within reach, and walked towards the door, glancing to both sides, trying to blend in.

He seemed to stroll as casually as possible through the nearly empty parking lot. I had preferred to make the short trip to the market at night, because I swore it would be a bit more discreet.

Then I became the hunter, following him until I reached a point where I could approach and grab him from behind, pinning him against a wall, throwing him into it from the front. His face probably hit the concrete because he grunted in pain.

"I... I don't have any money with me, just a card!" he stammered, raising his hands. Without even thinking, sure that I was dealing with the right person, I pulled the gun from my pocket and pressed it against his head. He moaned in fear, which made me a little worried.

BOUND BY BETRAYAL

"Don't play dumb. Was it *The Westies* who sent you here? Are they working with Cipriano?" My voice sounded heavy, severe. If I found out he really was following me, I would need to take another approach.

Would I kill the guy right there or take him somewhere else to extract information? I needed to decide.

"What? What are you talking about?"

His fear seemed genuine, but I couldn't hesitate.

"Answer me. Why were you following me?"

"Me? I wasn't... I have no idea who you are... I just came to shop."

With a swift motion, I yanked the scarf from his neck, tossing it on the ground, searching for the tattoo. There was none, nowhere.

"Sir, please. My kids are in the car with my wife. Just let me go back to them. If you want, I can pull out some cash, but I don't have much. I don't know anything about what you're asking, just for God's sake... don't kill me. I have a family."

That broke me.

I took a step back, immediately releasing him. It could have been a ploy to convince me, but I stepped back, distancing myself from the man as if he could pass some contagious disease onto me.

But it was the opposite. I was the monster who had forever tainted his simple, mundane reality—in the best sense of the word.

He would never forget that night when he had a gun pointed at his head.

"Go," I whispered, still holding the gun, not looking at him, gesturing for him to leave.

The man didn't think twice; he just ran toward a car. I followed him with my eyes and saw that there were indeed two children around the vehicle, running while a woman watched them closely. They looked to be about twelve and ten years old. A boy and a girl.

I had misjudged and cornered a family man.

This was the kind of shit my life forced me to do.

I stood there for a while longer, after putting the gun back where it should never have come from; before finishing my shopping so I wouldn't return home empty-handed.

But I couldn't shake the image of that man from my mind.

I had said I would haunt him for a long time, but I could say the same about him. We would never forget.

CHAPTER ELEVEN

Luna

It was the first time he had left the house. It was the first time I was alone.

Not just since I arrived in Scotland, in the company of the two men from the Cosa Nostra, but... in my life.

It was different from being left in a room or locking myself in a space for privacy. For the first time in my life, I was completely on my own.

I wondered if I was scared or relieved. I had no idea how long Alessio would take to return, but I imagined it would be more than an hour. What could happen in those sixty minutes?

Lost in a desolate place, I should have been terrified, but the feeling of peace was much greater.

It was as if anything I did while alone, as long as it wasn't witnessed by anyone, immediately ceased to be forbidden or a sin.

I imagined that God was always watching everything and everyone, but when I entered Alessio's room, without even knowing why, I decided to push those thoughts aside and focus on my mission: to find any information I could use to understand the reason for my stay in that place.

And no, I wasn't that naïve. Especially after discovering that my father was a traitor, my certainty that I had been made into a pawn grew even stronger.

But hadn't that been my role since I was born? When I was promised in marriage to Alessio himself, wasn't it for a greater good? To become the wife of a Preterotti? And since my father's intention was to betray the Cosa Nostra, wouldn't I be a tool for that plan? Or perhaps I underestimated myself enough not to even consider that possibility.

Since it was an investigation with a noble cause, I figured it wouldn't be a sin, but a matter of survival.

The door was ajar, so I pushed it open as calmly as possible, becoming the clandestine person I truly was, still unaccustomed to the fact that I was never alone. It felt as though Alessio would appear at any moment to catch me in the act.

I didn't know where to start. Should I rummage through his drawers, his wardrobe, even his suitcase, which was on top of the closet? I could grab it and search it, but I wanted to begin with simpler places.

And I didn't have much time, because it had already been half an hour since Alessio left. Thirty minutes in which I pondered what I should or shouldn't do, scared, like the timid girl I knew I was.

I followed from corner to corner of Alessio's room, looking for anything. Any papers, documents, something signed, a recording. A cell phone, a laptop that I could access.

It was probably naive to believe that an experienced man, a ruthless mobster, would be so careless with his secrets.

I also entered the bathroom, but I was already fully aware that my intentions were no longer just to continue my search. When I opened the door, I was drawn in by the scent of a masculine cologne and aftershave, and I was surprised to find it already familiar. The shower was still a bit wet from his bath, and he had left the clothes he wore earlier hanging on a hook, but other than that, it was quite organized.

BOUND BY BETRAYAL

I felt a bit embarrassed by my own behavior, but I picked up the white shirt and held it close to my nose, inhaling.

I took a deep breath, feeling as if it were a hug. The fabric was soft, and it was so masculine that I almost felt dizzy. I closed my eyes, imagining that perfect face, beyond the body I saw when he emerged from the pool, even biting my lip at the thought of what Alessio's touch would feel like.

The kiss.

Would he wrap me in that scent, and would I feel protected in his arms? Or would I be frightened by my body's new reactions?

Lost in those thoughts, I didn't realize that time was passing. I spent a little too long exploring Alessio's room, and when I heard the sound of the door opening and closing with a thud, I panicked and hurried to leave before he arrived and caught me.

I didn't know which would be worse: if he caught me rummaging through his things trying to discover something or if he saw me lost in a trance, clutching his shirt.

I put the piece of clothing back in its place and rushed to exit, leaving the door ajar just as I had found it. I ran downstairs to help him with the shopping, to put things away, and I saw him arriving with several bags in his arms, carrying them as if they weighed nothing.

I had no sense of how long he had taken, but I could see on his face that something was wrong. Just like that day when he was rude.

I began to formulate various theories in my mind, that someone else could have been hurt. Or that my father had been captured by Dominic and was in his hands, but it seemed something more personal.

It felt like a matter Alessio was dealing with himself. Something that had shaken him.

"Alessio..." I wanted to say something, noticing he was troubled to that extent, but I saw him raise his hand, stopping me from speaking.

"Please, *dolce angelo*. I don't want to say something I'll regret later. Not to you."

I hesitated for a moment but nodded, watching him leave all the groceries in the kitchen and walk away, up the stairs, slamming the bedroom door.

The same room I had just left.

It should be a passing outburst that wasn't my concern.

Or maybe it was, but I wouldn't discover it by pressing him to talk. We weren't friends. In fact, I wouldn't even know how to define our connection.

Theoretically, we were promised to each other. There was a chance we would marry. Maybe we would have to spend the rest of our lives together. Yet at that moment, he was little more than a stranger. Someone whose intentions I didn't know.

I organized the products, putting away what needed to go in the fridge and what was for the pantry. There were far fewer things than I had imagined, which gave me the impression he had interrupted the shopping for some reason.

I took the opportunity to clean the kitchen a bit, wiping down the countertop, and when I realized, it was already past nine at night.

Since leaving the convent, I had started going to bed a little later, even while maintaining my habit of waking up before dawn. I wasn't sleepy, though. Perhaps I was still too worried about Alessio's closed expression, curious to know what had happened.

I made myself a sandwich and prepared a juice, leaving a little for him in the fridge in case he woke up later and was hungry. I, on my part, would head to my wall, the one from where I could get the prettiest view and feel the most freedom possible.

BOUND BY BETRAYAL

I thought I would be alone, but it hadn't even been fifteen minutes when Alessio appeared. He still didn't seem well, showing signs of melancholy, but apparently wasn't seeking solitude.

I accepted his company, but also his silence, as for a few moments, he simply didn't say anything, just stood by my side, quiet, looking at the same spot I was, even though there was nothing in front of us but an obsidian sky, sprinkled with golden, shining points.

"I guess I stole your hiding place, didn't I?" he spoke out of nowhere, but without looking at me. He continued to gaze at the same point lost in the sky, with that look of a helpless boy that could enchant anyone.

"I never meant to hide."

"Then why do you come here?"

"It's the closest point to the sky. At least in this house."

He shook his head and lifted it a bit more, as if he had seen something interesting above.

"With your faith, do you think there's something beyond death? That there's really a judgment for good and bad people, so they can't enter heaven?"

"That's a pretty deep question."

"I know."

Still, he didn't withdraw it. He seemed to need the answer almost desperately, as if it would change something in his thoughts.

"I think so. But I believe the concept of good and bad is very subjective. People don't have just one side."

"Some do. You're an angel, aren't you, Luna?"

I was surprised by the comment and even more by the way he looked at me. As if he truly believed what he was saying.

"I'm human, like everyone else."

Little did he know that I had spent some moments before thinking about what it would be like if he touched me. If he had any idea of all the things I had imagined since we started living together, he would understand that the last thing I had left was the purity of before.

He opened a half-smile, almost wicked, mocking, dark. I felt a shiver run down my spine because that reaction was unexpected. It made me realize there was a side of Alessio Preterotti that perhaps very few people knew.

A side he also hid, but if it came to light, it would be very, very dark. It was easy to see that he held many secrets.

"You're not safe with me, Luna. You shouldn't have been left under my care."

He seemed to be rambling, but his statement put me on alert.

What was he talking about? Where was he going with this conversation?

And why, for the first time, did I feel the urge to run from Alessio?

CHAPTER TWELVE

Alessio

I didn't smoke, but at that moment I would gladly accept a cigarette. Or a drink. Something strong, no ice.

My urge, when I got home, was to lock myself in my room and feel miserable for myself. But canceling out and trying to forget what had happened wouldn't change anything. It wouldn't change what I did.

And I had done a lot in my life. Much worse things, in fact, than frightening an unknown man on the street. But definitely cornering a complete innocent and pointing a gun at his face was a novelty on my list.

Somehow, it affected me.

The act of going close to Luna was a ridiculous attempt to feel more connected to something pure. As if being near that girl could protect me from feeling like a complete villain in the story.

I wanted her to say something that would calm my heart. Something that would make me feel better about myself.

The problem was that the spell turned against the sorcerer, and at that moment, I found myself desperate for a kiss.

She looked so beautiful under the starlight, with her hair down and blowing in the gentle breeze that cradled the night, that I found myself gazing at her, a bit foolishly, not knowing what to say.

With that same intention, somewhat clumsy—like I had never felt close to any woman—I reached out, touching a strand of her hair.

Luna jumped slightly, looking at me as if she hadn't expected that contact.

I didn't pull back, however.

"You just said I should stay away... but you're getting closer," she whispered, in a nearly bold move. Still, I could feel her shyness.

There was a restless soul inside Luna, and that was something I started to notice gradually. Although her behavior was that of an innocent girl with very little experience, not just with men, but in life in general, she wanted to rebel. She wasn't the type to swallow what she thought, even though she had probably been stifled her whole life.

"That means that of the two of us, the one who needs to be strong is you," I replied playfully, with a smirk, still toying with a lock of her brown hair between my fingers.

"My little life experience would make me an easy prey for you, don't you think?"

"Why are you saying that?"

She smiled, lowering her head, fidgeting with her fingers, looking at them as if there were something very interesting that deserved her attention.

"Because I know your reputation. I may have lived a long time away from the Cosa Nostra, but I attended events. People talk. You have a gift for seducing women."

"Do you think I could seduce you?"

Maybe I had been too direct in my approach, and it probably wasn't the right night to start thinking about that kind of thing with a girl who had never, at all, been touched by another man, but the truth was that it was exactly the fact that I felt so dark inside that stripped me of my modesty and control not to mess with her.

In any other situation, if she weren't who she was; if she weren't the sweet girl promised to me, virgin, innocent, and completely untouched, I would have already made a first move. She was beautiful and undoubtedly attracted me. If I was behaving as much like a gentleman as I could, it was due to all the circumstances surrounding us being completely out of the ordinary.

"Why are you asking that?" she was startled.

"Because I could strive for it. For real. I would like to try, since maybe we have a future together."

Luna seemed to hesitate. It was the first time we talked about that subject. Not the marriage itself, because neither of us was sure about anything anymore, but about me trying something with her.

If we were really heading to the altar, I didn't want to have a bad life with her. Since she aroused desire in me, and the way she looked at me indicated she wasn't completely indifferent to me, there was a chance that at least we would get along in bed, which would be much more than many couples in the mafia could share.

"And how would that be?" As soon as she finished speaking, the girl seemed to regret it. It wasn't the first time, since we started living together, that I noticed a spark of curiosity in her eyes. Just as I mentioned before, I had already realized that appearances could be deceiving and that she wasn't just the submissive flower they had led me to believe she would be. That woman could still surprise me.

I brought one hand to her face, touching it with my knuckles, fixing my eyes on her mouth.

When it came to women, there was no manual to follow, especially since each of them was completely different. There were those who liked to be swept off their feet, who enjoyed a rougher touch, and others who needed romance. With Luna, I didn't know how to act, but I preferred to take it step by step, discovering her and unraveling her like a mysterious book.

I caressed her cheek with my thumb, then traced it to her mouth very slowly, tilting my head to observe her reactions, not missing a single second, like someone watching a wonderful movie and unable to divert their attention from the screen.

"You really are an angel, aren't you, Luna? *Mio dolce angelo*" my voice sounded hoarse as I lowered it to a whisper.

Luna closed her eyes and allowed herself to be caressed slowly, almost lazily.

"Is this part of the seduction?"

I let out a silly laugh because the way she spoke was adorable.

"No, it's just my opinion."

"It's working..."

I laughed more loudly, bringing our faces closer. So close that I could feel her breath on my face.

I continued to admire her with my gaze and touched her as innocently as possible because I wanted her to feel safe. I wouldn't go further if I sensed she wasn't ready. More than that, I had no intention of taking her virginity until we were married. I would not ruin her, knowing how things worked within the mafia. If our marriage didn't happen, she would need to join someone else, and many men would reject her if she weren't pure.

I thought all of this was foolish. But some clung to those outdated convictions.

I was still smiling, looking at her, until that thought interrupted me.

Luna with another man. Luna being touched by someone who wouldn't treat her as she deserved. Her being hurt on a first time, because the son of a bitch who deflowered her wouldn't be careful or gentle.

Luna becoming someone else's wife.

Many people had told me that the day I met someone who would mess with my head, I would go crazy. That the feeling of falling for a single woman was both frightening and fascinating. I always doubted it, because the option to desire many had never seemed bad to me. I joked that there would always be space for

BOUND BY BETRAYAL

several in my heart, that I would never close the doors, because I also didn't imagine I would need to marry so soon.

Many men I knew were crazy for their women. To a nearly toxic level. Possessiveness was something that always scared me and that I didn't understand, but when the image of Luna in another's arms appeared in my mind, I felt my blood heat up immediately.

"What is it?" she asked perceptively, immediately.

I took a deep breath, fearing I had ruined the moment.

"Nothing, beautiful. I was just thinking if I'll be the first man to kiss you."

Luna's beautifully shaped lips parted in a look of surprise.

"You *want* to kiss me?"

Unconsciously, I ran my tongue over my lower lip, as if savoring each of her words, even more so with her reactions.

"I want to very much." She opened her lovely eyes again, as if surprised. "It's not a surprise, Luna."

"No, because you must say that to many, right?" I didn't have the courage to deny it. This seemed to make her a bit sad, as she lowered her head, avoiding my gaze.

I placed my hand under her chin, lifting it so we could look into each other's eyes.

"Let's do this. I want it to be different with you. I've never strived for a kiss. How about tomorrow I give you some special moments, and at the end of them, you decide if I deserve it or not?"

"Would you do that?"

"A man needs to fight for something worth it, don't you think?"

I noticed Luna's breathing became more rapid in anticipation, and I almost regretted what I had done.

I couldn't be that girl's prince because I wasn't one. Providing illusions in a scenario like the one we were in could be disastrous if things didn't go as planned. I didn't want to hurt her, but going back wasn't possible either.

So, when she agreed and gave me permission to strive for a single kiss, I decided I would take the story as far as it could go.

The ending? It still needed to be written. Happy or not, we would be part of it. This was just the beginning.

CHAPTER THIRTEEN

Luna

No one ever taught me how I should feel on a first date with a man. In fact, I was trained for many things, even living in a convent for much of my life. How to behave at the table, how to appear elegant, how to do my makeup, dress, and groom myself when necessary, without seeming too vulgar or exaggerated.

But there was no manual for controlling my emotions. I was never given lessons on how to ease my anxiety or the pounding of my heart in a moment of expectation like this.

They never did that because theoretically, I was only going to get married. No man would take me on a date; none would try to win me over, because I was already a possession. With much less value than a car or a luxury property that their fortunes could sustain.

Although I didn't have many nice clothes, I kept a dress that I wore to one of the Cosa Nostra parties, and I didn't even know if it still fit me, since I hadn't worn it in about three years.

When I put it on, its lilac color almost seemed strange against my skin tone, as I always dressed in black, gray, or white, which were the permitted colors in the convent. I turned from side to side, trying to see myself in the full-length mirror, analyzing if perhaps the neckline was too deep or if it was just an impression, since I rarely wore anything that left my shoulders bare.

The piece had thin straps and an off-the-shoulder detail with a slight ruffle. The rest of the dress hugged my curves interestingly.

It was probably a bit small, tighter than I would wear under other circumstances, but it was the best I had. The length was okay—not too short and not too long, falling to the middle of my thighs. On my feet, I opted for a flat sandal, as it was the prettiest I had.

I styled my hair as best as I could, washing and drying it, leaving waves at the ends. Makeup wasn't something I carried in my bag, especially since I never wore it while in the convent. Only at the parties I attended during my free time. Tizziana was the one with those things, and she had put an eyeliner and a lipstick in my bag, so I did what I could, but I genuinely felt beautiful, with my eyes a bit darker and a nude tone on my lips.

I took a deep breath before considering myself ready, and even more when I left the room, heading to the dining room where Alessio had arranged to meet me.

When I arrived, I noticed he had also dressed up. With his back to me, I admired him in a well-cut blazer that accentuated his broad shoulders, in a graphite tone. Despite opting for this elegant piece, he wore jeans. On his feet, probably Italian shoes.

I cleared my throat as discreetly as possible, but it was enough for him to notice my presence. He turned to face me, and I saw a smile on his face, but it disappeared the moment he saw me.

At first, I thought I might have done something wrong, but by the way he stared at me, his mouth slightly agape, all my questions were answered. He approved of my appearance, which made my stomach twist with anticipation.

"Where did this dress come from? I've never seen you in anything like it."

"It's the only one I have. I hope it's not too much."

"Too much? Not at all. I just think you look too beautiful for my own good. Maybe I should prepare my heart better for what I'm seeing."

Had Alessio already started the game of seduction? Because, in my opinion, he was already playing his best cards and our date had barely begun.

After taking my hand, he led me out of the house. I was confused for a moment, thinking we were going to have dinner, but I soon saw the table set outside, near the wall where we had talked the night before.

"I wanted to make the decor a bit nicer, but we didn't have many options out here," he explained, although it wasn't necessary.

"It's lovely. Thank you."

As a gentleman, he pulled the chair out for me, and I sat down, truly feeling like I was in a fairy tale. How could it be any different? Alessio really looked like a prince, and I felt like a princess, even if my dress wasn't the most elaborate. Besides, the setting helped, because the house we were in looked more like a castle.

Just thinking about all this made me feel like a very silly girl. It wasn't hard to conclude that Alessio could easily have me in his hands, without much effort. Since the beginning of our conversation the night before, I had no doubt he could kiss me whenever he wanted. Even so, I was anxious to see what he had prepared for me.

He opened the serving dishes, revealing a risotto that smelled wonderfully good. To be honest, I wasn't very hungry, which was probably a result of my nervousness, but I didn't want to be rude, so I allowed him to serve me.

Everything seemed to conspire in my favor, because the food was delicious. There was also wine, but neither of us seemed very interested in drinking too much, as during the meal we sipped slowly from a single glass, taking our time.

Knowing that I went to bed early, Alessio chose a time just before sunset for us to eat. It was unconventional, and perhaps less romantic than he had planned, but it was thoughtful. I couldn't complain about anything.

Up to that point, the topics of conversation had been trivial, mainly Alessio telling me about his childhood and family, basically trying to change my bad impression of Enrico. It was easier that way, especially since he was much better at socializing than I was.

But I knew I would be in the hot seat at some point. Yet of all the topics I thought Alessio might try to bring up with me, discovering my tastes, dreams, and preferences never crossed my mind. When I tried to imagine my conversations with my future husband—if he would even be that—I couldn't conceive a scene where my thoughts would be relevant enough to become the subject of conversation.

"Do you miss the convent?" he asked after a bite of risotto. We were almost finished eating.

"Like anyone would miss the only home they've known," I answered without a trace of doubt.

"Wasn't it lonely?"

"Never. I was always surrounded by people. By those who have known me since childhood. Women who grew up with me, who taught me everything I know."

"And inside, didn't you feel the absence of something? Because it was a world of deprivation, wasn't it?"

"Not really. Considering I never had much to miss..."

"You're a mafia princess, Luna. Your family is one of the richest in the Cosa Nostra."

"But I never enjoyed any of that. My life has always been very simple. Dresses like this one, for example," I pointed to my own outfit "weren't part of my reality. The clothes we received in the convent were always donated or sewn by the nuns themselves."

"And you lived their reality completely?"

"It was a rule in there. No one could have more or less than the others. Even if I'm a mafia princess, in there I was just another girl with the same rights and duties as everyone else."

"A lesson in humility, I imagine."

BOUND BY BETRAYAL

"Yes. But I believe that wasn't my family's intention. Perhaps they wanted to preserve me and keep me innocent."

"I suppose so. Either way, if you really become my wife, you'll have to get used to a different reality," he said seriously, taking a sip of wine. I felt curious, maybe even worried.

"What reality, Alessio?"

"You'll have everything you want. I can give you everything. Dresses, jewelry... the princess life you never had. In fact, if you become a Preterotti, I'll need you to act like one. You'll be the wife of a capo, the daughter-in-law of the boss in Los Angeles. It's an important position."

I forced a smile, almost bitter.

"Since when do women have any importance in the mafia?"

That question seemed to make him uncomfortable, enough for him to shift in his chair.

"I don't agree with that, Luna. I don't want my woman to be an object."

My. Why did that pronoun, spoken with such intensity, send a shiver down my spine, making me wish he was indeed referring to me?

"That's good to hear."

I smiled and took a gentle sip of the wine, hoping to appear casual. I wasn't used to drinking, but on certain occasions I would risk a bit of wine. Never more than half a glass, and it wasn't in this moment that I planned to get drunk.

"Soon we'll have to go back to the United States. We can't stay here much longer. I need to talk to your brother, too."

At that, Alessio swallowed hard. I knew the reason. He was thinking about my father. I hadn't asked until now, but something told me Dominic had already found him.

I didn't want to know. Not tonight. Not whether my father had been captured, nor whether my brother was in charge.

I didn't know which was worse.

CHAPTER FOURTEEN

Alessio

We started the night in a certain mood. Both a little nervous, which was rare for me, trying simple conversations, safe topics, but there we were: in an undeniably magnetic aura.

I hadn't drunk much of the wine, and neither had Luna. It wasn't even necessary. There were smiles, laughter, and even though she still seemed quite shy, she was gradually opening up.

And I felt like a fool for her.

It wasn't uncommon for me to be attracted to a beautiful woman. They came and went in my life every night, filling my bed and giving me pleasure, as if I needed all of that to fill the void that never left me.

Every night I fell for a different person. But the next day that feeling disappeared, and I was ready for a new journey.

With Luna, things were lasting. Maybe the fact that it hadn't been overwhelming since the first time I saw her, that it was being built little by little day by day, felt a bit more genuine. I didn't want to believe my heart had been captured, because that was something that terrified me.

Few things scared me. The idea of wanting just one person for the rest of my life and no one else was a mystery to me. I didn't know if I was ready to embrace it and take the risk.

But I started to ponder that maybe Luna was worth it.

It was the early hours of dusk. The days were ending later; night always arrived late. Under the flames of the setting sun, illuminated by a golden light, the girl embodied the image of an angel that I had associated with her from the first moment.

So beautiful she hardly seemed real. And I was dying to kiss her, but I promised I would make it special.

"Why are you looking at me like that?" she suddenly asked, curious.

That was a simple answer.

"Because you're beautiful, and I'm trying to find a way to keep my promise. But to be honest, I barely know how I'm going to control myself until then."

Once again, the girl was left speechless. It wasn't surprising that she was so taken aback by my responses, especially since she wasn't used to dealing with men, much less someone who courted her, if that word still existed.

I reached out my hand and touched hers across the table, intertwining our fingers.

"Tell me, *sweet angel*... am I close? Do you think I have a chance?"

"Chance for what?"

As I had done the night before, I leaned closer to her, holding her chair and pulling her nearer to mine, positioning her beside me, within reach of my hand. I brought my fingertips to her cheek, touching her gently and reverently.

"To get a kiss."

Luna sighed, seeming flustered by my lack of hesitation. Even though I didn't intend to play with her, seduction was always a game. Most of the time, both parties ended up winners.

I hoped that would be the case here.

Luna ran her tongue over her lower lip, lowering her eyes, shy and sweet as always. It was impossible to think that girl had any connection to her father's betrayal.

BOUND BY BETRAYAL   **81**

"You're not going to hurt me, are you, Alessio?"

"Why would I do that?"

"Just like I heard stories about your brother, they also told me about you; the Don Juan of the Cosa Nostra. A seducer. Why would it be different with me?"

I became very serious, my eyes narrowing, fixed on hers. It wasn't a type of response I was willing to give. Not that she didn't deserve it, but because it was real. My reputation preceded me. I could never deceive someone, pretending to be a saint, especially not that girl. And no matter how much people were reluctant to believe, when I got married, I intended to be faithful.

I just thought I wouldn't be marrying anytime soon.

"I will be your husband, Luna. We have a commitment."

"I don't want you to feel obligated to stay with me, but I know things will be that way, won't they?"

"You'll also be obliged to stay with me."

"It's different. I don't have much to compare. You've had several women; I have no experience. How am I supposed to please you?"

"That's not how it works. There's chemistry, touch, skin. Not always do the most experienced people understand each other. If you allow me, I think we can put it to the test."

She hesitated for a moment, looking at me. At least she didn't look away this time.

"I allow it. I want to discover too."

Her innocent face flushed with that response. She was clearly embarrassed, but she handled it quite well, surprising me. I hadn't expected that kind of personality from the girl who was my fiancée. Since I met her, I had been afraid she would behave like a frightened little creature, but Luna was a contradiction from head to toe.

I stood up, keeping my gaze fixed on her throughout the movement. I reached out my hand to help her stand as well. Luna accepted, and then I took an unexpected step: I squatted down and lifted her into my arms, as if she were a bride, starting to carry her toward the house.

"What are you doing?" she asked, seeming a bit flustered at first.

"I'm giving you romance. I want it to be special."

It was simple. I wasn't trying to act like the seducer everyone said I was. I was just interested in meeting the expectations of that amazing girl who had been placed in my path. If I was going to be the owner of someone's first kiss, I wanted to be remembered sweetly and perfectly.

I even trembled seeing Luna's eyes fixed on mine. I didn't want to confuse things; I didn't want to think she was looking at me in a passionate way, but that was the impression I had at that moment. Just as it was when she wrapped her arms around my shoulders with a smile on her lips.

It was a dreamy smile.

The sun was sending its last rays that evening, sprinkling all the greenery around us with small golden lights. I used my foot to push open the heavy wooden door, which I had left slightly ajar. I entered, walking with the woman in my arms, climbing the stairs and heading to her room.

When we entered, I gently placed her on the ground, slowly, carefully, positioning her in front of me. It could have been a delicate kiss, but I also wanted it to be intense, so I placed my hand on her neck, tangling my fingers in her hair, pulling her toward me as I leaned in to find her lips. There was a significant height difference between us, which made me wrap an arm around her slim waist and lift her off the ground again, to make things easier.

Luna immediately embraced me, and I felt her small body tense against mine. I opened her mouth with my tongue, hoping it wouldn't be a move that scared her. But as much as her innocence was evident, it didn't take long for her to respond.

BOUND BY BETRAYAL

I didn't know how to kiss subtly. I had never needed to, really. I loved to explore lips, to devour, to make love with my mouth. I didn't even think that maybe I should take it slower just because it was her first kiss. I imagined she would want to be swept away too.

However, I didn't expect that *I* would also be swept away, in some way.

Keeping her off the ground, I took Luna to the dresser, gently pushing her to sit on it. Every movement seemed to take her breath away, as the girl gasped constantly, and I needed to remember that this was all a big novelty for her.

With her in that position, I lost all control. The kiss became overwhelming in a way that I could lose my head very quickly. I even grunted against her mouth, holding her tightly in my arms, possessively. I didn't even understand what was happening.

It was supposed to be just a kiss, but when I realized it, all I wanted was to stay there tasting Luna more and more and more.

When we finished, we looked at each other, and all I could think was: what will happen to us from now on?

CHAPTER FIFTEEN

Luna

I didn't want to fall in love. I didn't want Alessio to enter my heart, because even though he insisted on the theory that there was a commitment between us, there still existed a maybe. Nothing was certain, especially with the whole story of my father's betrayal.

But at the moment he pulled away from me and we got lost in meaningful glances, I knew. There was nothing I could do to prevent it. My heart had been given away.

"I don't know what to say," he began, in a deep, husky voice.

"Neither do I. I don't know what kind of thing to say after a kiss," I tried to sound playful, hoping Alessio wouldn't notice how unsettled I was by what had just happened.

"No, that's not it. It's just that it wasn't just any kiss."

"What do you mean?"

"I think that..."

I had no idea what Alessio intended to say, but we were interrupted by the sound of the phone. I was still sitting on the dresser in the room, and we both stood still, taking no action.

"Aren't you going to answer?" I asked, knowing the phone was in his pocket.

"Maybe I don't need to."

"But maybe you do."

I was being foolish, for sure. I should have let him speak, but I wanted to buy some time. I wanted to catch my breath and not feel so vulnerable. I wanted to collect my thoughts.

Alessio seemed a bit disappointed by my response, but he reached into his pocket, nodding, and took out the device. He glanced at the screen, and when he looked back at me, his brow was furrowed.

"It's your brother."

I immediately froze.

"You have his number?"

"Dominic gave it to me recently, after he offered to..." I knew what Alessio was going to say. He was going to mention my father. At least he had the delicacy to change the subject. As long as we didn't speak it aloud, I could continue pretending it wasn't real. "Well, he left it with me in case we needed to keep in touch. Apparently, he passed mine to your brother too."

In seconds, he tapped on the phone's screen and moved a bit further away from me to answer. He gestured for me to wait because he was going to speak in another room.

Of course, they were going to discuss something I couldn't know. Or, more than that, I might say something wrong. As if I were the damsel in distress who needed to scream for her brother's help.

I would never call for Mattia. I would never ask for his help with anything.

I got off the dresser while Alessio remained in the other room, and I could almost hear murmurs of his voice through the walls. I stood still, hands clasped behind my back, restless, as if I were waiting for something I didn't even know what it was.

Then Alessio raised his voice. He cursed something in Italian, looking very displeased. He returned to the room, still speaking on the phone.

"That's not negotiable. She's going to marry *me*.

Not that I knew him very well, but I had the impression that Alessio rarely lost his temper like that. I never imagined I would see him so upset, with such a closed-off expression. His brow furrowed, his jaw clenched... he was pure fury.

"I don't want to know if it was your father who arranged the marriage and he's no longer of your interest. The choice is Luna's."

My heart stopped at that moment. Of course this would happen. Mattia had always been against my father's idea of me marrying Alessio. He always said I could do "better." He had always intended to unite me with a boss or at least a consigliere. Even though Alessio was a prince from Los Angeles, he had always been voted "no" by Mattia, especially because of his behavior.

"I'm not giving her back, then."

Alessio looked at me and finally put the call on speakerphone, signaling for me to remain silent.

The word "give back," however, lingered in my mind, as if I were a piece of merchandise.

"You'll regret this, Preterotti. Especially if you touched my sister. I'll kill you."

Alessio opened a wicked smile that almost frightened me.

"You'll have to catch me first. You won't take her from me. Not to fulfill your plans."

What were the plans, my God? I was starting to feel anxious.

"You'll regret it, Alessio. You don't want me as an enemy..."

"And neither do you. Don't underestimate me, Mattia. None of you know me."

In a clear burst of anger, Alessio hung up the phone, tossing it onto the bed. He remained silent, pacing back and forth, but without including me, without sharing his thoughts with me.

I didn't know what to do. I couldn't decide whether it was better to ask something, to remain silent, or to leave the room and let him be alone. I had witnessed two moments of tension from Alessio, and he had behaved differently in each of them. This time, I thought it best to wait.

"He wants you to marry Horatio Nuttini," was all he said, in a voice that was almost guttural, with his hands on his hips, facing away from me. I could feel his shoulders tense, even beneath his jacket.

The name exploded in my mind like a gunshot. I flinched, bringing my hand to my chest.

"Horatio Nuttini?" I almost shouted. "Alessio! He could be my father!" Or older, since he might be nearly seventy. Sixty-five for sure. "Is that really who you're talking about?"

Horatio was the consigliere of the Pellegrini in Florida. He had recently become a widower from his second marriage. He had about five children, the oldest being at least fifty. The youngest was my age, or even older.

"That's him." I staggered at that information, holding onto the same dresser where I had just been kissed. Noticing my distress, Alessio approached and held me. He placed his hands on my arms, with a bit more force than necessary, but it was clear he was irritated and didn't have much control over his actions. Still, he wasn't hurting me. "You're not going," he asserted with great conviction.

"But my brother is in charge now. My father..."

Alessio's shoulders dropped, and I didn't need much more explanation to understand. My father had been captured, of course. He had fallen into Dominic's hands. I didn't want to imagine the damage.

But I also couldn't pretend I loved him. He had never mistreated me, but as a girl, I had never attracted his attention. He always had other children far more important than me, and even so, none of them were ever loved. They were his soldiers, heirs, and I was just a burden. Someone he would need to protect, who might make a good marriage one day.

I lamented his fate and would pray for his soul, but I felt from the start that it was a lost cause.

"You're not going," he repeated, with an even more feral voice.

I stood still, trying to control my thoughts. What if I really were forced to marry that man, whom I didn't even know and who was so much older than me? Just the thought of having to give my virginity away like that made me regret all the times I had lamented my fate of being promised to Alessio, especially before I knew him.

I started to tremble, terrified, and Alessio held me tightly enough to shake me.

"Are you listening to me, Luna? I'm not going to hand you over to them. We're going to fight one hell of a war together, but you're not marrying anyone but me."

I wanted to believe him; I wanted to surrender when he pulled me into his arms and rested my head on his chest. But could I trust him? From that moment on, Alessio was free from his commitment to me; he could be free to be with any woman or continue his single life, as he always had.

What did he owe me?

What would happen to me if he decided to leave me behind?

I closed my hand around his shirt, sensing one of those feelings. Something wasn't right.

Something very bad was still going to happen.

CHAPTER SIXTEEN

Alessio

I had to shove myself under the shower to try to calm down. Anger bubbled inside me like lava. It felt like something was boiling as I thought about that son of a bitch.

Who did he think he was to negotiate Luna like she was a pawn in some twisted game? How could he even consider the possibility of Luna being handed over as a wife to a man like Horatio Nuttini?

I didn't want to scare the girl, but it wasn't just the fact that he was much older; the problem was that the reasons for the deaths of his two previous wives were unknown. Both had died in suspicious accidents, and he always had multiple mistresses during the marriages, some of whom had simply disappeared.

The man was a monster. If he thought he was going to lay a hand on my *dolce angelo*, he was sorely mistaken.

I returned to the room, got dressed, and went to find Luna. I needed to talk to Dominic and my father, even Enrico, and try to figure out what they thought about all of this. I had to ask them to stand by us or Luna would be in real danger.

I couldn't let that happen.

Despite this urgency, I needed to find her first. When I hugged her, I immediately felt how terrified she was, and I wanted to stay close to her, but I felt like I was about to explode. I wouldn't be able to comfort her, let alone say or do anything worthwhile.

But after clearing my mind, I regretted not sticking around, because I couldn't find her anywhere. Not in her room, nor in the living room, kitchen, or hallways.

I even went to the wall where we talked the night before—it felt like it had happened an eternity ago. I didn't find her there, which soon worried me.

I began walking around the property, but she seemed to have evaporated into the night.

"Luna?" I called, even starting to run, thinking about what I should do if she had left. How would I find her?

I went back inside, climbed the stairs, and headed to her room once more. We could have just missed each other. I didn't need to feel so desperate.

And the truth was that I wasn't just anxious about the possibility of her being out of reach, defying the instructions I had received, or fearing that she might get lost or even run away, although I wanted to believe she no longer felt like a hostage in there. The problem was my concern for her. How much I wanted to find her, because I couldn't bear the thought that *she* might want to disappear.

"Luna?" I raised my voice, calling her more forcefully, hoping she would hear me and respond.

I was about to leave the room again when I realized that, very faintly, I could hear the sound of crying, along with the water that was probably falling from the shower. I stopped mid-step, before exiting, and turned back.

The bathroom door was ajar, and I didn't want to invade her space, but I also didn't want to neglect it if something bad had happened.

"Luna, I'm coming in..." I announced, hoping she wouldn't be embarrassed by my presence.

I only heard another sob, but she didn't respond. I continued entering, step by step, slowly, and realized she wasn't naked, but

BOUND BY BETRAYAL 91

almost. She wore a long, loose white nightgown made of cotton, which the water soaked, drenching her hair, and I could see, through her legs, that the garment had become completely transparent.

She was crouched down, arms wrapped around her knees, hugging herself, sitting on the floor.

I could see her through the glass of the shower, and the way she was curled up like a baby truly frightened me.

"Luna?" I softened my voice, and my eyes filled with compassion as she lifted her head and turned to me, looking frightened, almost like a little creature turned prey.

I opened the shower door, turning off the water because it was splashing everywhere, and knelt down, pained to see her crying like that.

I held her arm, brushing her hair away from her face, looking at her red and swollen eyes.

"My brother hates me, Alessio. He's going to force me to marry that man. I can't... I can't," she barely seemed to have the strength to speak.

I wanted to respond, to say something inspiring to make her feel less afraid, but first I needed to get her out of there.

"Come on, sweetheart. Let's take care of you," I said softly, grabbing a towel and wrapping it around her small body. She was soaking wet, but I didn't care; I just lifted her into my arms, taking her off the floor.

She trembled violently, but clung to me as if I were her lifeline, and I felt myself losing control a bit because I didn't know what to do. I didn't know how to help that girl calm down. As much as my promises came from my heart, that I was willing to protect her and do everything to prevent her from being handed over to that man, I knew that in that moment she wouldn't be able to believe it. Her mind would sabotage her, making her see only the worst of the situation.

I took her to the bedroom and sat her down in the leather armchair in the corner, kneeling in front of her, drying her off. First her hair and then her clothes. I wanted to avoid looking at her because I knew she was practically naked; that the thin fabric was transparent and that every contour of her body was revealed.

I didn't want to think about anything other than how much she needed to be taken care of. Her moment of vulnerability would not be neglected by me.

"Mattia is cruel, Alessio. He's not a good person."

I frowned, surprised by her revelation.

"Why are you saying this?"

She shuddered even more.

"He used to hit me when I was little. He hit all of us."

"Sometimes older brothers..." I was saying that, but as bad as Enrico's training with our father had been, he had never hurt me, never been violent. I knew he had a very dark side, but it had never affected me. Still, I understood that a sibling relationship could be complicated; it wasn't always a fairy tale. Besides, we were all mobsters. None of us were saints.

"No!" she whimpered, raising her hands to stop me from continuing. "That's not it. He enjoyed it. He's a sadist. When he hit me or my sister with a belt, I felt like he was... happy."

I took a deep breath, watching the panic in her eyes.

"He'll want a husband for me who does the same thing." Luna clutched my shirt with her small hands. "Alessio, I need to disappear. You have to help me."

"You're not going to disappear, Luna. We can get married. We're in Scotland. It's easier here."

"I can't do that. I'm a religious woman. I grew up in a convent; I want a decent blessing, a decent place. I want my other brothers near me. Tizziana as my godmother... I want..." She spoke without stopping, gesturing, until she seemed to crumble, and I stood up,

BOUND BY BETRAYAL

93

lifting her from the chair and placing her in my lap, cradled like a child. "I know I'm acting like a fool, Alessio. You're being good to me, and I'm not appreciating your protection."

"No, *dolce angelo*. You are pure. You are good. I respect that. But no matter what happens, I will be by your side. We will fight together."

"You don't have to. You can go on with your life. You're free of me."

I held her face between my hands, pulling it away from my chest, making her look at me.

"I will never be free of you, Luna. Somehow, you're already inside me."

We exchanged glances, and I leaned my lips toward hers, touching her with a soft kiss, just to seal the promise.

We stayed together, sitting there, until Luna seemed to feel a bit better, and I encouraged her to take a shower and change.

The long hours that turned into days were filled with tension because we knew we should have taken a flight back to find her brother and my family.

We exchanged glances at night when my phone started ringing because I simply hadn't shown up, as planned. We had been talking among ourselves, with Luna a bit more lucid after the scare, thinking of ways to bring the Preterotti to our side. Hopefully, Dominic and Giovanni would also back our fight and support me in protecting Luna.

As much as her father was a traitor, she was not to blame.

But I didn't expect, in any way, to receive the news I did.

My brother was getting married. To Sienna Esposito.

The woman everyone thought was dead had not only resurfaced but would become my sister-in-law. The traitor of the Cosa Nostra would return as the princess of Los Angeles, wife of the future boss.

I didn't understand anything anymore, but one way or another, I would need to return. Even if secretly, for a clandestine wedding.

So that's what we would do. We would come out of hiding and reunite with my family.

CHAPTER SEVENTEEN

Luna

Because it was something so unexpected and quick, I had to wear the lilac dress again, as it was the only one I had. Under any circumstance, it wouldn't be ideal for a wedding, especially not between a future boss of the Cosa Nostra and a woman like Sienna Esposito, but given the circumstances and the fact that even the bride hadn't worried about a grand dress, I thought it was fitting.

I had attended few weddings. Deanna Ungaretti's was one of them, and it was completely different, especially since the bride appeared in a vibrant red dress, which shocked everyone. Although I was also very, very surprised, not knowing anything about that woman, my first thought was: I wanted to be like her. Bold, rebellious, and with my own opinions.

Without even realizing it, Deanna, before we had a chance to talk, had flipped a switch in my mind. Even though I still had much of the innocent girl in me and would never be that insubordinate, some kind of determination began to rise within me.

Meeting her in person, even more so. Or rather... both of them. Sienna was an example as well.

I learned a little of her story, how she had been belittled by everyone and had to survive to fight for herself. It was a kind of strength I imagined all women had within them. So I should have mine too.

The three couples looked happy—Dominic and Deanna, Giovanni and Kiara, but especially Enrico and Sienna. It wasn't just joy and passion that they exuded, but some kind of relief; as if that moment was a truce in the number of obstacles they had to overcome to be together.

It wasn't the end, without a doubt, because we knew there was never complete peace in the mafia, but they were together. Probably, for both of them, at that moment, that was what mattered.

She shone. The most beautiful woman I had ever seen in my life. Since I was younger, I had always placed her on a pedestal in terms of appearance. I wanted hair like hers, a body full of curves, that timeless face, and her elegance. All the Cosa Nostra mothers used her as an example of good behavior. Some girls envied her; I admired her.

And Enrico... well... he was Enrico. A man as handsome as he was dark.

I looked at him for a while, trying to find similarities with Alessio, and I saw a few. The eyes were the same, although the ways of looking were completely different.

The younger of the Preterotti brothers smiled easily, oozing charm, and had a slightly more tender way of behaving. Enrico was the embodiment of mysteries. Dressed all in black, even at his wedding, he maintained a rigid posture, never smiled, and seemed to observe everything with the attentiveness of a suspicious watchman. Whenever he touched Sienna, he did so in an extremely protective way, and he seemed to feel the same kind of sentiment toward Deanna.

Underneath the layers, one could understand that this man would be capable of killing and dying for those he loved. The problem was finding lost emotions within his warrior's body, filled with mysteries.

The knight of shadows.

BOUND BY BETRAYAL

And Alessio, to me, was the Fallen Angel. Beautiful as an angel, but with a soul tainted like Lucifer.

Dominic and Giovanni joined them, forming a very powerful quartet.

Of course, I wasn't the only one to notice.

"Quite a group, don't you think?"

I was surprised to realize I was no longer alone. Deanna had positioned herself next to me, a drink in hand.

Deanna didn't have Sienna's classic beauty, but she was stunning. The kind of confident woman who, even if she weren't as beautiful—which she was—would still be sexy and attractive.

"They're handsome men."

"Yes. And they know it." She rolled her eyes. "But they know our worth too. Or we find a way to make them understand it."

I smiled shyly.

"I'm not like you, Deanna. I wish I were. You're inspiring, but my soul is restrained."

She turned to me, very serious, taking a sip of her drink.

"Well, I think that's a load of nonsense. You have everything inside you, girl. You're trapping that soul because you were taught to be this way. Let yourself go just once. Just once. It will be a gift for yourself and will open a door that can never be closed again."

That was what I was afraid of. I chose not to say anything to Deanna, especially when the other women came closer to us, and I felt embarrassed to keep the subject going. But I was terrified at the thought of liking to make my own decisions and not being afraid to be who I wanted to be, yet I still didn't even know who that woman inside me was.

Moreover, in the world of the Cosa Nostra, being bold like Deanna could lead to severe punishments. As much as Dominic scared me a little—just like Enrico did—I had to give him credit for being kind to his wife. Open-minded. Not every woman would have the same luck.

I had witnessed the changes in Olena from the start. She was cheerful, lively, spoke her mind. After she married Mattia, she visibly wilted. He had tamed her, cornered her, and turned her into a quiet, scared wife who demanded strict respect.

None of the women surrounding me that day seemed like that. Not even Kiara, who was a bit sweeter and quieter than Deanna and Sienna. She seemed very at ease with Giovanni; very secure in her marriage. They had left their little boy at home with the nanny, but I knew she was also a happy mother.

That group was an exception to the rule, but I didn't know if I would have the same luck. With Alessio, probably yes. But nothing was certain.

The conversation with my brother was still very recent, and we hadn't even had time to process everything. It took us a few days to understand Sienna's story and to prepare for the trip, but everything was so rushed that we couldn't sit down and talk about what had happened.

We would end up doing that with everyone at the secluded cabin that was Sienna's refuge, after the small ceremony, when we paused to have a meal.

I felt Massimo Preterotti's gaze on me and Sienna. One of us had already become his daughter-in-law; there was nowhere to run. As for me, I was still being scrutinized. From what I could gather, he didn't seem very pleased with Alessio's decision not to hand me over.

"I have two unruly sons," he grumbled, and soon received a sideways glance from Mrs. Cássia, Deanna's mother.

"Be careful what you say, *papà*." Enrico probably didn't mean to threaten him, but it sounded that way. Everything he said had a very dark tone.

BOUND BY BETRAYAL

"No, but it's the truth. My heir decided to marry the most unlikely woman of all. The one who could cause real chaos." After speaking, he turned to Sienna. "Don't take it the wrong way, girl; I believe your story, but things won't be easy."

"No hard feelings," Sienna replied, trying to sound indifferent, but it clearly hurt her.

"I talked a bit with Enrico about this, and although I don't know if it's the best choice to make, I will support you. I'll try to talk to Mattia, because I think that depending on how your marriage is negotiated, he might agree. I can offer you a profitable business partnership and a bit of blackmail, considering your father died a traitor."

I had to hold my breath, as many emotions overwhelmed me upon hearing him speak.

I couldn't pretend it didn't shake me how he spoke of my father. It would always cause me strangeness, but also pain. Just like Sienna, who, no matter how accepted she was—and I hoped she would be, throughout the Cosa Nostra—would always carry that stigma; people would still look at me and whisper about my father.

Not to mention I still needed to come to terms with the idea that he was gone, probably amidst great suffering.

I even shuddered at the thought, controlling the urge to cry.

But aside from that—for which I still needed to allow myself to grieve a little—I could and should focus on the main point of that speech: he was going to support us.

"Are you serious, *papà*?" Alessio asked, looking very pleased.

"Yes, I'm serious, but I need to know if you're really willing to get married. Not just the girl, Alessio, but you too. Know that it will be your choice. Will you be faithful to your wife?"

I froze completely at the question and turned my eyes to Alessio, who also turned to me.

He was an experienced man and had only kissed me. He hadn't even managed to go further than that. How would he swear fidelity to a woman he didn't even know if there was chemistry; if it would work physically?

I knew this would linger in my mind, alongside what Deanna had said.

"Yes. I will be not only faithful but loyal." Alessio extended his hand to me, placing his over mine, sharing a look much more tender than I expected. "We will be happy."

Would it be another promise?

How many more would Alessio make to me, and how many of them would I be able to believe?

CHAPTER EIGHTEEN

Luna

None of us stayed at Enrico and Sienna's cabin because we wanted to give the newlyweds privacy. But Alessio and I also couldn't go to any of the others' houses, as our mission was to remain hidden. So, Enrico arranged for us to have another chalet nearby, renting it for two nights, but it could be extended since Massimo would talk to my family.

First, they needed to resolve Sienna's situation and her reintegration into society, but soon it would be time to decide my future.

I didn't want to think about it, but it was inevitable; especially after the conversations we had.

We were followed by the Preterotti family's security, and one of them was left nearby in case we needed reinforcements, although I knew Alessio was always armed. We parked in front of the location, and I couldn't hide a smile.

Completely different from the opulent and oppressive property where we had been staying, this chalet was the purest representation of romance. Small but comfortable, it smelled of wood and wet grass, and there were sounds of crickets around, making me feel like I was indeed in the middle of nowhere, but in a good way.

"Enrico told me it only has one room, just one bed, but I can manage on the sofa, no problem. It looks pretty comfortable," Alessio said, in a tone of apology, but I just nodded, still looking around while tightening my heavy coat around my dress, feeling the night less warm.

The gray suede piece, with rough and cheap buttons, didn't match at all with the delicate dress I wore underneath, but it warmed my body. And I knew the chill was not just about the temperature of the place, but also about my emotions.

Even though I had been living alone with Alessio for quite a while, the situation was different. One thing was to be with him in a huge house, where we could spend one or more days without even bumping into each other. Another, completely different, was to spend hours in a small, cozy chalet with an almost sensual atmosphere.

But it wasn't just that. I was filled with very dangerous thoughts.

He moved away a bit and took off his black jacket. Underneath, he wore a petrol blue button-up shirt, and I saw him unbuttoning the cuffs, revealing patches of skin. It was a simple gesture, but it seemed sexy and very natural, almost as if we had intimacy.

I couldn't look away. Especially when he crouched down to light the fireplace, stirring the pieces of wood that were already inside.

He had very graceful movements, especially when one of his rebellious curls fell into his eyes and was brushed away with a careless shake of his head.

Alessio was the embodiment of a prince, but with the dark touch that all mafia men seemingly had. How could I resist?

"Alessio?" I called softly, making him turn to me immediately, as if he only needed one word to rush to my aid in any situation.

He stood up, having been crouched by the fire, and approached me.

"Do you need anything?"

Sighing, I thought of what Deanna had told me about giving a single chance to the Luna I wanted to be, not the one I had been trained to become. I just needed a gesture. A phrase. An affirmation.

BOUND BY BETRAYAL 103

"Kiss me," I whispered softly, still very shy. I almost regretted saying it, almost swallowed the words halfway through, but it was an attempt.

I wanted more than just a kiss. I wanted a special night.

I had no idea if Massimo would manage to convince my brother of what we wanted, but if Alessio was to become my husband, that would only be our first time, and he could have more certainty about fighting for me or not. If I married another man—especially Horatio Nuttini—I didn't want to go to his bed a virgin. It didn't matter if he would mistreat me for it or if he would hurt me for not being the pure wife he probably desired. I wanted to at least know pleasure. To experience the feeling of being loved by a man I also desired.

Who knows, with luck, upon discovering I wasn't untouched, that monster might give up wanting me as his wife.

Alessio didn't ask questions; he didn't hesitate. He threw down the tool he had been using to stir the wood and came to me. He held both sides of my coat by the lapels and pulled me closer, but he didn't take my lips immediately. He was building anticipation.

He was an experienced man. A man who knew how to envelop a woman in a haze of seduction; how to ensnare her with a simple look.

Our faces were very close, and the seriousness in his expression, with narrowed eyes, completely dominated me.

"Do you want to be kissed, *dolce angelo*?"

"Y-yes," I responded, feeling my voice falter, stammering but determined to maintain my conviction.

"How?" It could have been on purpose, but Alessio let a slight rasp creep into his voice as he tightened his grip on the heavy fabric of my coat, as if he wanted to pull me closer but was holding back.

"I-I don't know. I don't know much about this."

"I can teach you everything. I'll be a good teacher. But I need you to tell me, Luna: how do you want me to kiss you? Like a gentleman or like the man full of desire that I am for you?"

It was hard to believe he felt that much desire. To me, it was all part of the seduction.

Not that I didn't consider myself a beautiful woman, but the truth was I didn't know what to do; I didn't know how to involve him the same way he was doing with me.

"I can kiss you both ways, and then you'll choose how we'll continue..." He brought his face closer to mine, almost touching my lips. As he spoke, his warm breath intertwined with mine, swirling together and creating what I could swear were little flickers of fire, if only we allowed it. "Is this how you prefer it, Luna?"

I nodded, agreeing, simply because I had no clarity for much more.

Then he didn't say anything more; he just leaned in a little more and joined our mouths in such a gentle, subtle way that it really felt like just the action of a whisper of wind.

There was no tongue this time; it was just an innocent contact, very, very sweet, but I could feel him breathing deeply. Not even what could be called a peck with Alessio was trivial.

He pulled away, quietly, and those deep eyes locked onto mine, with the hint of a sly smile, light and mischievous. A look from someone who knew exactly what he was doing to me.

"I can do better than this."

"I know you can..."

But I didn't know anything at all.

With all my inexperience, I had no idea that kisses could be different from one another. I didn't know that a man didn't have to kiss just with his lips and tongue.

Alessio slipped one hand inside my coat, placing it flat against my back. The other held one of mine, trapping it between us, our fingers intertwined. The way he pulled me closer, fitting me against his body, made me gasp. The way he devoured me, with few words, with no preparation, left me dizzy.

I leaned back as his tongue claimed mine, and we began to find each other in a rhythm that was anything but slow, anything but calm.

There was no calm in that kiss. If, with the first one, I felt swept away, Alessio was marking his territory with me once and for all.

He tore off my coat, throwing it to the floor, and then crouched down, grabbing me by the thighs and lifting me, leaving my legs wrapped around his waist. I was surprised by that movement, but to be honest, anything that happened was new to me. But the way he managed to manipulate my body effortlessly was disconcerting.

I was placed on the dining table, which thankfully looked to be made of sturdy wood, and he stepped back for a moment, bringing two fingers to my chin, holding it firmly.

"Can I go further? I promise we don't have to do anything you don't want. I just want to show you... show you some things."

"Y-you can. Yes, you can." I wasn't completely sure, to be honest. But again, I thought about what Deanna had told me and the missed opportunities.

I wanted to have control over myself, over my body, over who would touch me and when. So I just let myself go...

CHAPTER NINETEEN

Luna

I needed to confess that I was nervous. I became even more so when he pushed my body down, making me lie back on the wooden table, pulling me to the edge and spreading my legs.

He was going to do...?

Oh, God... I knew, in theory, what he was going to do, from the books Tizziana had hidden and showed me. But... what would it feel like? How would it work in practice?

Alessio slowly lifted my dress, making it slide down my thighs, and did the same with my panties, which ended up on the floor. He positioned himself between my legs, placing them on his shoulders, leaving the backs of my knees resting while my feet hung over his back.

I had never, in my entire life, been touched there, right in the middle of my legs. Except for my own hands, in the shower, not even a doctor had seen me like that, so exposed. But the first time someone had access to that part of my body, it was like this. With his tongue on me, licking without any shame.

I couldn't help but let out a moan; a sound completely unknown to me. The tone of pleasure – and the sensation too – was utterly unreal. It was... sublime.

"Luna... Luna... Holy shit...!" Alessio had never sworn in front of me. I wasn't that sensitive, but I didn't expect him to do this, especially the first time we were having more intimate contact.

"Did I do something wrong?" I asked, worried, but I let out another moan when he did something with his tongue, swirling and sucking.

"No, sweetheart. Absolutely nothing wrong."

Then Alessio abruptly pulled me off the table, standing in front of me and tearing my blouse open in a rush. It wasn't the first time I had seen him like this, with his bare chest, but the feeling was the same. I could swear that there was no man more beautiful than him, with more sculpted muscles, or one sexier.

I was probably giving in too quickly, but who could resist? Not even if I had truly become a novice could I close my eyes and say no to him.

He suddenly turned me around, positioning my torso against the table. My butt was raised. I felt embarrassed by the exposure, but curious about what he was going to do.

As he positioned himself behind me, I felt his finger playing at my opening, threatening to enter, but moving side to side along the length of my slit.

"Can I go deep, princess? For now, it will be my finger, but soon it will be me."

I controlled my pride to not faint right there with that voice and the way he held me. I could almost feel the tension surrounding us, as if it were something I could grasp in my hand.

When I nodded, gasping with anticipation, he penetrated me with one finger, slowly, and I felt him playing, twisting it inside me, moving leisurely. He would pull it out and push it back in, as if stocking, until it couldn't go on anymore, and he thrust more forcefully. While he was pleasuring me, he used his other arm to wrap around my shoulders and slipped his hand through the modest neckline of my dress, invading my bra and finding my nipple.

I let out a little squeak of surprise because... What was all this? How was it possible that my body could feel so many things at once? How could parts of me provide such intense emotions?

Something was building up, building up, and I knew, in theory, what it could be. I even knew the name: orgasm. But I never expected it to be *like that*.

My legs could barely support the weight of my body, so much so that Alessio held me up. I had forgotten how to breathe, and everything seemed to explode, filling my eyes with silver dots, racing my heart, and leaving me out of orbit.

I was lifted into Alessio's arms, who carried me to the bed, laying me down there.

He positioned himself next to me, cuddling me against him, asking nothing more. Not demanding that we continue.

But I wanted to.

"Are you going to show me the rest?" Once again, that embarrassment, but I couldn't expect much more from myself, having been raised as I was. I was actually doing quite well at expressing what I wanted.

"Do you want to?"

Once more, I nodded, and he positioned himself over me.

"It's an honor, you know? Knowing that you're choosing me. But I'm afraid you might regret it."

"I won't. I want it to be you. No matter what happens."

It was a clear message. It didn't matter that we wouldn't get married or have a future together. That moment was a salvation for me. If I ever had to marry someone who wouldn't care about my pleasure at all, I would always have those memories to hold onto, that life could be much better.

Understanding what I meant, Alessio slowly took off my dress, admiring me in my lingerie. It wasn't anything sexy, just a simple cotton set, but the cutest I had. That didn't seem to matter to him,

BOUND BY BETRAYAL

who also slowly removed it, looking me up and down as I had never been looked at before.

"Funny that looking at you like this, I can no longer associate you with the image of an angel," he said playfully, trailing his fingers over my body as he looked at me. The expression on his face was pure lust.

"Oh, really?"

"No, beautiful. You are pure sin."

As he said this, he stood up, rummaging in his bag to get what I soon realized was a condom. Then he slowly took off his belt, pants, and underwear, revealing his very hard member and...

Wow. I didn't have much of a sense of size, but from what I could see, he was very large. Bigger than I thought.

I curled up on the bed, a little scared, and Alessio smiled as he put on the condom.

"I'll take care of you. You can relax."

"It hurts, doesn't it?"

"They say so. But it's good, I can swear that."

With the condom in place, he lay down, supporting himself on his hands, taking my mouth in another kiss. While he focused on my mouth, I felt him seeking my entrance, but gently, really with the care he promised.

No man would do it like this. So much so that when he entered, and I felt him opening me, stretching me, and the pain came, I realized I was making the best decision. With anyone else, it would have been torture. With Alessio, it was something that filled me with anticipation.

His kisses and hands, the fingers that twisted my nipples, everything contributed to shifting my focus away from the pain I felt. So much so that gradually, the movements began to cause me more than just discomfort. It felt good.

Suddenly, it became very good.

"You are heaven, Luna. I'm among the stars and the moon here, in your body. I'm floating with you."

It could be just a poetic line from a man who knew how to use words to seduce, but I wanted to believe. I wished to pretend there was nothing bad surrounding us.

So when he also reached his orgasm – which I didn't expect to achieve with my first time – I decided to cling to the illusion that he was mine. That we were just two lovers discovering each other.

I could have nurtured that illusion longer if one of those premonitions hadn't taken over me.

Once again, I knew: sooner or later, something very bad would happen to us. Something I wasn't prepared for.

CHAPTER TWENTY

Alessio

I knew I would find her there.

It had been five days since we returned to Barrhead, our refuge that had become a home for both of us, and Luna seemed very restless, yet at the same time quieter than usual. I could see her hands tangled together, her gaze lost, wandering around the room to any point she thought deserved her attention.

I knew that, even after some time away from the convent, Luna still felt the need to pray every morning and before sleeping—although she did this from anywhere, not necessarily in the chapel. Since we returned from Los Angeles, she had been spending more time in seclusion, praying her rosary and talking to God.

I didn't share her faith. I wasn't as devoted, and often, after seeing everything I had, I questioned the existence of a higher power, because I didn't always believe there was someone looking after us.

Regardless, I respected her moments, but I was still intrigued by the reason for so many prayers. Sometimes I wondered if she felt guilty about us having sex at night, every day, without being married. Maybe that was important to her. But possibly, there was some other reason she didn't want to share.

That morning, she had spent more time than usual hidden in the chapel, behind closed doors, with her candles burning. I was worried because I saw her on her knees, practically fasting, since very early.

112   AMARA HOLT

This time I knew the reason. That night, in a few hours, we would return to the United States—once again—but we could no longer escape the inevitable. We would have to find Mattia to negotiate the marriage.

My father had assured us that he was willing to accept the deal, flexible and interested in the proposals we had to offer.

I had talked to my family earlier and could barely find words to thank them.

"Not that it's not something good for me, Alessio, because we have business in Texas, and this partnership I'm proposing to Mattia will benefit us as well, but we will really open ourselves up to them in Los Angeles. Do you really think it's worth it?"

For Luna? Of course it was worth it. But I decided to control myself and use more valid arguments with my father.

"It's a good marriage. Besides, I don't think I could lay my head on the pillow and think that Luna would be in that madman's hands."

"That's undeniable. He would mistreat her," Enrico corroborated my thoughts, and I looked directly at him, grateful.

My father remained silent, looking at me as if he were analyzing me.

"You're in love, kid. I thought that would never happen."

"I thought so too, Dad."

"Does she know? Have you told her? I don't know her, but she seems like a very innocent girl. That might be important."

I had never said that kind of thing to anyone. I barely knew how to start. Not to mention that, being for Luna, I feared I was rushing things because I didn't truly understand my feelings. One thing was telling my father and brother that my heart had finally been occupied; another, completely different, was confessing to the woman in question and giving her some hope that could be shattered later.

Maybe it was something very scoundrel, but I didn't trust myself and didn't want to disappoint that girl.

"I haven't said anything, but I will. We're getting married, after all. I'll have plenty of time."

Or so I hoped.

The conference had ended a few minutes ago, and I needed to give Luna the good news. At least I believed it was good that we had the certainty that Mattia would give us a chance to talk. That marriage wouldn't be such an impossible condition.

I headed to the chapel, finding her on her knees as always, with her hands clasped, the rosary between her fingers, and her soft voice murmuring the Our Father in Italian.

I approached slowly, carefully, because I didn't want to break her trance. Still, I kissed the top of her head, which startled her.

She raised one hand, asking me to wait, and she finished her prayer, making the sign of the cross and beginning to rise. Having been in that position for hours, I needed to help her, and I saw her wince in pain.

"What are you doing? You barely ate, you haven't left here all day." I lifted her long skirt, finding her knee slightly injured. "Damn it, Luna! Look at this! You're hurt."

"Don't blaspheme in God's presence, Alessio!"

"He'll understand, for sure." I stood up, extending my hand to her, starting to get nervous because I simply didn't understand her thoughts. "Come on. You're not staying here. You can pray from your bed, and the intention will be the same."

"I haven't finished yet."

"You're going to come willingly or not. I'll throw you over my shoulder, and God certainly doesn't need to see this scene."

Luna, compliant and without an alternative, got up, still grimacing in pain, but taking the lead to leave the chapel. She limped a bit, and I was anxious enough to pull her to me and carry her in my arms, which didn't please her much, but seeing her in pain stressed me even more.

I sat her down on the couch and went to grab the first aid kit from the kitchen. I returned to the couch and found her looking at me, a bit surprised by my actions. I didn't want to come across as authoritative or rude, but the truth was that I was also a little nervous about all of this.

Opening the kit, I knelt in front of Luna, lifting her skirt and exposing her knee. She had beautiful legs, naturally toned from the hard work at the convent. They were very pale because they were always hidden under those long, heavy clothes, but I loved kissing and nibbling them during our most intimate moments.

I soaked a cloth with some alcohol, looking at her before using it.

"It's going to sting," I warned.

She smiled in a way that almost unraveled me.

"I know that. I'm not a child. I've hurt myself before."

I ended up smiling too and pressed the cloth against her wound, which made her hiss a little, but she held up well.

Ready to be the wife of a mobster. Strong, brave, and admirable.

Thinking about all that made me want to kiss her wildly, so I lifted myself up and pressed my lips to hers, looking into her eyes like the lovesick fool I was.

What an irony. I had never given my heart away, but when I finally did, it was to the most unlikely, innocent, and unusual girl who had come into my life. My future wife.

"Why did you hurt yourself like this? Is it some kind of penance?" I asked, concerned but truly wanting to know if that was the kind of thing she sought. I didn't know how things worked in the convent; if they had such practices, but I hoped not.

"No. I just... lost track of time. And I didn't want to see it, anyway."

"Why?"

She took a deep breath, and I saw her eyes take on a pleading expression.

"Because I don't want to go back, Alessio. Can't we stay here? Forever? We can find a way to work, to hide in the city. We could go somewhere else, where no one would find us. It would just be us, without the Cosa Nostra dictating our lives." Luna spoke with such desperation and conviction that it was hard to deny her request.

Especially since it wouldn't be the first time that idea had crossed my mind. Whenever I felt belittled or diminished by my father or others who thought I was useless—unaware that behind the scenes, I was the one solving many problems—I wondered if it wouldn't be better to take a different path. I had plenty of money; I could disappear and start a new life anywhere in the world.

When those thoughts crossed my mind, the image I had was of doing it alone, but at that moment, I had Luna.

The idea was tempting, but I couldn't put my father and brother in that situation. It would ultimately fall back on them.

"Sweetheart, we can't. But everything will be fine. We'll go back, talk to your brother, and get married. I'll take care of you, and we'll be happy. What could go wrong?"

I couldn't even convince myself of that story, so when I saw Luna tense and didn't know what to say to comfort her, I decided to do what I knew best: seduce her.

I pulled her to me, laying her on the couch and positioning myself over her, kissing her, hoping that this would make her forget the shit that was happening between us.

CHAPTER TWENTY-ONE

Luna

I didn't expect to be swept away in that moment. I had no idea Alessio would start kissing me, laying me back on the couch. Dazed, I began to respond, especially when his hand started to squeeze my bare thigh, as my skirt, already lifted, had bunched up around my waist, giving him free access.

"Alessio... What...?" I tried to speak between kisses as he nibbled my jaw and moved down my neck. As far as I knew, our flight was that night; we didn't have many hours left until we had to leave.

All our things were already packed, but I still felt a bit confused.

"I'm going to make you forget, *sweet angel*. I'm going to make you come until you pass out from pleasure, and then I'll start all over again. I won't stop giving you pleasure until it's time to go. That way, you'll forget your problems and won't be able to think about anything other than me."

It was a tempting proposition, and why would I say no? I had just knelt before an altar, immersed in my faith, so it felt almost contradictory to have those same knees open with a lustful man between them, kissing me as if the world would end tomorrow.

It was certainly wrong, but I would silence my thoughts and let him use my body, because it was the best we could do to intoxicate our minds.

The couch we were lying on was large and reclined, almost like a bed. Taking advantage of the space, he slipped his arm around my

BOUND BY BETRAYAL 117

waist, spinning me with a quick motion and laying me face down effortlessly, using only the strength of that arm. I gasped, not just from the movement but from the roughness, which I hadn't expected.

Since we made love for the first time, Alessio had always been very gentle and romantic, but I could feel, from the energy we were emitting, that this time would be different. He was going to let loose; I would be surprised by something much more intense.

Once I was on my back, Alessio tore open the buttons of my shirt with a ravenous urgency and also unfastened my bra, exposing pieces of my skin that he took to his mouth and tongue. He even bit my shoulder as he lifted me with one arm, arching my back to rip away the garment and leave my upper body bare.

He had such skill with his hands, arms, and mouth. His experience handling a woman's body was undoubtedly something to consider.

The skirt was torn off next, and he also removed his shirt, leaving only in sweatpants, which I caught a glimpse of over my shoulder as I lay on the couch.

I let out a long, gasping moan when he slid two fingers inside me. I reached out and gripped the arm of the couch with claw-like fingers. I moved my head too, resting my forehead against the seat to breathe a little more freely.

Alessio grabbed one of my buttocks, squeezing it tightly, even giving it a light smack. I gasped, surprised, but not displeased. On the contrary, the feeling that I was doing something different, that I was becoming someone other than the Luna I had always known, made everything even more exciting.

"You know you're mine, don't you, *sweet angel*? From the moment I touched your body and possessed you, no one else... " Alessio gasped, leaning in and whispering in my ear as he stimulated me—"absolutely no one else will do the same. I won't allow it. And you can be sure I'll fight until the end so that no one else lays their hands on what's mine."

It was possession, not love. That's what I understood from the way he spoke. At that moment, it should have mattered a bit more, but I was caught up in the aura of sex and forgot everything else. I could think more about his statement later.

Besides, considering the size of my problem, it didn't matter at all what his motivation was for helping me. Whether we were getting married because he loved me or because he thought he owned me, I just wanted to be saved from the horrific fate they had planned for me.

I screamed when I felt him stimulating me with both hands. One of his fingers began to play with my clitoris, and in an involuntary reaction, I found myself grinding against his hand. I wasn't a lifeless doll while Alessio and I had sex, but I still had my modesty and limitations. He didn't seem to mind, especially because he enjoyed it and always wanted more; he always appeared satisfied. But at that moment, I wanted to feel him too. I wanted more.

Leaning forward again to speak closely in my ear, he paused in his ministrations for a moment.

"I wanted to take you from behind, but I know you're hurt. When you kneel next time, sweetheart, let it be for me."

It was a blasphemy, no doubt, and I would have been outraged, but Alessio was clearly joking. More than that, he took another action that didn't allow me to think.

I was spun around once more, and he lifted me into his arms, intertwining my legs around his waist. He was already without pants too, which made me feel his hard member against me, announcing what was to come.

When I lost my virginity to him, I was scared at the thought of the pain he might cause, but once I discovered how much pleasure he could give me, I trembled with anticipation as my body ignited.

BOUND BY BETRAYAL

"Is it going to be like this?" I asked, half surprised and half scared, as he pressed me against a wall, supporting my body against it. Not in a bad way, definitely.

"It is, sweetheart. I'm going to fuck you like this," Alessio almost growled, and I was swept away by the way his penis entered me like that. He just needed to position me.

I felt even more filled, and the fact that I was suspended in the air seemed to make the sensations much more intense.

"I hope you're really ready, *sweet angel*. I won't stop. Until we leave the house. Once we finish here, I'll take you in the shower. And then in bed. Then we'll go back to the living room."

With that, he thrust for the first time, and I let out a scream, wrapping my arms around his shoulder. Alessio wasn't going to let me fall, but I wanted more and more closeness.

"My God, Luna... you feel amazing. Damn... I can't control myself."

"Don't control yourself."

With my consent, he brought one hand to my breast, practically squeezing it in his palm in a rough way that made me gasp. When he twisted my nipple between his fingers, I had to lean my head on his shoulder, muffling my moans against his skin, knowing that my orgasm was approaching.

My whole body tightened, and he held me more firmly, thrusting harder, growling as he prepared to come as well.

We reached climax almost together, and as soon as we recovered, still joined, Alessio whispered in my ear:

"Get ready for more. I won't stop... I won't."

And so it went, until we had to leave.

Alessio truly managed to calm my anxiety, and I lost myself in his arms for hours, surrendering and belonging to him more and more.

CHAPTER TWENTY-TWO

Alessio

Luna spent most of the flight sleeping, after I had exhausted her with rounds of sex. Smiling, I looked at her as we were about to land, before waking her up.

I brushed a strand of hair from her face, watching her and thinking about how it was possible that I was so wrapped up, so in love with this girl? And until then, we hadn't talked about it.

She knew I desired her, that I wanted to marry her, but we hadn't really spoken about our feelings. Most of the time, I considered myself very arrogant for believing that she was in love with me too, since she had given me her virginity. But that didn't mean anything, right? She was a woman with her own desires and was discovering life after years of confinement. Her freedom of choice needed to be taken into account.

Having her like that, all curled up in the airplane seats, reminded me of our first trip when I took her from the convent and brought her to Scotland. The difference was that our closeness was completely different. Her head rested in my lap, and I was stroking her hair. Not to mention that it was my jacket serving as a blanket for her.

I gently woke her up, and we prepared for landing.

We wouldn't have much time for anything because we were delayed, so we would only take our things to my father's house after the conversation with Mattia. I knew Luna was terrified at the possibility of her brother wanting to take her away from me immediately, whisking her off to a hotel or wherever they were staying.

We would already be starting a fight with that, but if everything went wrong, I already had in mind that my course of action would be to grab Luna and take her far away from there. I would kidnap her and hide her with me, whether in Scotland or the far corners of the world, but I wouldn't let her be thrown into a violent marriage with a monster like that.

We got into the car, recognizing one of my father's men who had come to pick us up. He helped us with our bags, and I sat next to Luna in the back seat, taking her hand and holding it, hoping she understood that we were united, no matter what would happen.

"Everything will be fine," I said in a low voice, not sure if I was affirming it for myself or for her.

"I don't know, Alessio. Something feels wrong," she replied without looking at me, placing a hand on her chest as if trying to soothe her own heart.

"What do you mean?"

"It's a feeling. I always have these kinds of feelings, you know?"

I reached out and placed my hand on her face, turning it toward me so she would look at me.

"Don't torture yourself like that. We have advantages on our side. There's no reason for Mattia not to want us together. It will be beneficial for him."

"I know. Still... something feels wrong," she repeated, turning her eyes away from me again. It would be impossible to convince her otherwise, considering how nervous she was.

The only thing I could do was try to comfort her, so I pulled her to me and rested her head on my shoulder, staying that way for the rest of the ride in silence. What could I say? Her somber tone worried me a little, no matter how skeptical I was about these feelings and intuitions.

The agreed-upon location was a restaurant in New York: neither in his territory nor ours. Plus, we would have Dominic as an ally, which was a significant strength.

When we entered, still holding hands, I noticed that everyone was impatient. My father, especially. He probably thought I wouldn't show up, as I had done last time. No doubt, feeling the tension in the air, that was my instinct. Or just to flee from there and never return. Exactly how I had planned to do if things didn't go the way they hoped; I would grab Luna and disappear.

But it was my duty to be there, to introduce myself to her guardian and show my intentions. What would happen next was up to fate.

At the moment everyone stood up, Luna clung to me tighter, and I tried to exude confidence for her, even though I wasn't exactly a picture of security.

"We're here," I said confidently, looking at my brother, who was, as always, very serious.

Despite everything, I trusted Enrico. He wouldn't let me down. If he was there, beside our father, and had promised me that everything would be okay, I knew he wouldn't allow any surprises to occur.

Mattia Cipriano flashed a smile that made me furrow my brow. It wasn't a kind or natural expression. It was a twisted kind of smile that made me understand why Luna was so reticent with him.

When he kissed the top of her head, I wrapped my arm around her shoulders in a protective gesture.

"We understand your interest in marrying my sister, is that correct?" he asked, completely ignoring Luna's reaction to his kiss.

"Where are your other brothers? As far as I know, the decision should involve everyone, right?" I inquired firmly, since Luna seemed much closer to the other two than to Mattia. They could help us if my father's and Enrico's opinions weren't enough.

"My brothers have nothing to do with this."

It was with that answer that I started to feel a bit tense. It was then I realized that things wouldn't be so simple and that Luna's feeling was indeed correct.

"Of course they do. If it's Luna's wedding and your father is no longer alive, everyone can have a say. Including her," I tried again, but I looked at my father, and he gave me a look, as if he didn't want me to continue speaking.

"Only *I* am interested in this. Neither Lorenzo nor Giulio want anything to do with it. And Tizziana is just a child."

"Shall we shorten the conversation?" *Dad* interrupted, clearly fearing that I would say something else stupid. "It doesn't matter who resolves this matter, as long as it gets resolved. We trust that your family is still worth considering, because it was mutually agreed upon among members of the Cosa Nostra that your act of turning in your father was honorable enough to give you a chance."

Mattia smiled.

"If my family has a stain on its reputation, yours does too. Just look at who your son is marrying." Of course, his intention was to provoke Enrico, but I knew my brother well enough to know that this kind of thing didn't affect him.

"Why do you think I should agree to this marriage? Don't you think my sister is worth more than a union with a clueless boy who contributes nothing and can't see past a skirt?"

I stepped forward in a protective manner, leaving Luna behind me.

"I'm willing to be a good husband for her. That should be enough," I said angrily, and once again received a furious look from my father.

"They are in love, Mattia. I don't think it's wrong to have a marriage that isn't just about power interests."

Another chuckle from Mattia, and I continued to feel that dark atmosphere around us.

"You say that because your daughter married one of the most powerful men in the Cosa Nostra."

"And another died for it."

"Don't you think some people die in the name of a greater cause? Tonight, for example... We came to discuss a marriage, but things can't always be as we wish, can they?"

I couldn't foresee the next moves. If I could, I would have stopped it. I would have jumped on the bastard and spared my father.

Mattia pulled a revolver from inside his vest, aimed it at my father's forehead, and simply pulled the trigger.

Just like that. As if the life of the Los Angeles mob boss meant nothing. As if it were simple.

Damn... if I could control time, I would go back and make different decisions. About everything.

When you die, people say you see your life flash before your eyes in four seconds. All the events, especially the most significant ones, but at that moment I had a glimpse of my entire existence as I watched my father's eyes widen, and he stood there for a fraction of a second, absorbing the impact of the bullet.

I started to think: what if I had been a better son? What if I had tried harder to be the man he always wanted me to be? If I had trained like Enrico, to give him more pride?

What if I hadn't insisted that this moment happen?

If I hadn't fallen in love with Luna, all I would have done was accept the new directives and take another woman as my wife.

My father's life was the price for all my rebellion. Something built over years and years, and I would never be able to shake the guilt from my shoulders.

BOUND BY BETRAYAL

I needed to act, to run to hold him or to retaliate and also kill the bastard, but I just watched him fall, as if I couldn't believe it could be true. That that bullet had really taken his life.

When he started to tumble to the ground, things became more real.

"Dad!" a scream escaped my throat before I even realized it. I ran toward him, not even thinking that Luna was still there, standing, scared and vulnerable.

I managed to catch him in my arms, with that strange impression that he would get hurt if he hit his head on the floor, but he was already dead.

"Dad!" my voice came out choked, amidst sobs, in a tone I could barely recognize.

I couldn't distinguish anything else around me. I heard Mattia's voice coming from somewhere, but I had no idea what he was saying, because it didn't matter.

Nothing else mattered.

My father lay dead in my arms. His blood began to stain everything around, trickling down his face, and I didn't even want to think about how grotesque the scene was. I heard another gunshot, and I wanted to move to protect Luna, but I couldn't.

I couldn't. It was as if that bullet had hit me too, but instead of killing me, it had taken my soul away, leaving me with a lifeless body I couldn't control.

The only thing I managed to do was lift my head and look at my brother, without really being able to see him.

"Enrico! Our father! What have I done? It's my fault! If I hadn't insisted on all this... If not... If I hadn't...

I managed to swallow my own words, because I was about to blame my feelings for Luna for the loss, and I knew that would hurt her, destroy her.

How would we recover from this?

How *would I* get over it? What would things be like from now on?

How...?

CHAPTER TWENTY-THREE

Luna

It felt like my chest had exploded. Not only from the sound of the gunshot that burst my eardrums and made my ear ring, but also because of how unexpected my brother's action was.

Or better... who was I trying to fool? Of course I knew Mattia was capable of killing someone in cold blood. But like that? In the middle of an official assembly, with soldiers and bosses gathered?

To kill an important man like Massimo Preterotti?

My God... what would that mean for our family?

I could still hear the echoes of the shot in my memory when Mattia passed by me. For a moment, I swore he would grab me and take me with him, but of course I wasn't important to him. His intent in that chaos and his insistence on the marriage story was merely a ploy to gain access to the Preterottis.

I didn't need to be a genius to understand that, but in the midst of the daze caused by the confusion, I started to wonder: how did I not deduce this earlier?

My relevance to the family had always been nearly zero, but to my older brother? He ignored me as if I were a fly he could swat away. He hated me for being a woman, just as he hated Tizziana and even his ex-wife.

I could only look at Alessio, sprawled on the floor, holding our father as if he could transmit a bit of life to him. He shouted his brother's name and began to cry. That shattered my heart.

And there was that unfinished sentence he had uttered, but I understood its meaning. Somehow, he blamed our history for their father's death. It was my brother who had killed him. That would always linger between us. It would be a stain on our relationship.

The scene was horrifying. Knowing who caused it, that it was blood of my blood, left me dazed. I tried to feel the air, searching for some solid surface to hold onto, but found nothing. My legs could no longer support me, but a firm hand grabbed my arm, steadying me.

I looked to the side, and the shadowy figure of Enrico was what I saw.

"I'm going to get you out of here, okay?" a velvety voice said. I was afraid of that man, because of all the stories I had heard in my life; that's why I didn't move when he tried to pull me somewhere.

"Alessio... he..."

"I'll go back to him. And to my father. I promise."

It didn't matter what he promised, I felt completely out of myself. So much so that I stumbled again and felt myself being lifted from the ground, before I simply let myself be taken by darkness, not caring about anything anymore, knowing I would be taken somewhere but having no idea where.

I woke up sometime later, lying on a bed, and the first face I saw was Deanna's. Then Sienna approached as well, and they treated me like a child in need of care. They helped me take a shower, change clothes, and practically forced me to eat.

I felt useless, a coward, but what they always repeated was that I had seen more than anyone should see, not to mention that I had always been very sheltered from reality, which only aggravated the situation.

I didn't agree. If it had been any of them, they would have shown their strength. They would have rebelled and demanded to see Alessio. He needed me too.

But they barely let me leave the room. I didn't know what was happening. I didn't know how he was, what he thought after my brother killed his father. This was one of the reasons I felt so anguished.

I didn't know anything. It was like walking aimlessly, with a blindfold over my eyes, not knowing if there was or wasn't a cliff in front of me.

The first time I saw him was at the funeral, which took place two days after Massimo's death. Deanna lent me one of her elegant, but discreet, black dresses because all the clothes I had brought from the convent were torn and patched. The ones that weren't, weren't suitable for the funeral of someone so important.

They fixed my hair and helped me with light makeup, but I didn't want to hear any of it. I didn't even want to look in the mirror.

Why would I want to look pretty? Why would I want to beautify myself when everything around me was crumbling?

I walked arm in arm with both of them after we got out of the car. I had asked about Alessio several times, frightened that we hadn't seen each other for days, that he hadn't spoken to me until that moment.

When I saw him, I understood.

I didn't know him that well. We had spent two months together, living daily together. Months during which my feelings for him had grown, until I realized I was in love with the man I had been promised to.

And that love had developed as I realized that Alessio was much more than just the Don Juan of the Cosa Nostra, who couldn't see a pretty face and had no future. He was a man with layers, with a heart that had been preserved as much as possible, even amidst the dark life he led. He was fiercely loyal and protective.

With just one look, I understood that much of the sweet boy I had known had been lost in an instant. The moment his father died in his arms, Alessio embraced a melancholy that had never belonged to him. Next to Enrico, it was hard to tell which of the two seemed darker.

Because he felt guilt. And one of the reasons for that was me.

His always rebellious curls were tamed, slicked back, and held with some kind of gel. The stubble that usually shadowed his face was gone, and his skin was smooth like a boy's.

He remained devastatingly handsome, but he no longer looked like my fallen angel. He looked like a mobster.

Which he, in fact, was.

Perhaps the image I had created in my mind was just an illusion. This was the true Alessio Preterotti.

Next to him, practically supported by one of the soldiers, was a middle-aged woman who looked a lot like Deanna. As she quickly moved to her side, leaving me with Sienna, I suspected it was his mother.

Sienna confirmed this shortly after.

"They seemed to be getting along again, from what I saw," she whispered to me. "What a shame. She's an amazing woman. I think she would have softened Massimo's heart."

I nodded, understanding her words but not paying much attention. I felt sorry for Deanna's mother, but at that moment, I couldn't focus on anything but Alessio and the way he moved, his brow furrowed and his expression filled with bitterness.

It didn't seem to be a feeling he directed at anyone, but at the universe. At life itself. At fate.

Everyone fell completely silent for a moment, and I decided to approach. I didn't know if it was the wisest choice, but I needed him to say something. Anything. I wanted to know if he would push me away, if he would tell me it was all okay, or if he would just treat me with indifference.

I could handle all of that. Not knowing was far too agonizing.

I barely had time to say anything because I understood the reason for the silence: the arrival of someone.

My brothers, Lorenzo and Giulio.

It was a matter of seconds, because I felt Alessio's hand on my arm, pulling me forcefully behind him, as if he wanted to serve as a shield. Not just him, but several others—everyone was Preterotti soldiers—pointed their guns at the two. My brothers' men did the same.

A chaos formed as revolvers were drawn and aimed. If everyone fired, people on both sides would die.

"Give me a reason not to shoot you in the head like your brother did to my father."

It wasn't Alessio's voice. It was as if he had been possessed. As if another man were standing in his place. Someone violent, filled with hatred and bitterness.

Lorenzo raised his hands in surrender. He was young, far too young to be in that position. He probably wasn't prepared, as it had always been expected that Mattia would take charge.

"I come in peace. I'm sorry for what happened to your father."

"Your brother happened."

"I know!" I could see Lorenzo still trying to stay calm, but Alessio was ready for anything. The hand that held me gripped my skin tightly, almost to the point of pain, but he certainly didn't realize it. "Luna will confirm what I'm saying: we were never friends with Mattia. We would never side with him in a situation like this."

"DON'T PUT LUNA IN THE MIDDLE OF THIS!" Alessio shouted even more furiously, and I flinched.

But I was in the middle, wasn't I? One way or another, I would always be involved in this story.

"Fratello..." Enrico said in a reproachful tone. "Don't go too far."

"Alessio..." Giulio also spoke. He was even younger than my older brother, but he had always been more determined. "We'll fight alongside you. What do we need to do to make you believe this? We're willing to do anything."

Alessio and Enrico exchanged glances, and somehow, when they both turned to me, I knew I would once again be in the middle of the situation.

"Leave Luna with us," was Alessio's response.

"So she can be a pawn? You said you didn't want to involve her," Lorenzo tried to argue again, but Alessio adjusted the gun in his hand, and my brother raised his arms once more. "Promise you won't hurt her? Mattia might not care about her, but I do. I can agree to this because I know you two care for each other."

"I would never hurt her," Alessio asserted, and I believed him.

I believed he meant not only that he wouldn't physically harm me but that he would also take care of my feelings.

Maybe all of this was just an illusion, but at that moment, I truly believed it.

CHAPTER TWENTY-FOUR

Alessio

It was as if all my thoughts and memories had turned into a black-and-white film. I could no longer see life in color. I couldn't feel any illusion that things could be fixed.

I couldn't believe it could be fixed. It was like a broken object whose use had to be adapted so it wouldn't be discarded.

I had spent my whole life with a single purpose: to please my father. To be the son he always dreamed I would be. Worthy of the heir he needed.

To me, Massimo Preterotti was invincible. The most powerful man I knew and someone I wanted to emulate, even though I never found a way within my own nature to occupy the space the mafia required of me.

Every family has its black sheep, and I tried to play that role, pretending that everything was fine. With smiles, with lightness, even though inside I knew it was just feeding the spark for everything to explode.

And it exploded.

The guilt weighed so heavily that I couldn't see anything else, much less the truth before my eyes. At that moment, all I could comprehend was that I had killed my father. It wasn't my finger that pulled the trigger, but my recklessness, my desire to do everything I shouldn't. To transgress.

I wasn't a free guy who could use his rebellion as charm. I was a man with responsibilities. A man with a family and a name to uphold.

I needed to become that man.

Thinking about all this, I took a sip of the drink I had in my hand, sitting in his office.

Everything there reminded me of my father. The quality wood of the furniture, the sideboard full of his favorite whiskeys. The documents. Our photographs, including one of Deanna at her wedding, showcasing the controversial red dress.

He was an unyielding boss. He ruled his city with an iron fist, but deep down, he loved us. He had made mistakes but knew how to be just.

He was my father. My example. The man I loved most in the world.

I swallowed hard, holding back tears. There was no room for tears anymore. Only for revenge. Mattia Cipriano had to pay.

I heard the door creak open, announcing someone's entrance. There was only one person who could come in that way, without knocking, because he was the new owner of the space. I was just an intruder.

"I figured I'd find you here," Enrico said, approaching and standing next to me. I was literally sprawled on the leather couch in the office, my legs spread, still in the same suit I wore at the funeral, but without the tie and with two buttons of my shirt undone.

"I can leave if you need privacy," I said, my voice bitter.

"I would never ask that. This house is yours too."

"You're the boss now, Enrico. You can order me around as you please." That was me acting like a jerk. I knew my brother well enough to know that things wouldn't work that way with him, but I felt so exhausted and out of it that thinking about what I was saying wasn't an option.

BOUND BY BETRAYAL

"That's one thing I would never ask. To be the boss."

I was surprised by that statement but tried not to show it. I just shifted in my seat and took another gulp of my drink.

"You were trained for this your whole life."

"A training that destroyed me. Besides, I imagined I would take over many years later. When our father was too old for it."

My response was silence, but I was clearly uncomfortable, as my jaw clenched and I gripped the arm of the couch a little harder.

"I need you to understand that none of this was your fault," he asserted.

"But it was. It was with Luna's brother that we were negotiating. My insistence for that meeting was mine. I wanted, once again, to complicate things, as I always did."

"And I didn't complicate things too, *fratello*? I married the woman they considered the traitor of the Cosa Nostra. Do you know what could have happened if they hadn't believed in her? Many people would have died. But I did what I thought was right, and your motives are noble too."

I just grumbled in response and got up, ready to pour myself another drink.

When I turned my back, I heard my brother's voice asking the question I feared most.

"Do you love her?"

Of course, he was talking about Luna.

It wouldn't be a simple question even if the situation were normal, but after what had happened? I didn't even know how to deal with the girl.

"It doesn't matter what I feel. It's as if we're both cursed. Her father kidnapped my two brothers, and my brother-in-law killed him. Her brother killed my father. Do you understand that?" I asserted, impatiently. "I will fulfill my promise. I will marry her, especially because I imagine I would be cast aside if I didn't do it, but I won't be able to be the man she wants. I think..."

A sound manifested outside the office, as if someone had bumped into something. Enrico and I looked toward the noise, but I didn't even need to see to know who it was.

Of course, it was Luna. Of course, she would hear those things I said about marrying her out of obligation.

Because, apparently, things between us had the power to be destroyed in just a few seconds. It was as if our relationship were a sandcastle. We worked hard to build it again, but the sea kept coming and washing it away.

The door was ajar, so I could see her standing outside, still wearing her black dress. It was hard not to notice how beautiful it looked on her, almost as beautiful as the lilac dress she wore the night we kissed for the first time. It was definitely Deanna's, but it fit reasonably well because both of them were small and slender.

It was always stunning to see her in clothes that weren't the horrible ones she had brought from the convent. I hadn't had many experiences like that, since she only had those, but Luna was a very beautiful woman. Completely unaware of her beauty, which made her even more attractive.

The problem was that no matter how beautiful she was, and how much my heart still raced for her, my subconscious began to scream that it was wrong. Loving that girl was the same as ignoring the fact that my father had died at the hands of someone who was her blood.

Despite that, when she ran away with a hurt expression on her face, I slammed my fist on the table because it wasn't how things should be.

I lowered my head, taking a deep breath. What the hell was happening? Why did everything suddenly seem to have turned into a massive chaos?

What was I going to do? I felt completely lost...

BOUND BY BETRAYAL

"You should go talk to her," Enrico stated, his voice deep and serious.

I shot a look at him and saw him with his hands in his pockets, looking at me with a look of complacency.

I stood there, watching him, hoping to find the strength to be like him. He was certainly suffering for our father too, even though I knew he harbored some resentment for the past, for what he had lived through during his training—truths I was unaware of. Even so, he remained steadfast, like the powerful man he was. Someone to be followed and admired.

"Give me a few minutes. I'll go, but I need..." I took a deep breath, not knowing exactly what to say.

In truth, I needed many things. Surrendering to my sadness was one of them. So when Enrico approached, placing his hand on my shoulder and pulling me into an embrace I didn't expect—considering *who* he was and how he rarely showed his feelings—I allowed myself to crumble, falling into tears like a child crying for its early loss.

It would only be for a few minutes.

And then I would return to being the man I needed to be from that moment on.

Just a few more minutes...

CHAPTER TWENTY-FIVE

Luna

I wanted to disappear from that house. Why should I insist on staying there when my presence wasn't welcome? When they looked at me, they undoubtedly saw my brother and the way he shot Mr. Preterotti.

I couldn't get the scene out of my head. I would never be able to.

I was still running, descending the stairs as if someone were chasing me, until I heard a voice call out to me.

"Luna? Where are you going?" I glanced back and saw Deanna following me. It was only because of her that I stopped. When I turned toward her, she must have seen my puffy eyes because they widened. "I know this is a stupid question given the circumstances, but what just happened? What did they do to you?"

"It was nothing, I just..."

"What the hell do you mean, nothing? What did my brother do to you?"

I held my breath because I hadn't expected her to blame Alessio right off the bat.

"Don't look at me like that. Men are always to blame."

I almost laughed at the way she said it, but I ended up crying even more. This made her come closer and put her arm around my shoulders, guiding me back to the stairs.

"Come on, dear. Let's talk."

BOUND BY BETRAYAL

I ended up allowing her to lead me because I didn't even know where I could go. My brothers were in town, and maybe they would take me in, but I had to admit they hadn't pushed that hard to get me away from Alessio. Of course, the price of the agreement would be much higher if they didn't agree to the Preterotti's terms, but...

Yeah, I was dramatizing everything more than I should.

When I reached the room where I was staying in that house, Sienna was there too. I felt like I did before, like when the two of them took care of me: welcomed, even though we weren't friends.

They were two incredible, strong women, and I felt lucky to have them there, giving me the support I knew I wouldn't have if it weren't for them.

A support I always found at the convent.

"We're not going to ask you to talk about what happened, but know that whatever it is, we'll be by your side," Deanna stated, and Sienna nodded.

"He's your brother." I looked at the redhead. "And your brother-in-law."

"It doesn't matter. You're much more of a victim than he is. We all are, in this world we live in. Deanna and I were lucky to have better men than we could have had. Still, we suffer the consequences."

I lowered my head, thoughtful. They were right. It didn't matter how much better our fates were than most. There would still be stigma for being women. We hadn't chosen to be what we were, but many saw us as inferior, as burdens.

"It's not Alessio's fault, but my brother's. You should hate me, Deanna..."

"Why, Luna? Did you pull the trigger?" I fell silent because the answer to that question was no, which still didn't absolve me of the guilt. "I'm sad for my dad, but we didn't have much time together. Just because he's dead doesn't mean I'll consider him a saint and..."

"Dee!" Sienna gently and delicately reprimanded, and Deanna rolled her eyes.

"It's not that. I loved him, but he wasn't so nice to me. He got lucky because Dominic and I fell in love."

I knew the story of Dominic and Deanna. She had been kidnapped by her father to marry him. Apparently, everything had ended well, but I couldn't even imagine how that worked out, given that both were extremely stubborn people.

"What Alessio said is real. It feels like we're cursed."

"Luna..." Sienna placed her hands on my arms, and I looked at her, at that impeccably beautiful face, waiting to hear what she might say. "I fell in love with Enrico when I was nothing more than a girl. My brother didn't allow us to be together. We went through a lot before we reunited. If he and I could make it, you and Alessio will overcome."

"I'm not as strong as you. And I know he thinks that too. He thinks he needs to marry me because I can't stand on my own."

"I don't think that..." a familiar voice interrupted me.

Or rather, it was a familiar tone, but it sounded like someone else was speaking; no longer my Alessio, sweet and with that funny, rogue charm of his.

We looked at each other, and for a moment, I almost wanted to run to him and throw myself in his arms; to ask if he could forget everything and come back to me, like things were before—if we could ever be happy again.

I had overheard his conversation with Enrico because I was passing by the office by chance. Upon hearing my name, I did something I'd always been told was a sin: eavesdropping. Serves me right. I ended up being punished by learning a truth I would have been better off not knowing.

"Can you leave us alone?" Alessio asked the two women, who quickly nodded in agreement.

BOUND BY BETRAYAL   141

Sienna kissed my cheek after leaning in my direction, then followed Deanna, who closed the door, casting a glance at me as if to ensure everything was okay.

I settled on the bed, straightening up, trying to draw inspiration from those two women, who were strong and didn't back down from anything. I wanted to be like that too. No matter how devastated my heart was and how much Alessio affected me, I wouldn't let myself be swayed.

"You're mistaken," was the first thing he said, and his eyes barely met mine. He couldn't look at me.

"About what?"

"I'm not going to marry you because I think you're incapable of taking care of yourself."

"And you don't think so?"

"I think you do need protection, but that's not all."

I fell silent, taking a deep breath. It was just a slightly gentler way of saying I was the damsel in distress he needed to save; a responsibility he no longer wanted but couldn't shake off out of honor.

"Then what is it, Alessio?" I asked, tired.

"We're getting married because it's the right thing to do. I took your virginity."

I bit my lower lip to hold back tears, feeling it tremble. I knew he was hurt, that everything that had happened had changed him. I couldn't expect him to swear love after my brother had killed his father.

"I imagine I wasn't the first." Alessio was surprised by my response. "You have no obligation to me."

"I do. If you go back to your brother's house single, you'll be shunned. You won't find any husband. You know what a woman's future is in the Cosa Nostra in this case."

I swallowed hard again. I just wanted him to say he wanted to be with me. That he liked me.

Just that.

I also didn't want to fool myself by seeing him look a bit more irritated when I mentioned another man marrying me. He even clenched his fist and grew more breathless.

Still, it could just be in my head. An impression.

"You can take me back to the convent. They'll accept me. I can finally become a novice."

Alessio's lips parted, as if he wanted to show some kind of indignation, but at first, no sound came out.

I noticed he was trying to control himself, but it didn't work.

"Are you crazy?"

"Why? It's a safe place, with people who love me and where I'll be welcomed. Didn't I say I needed protection? I can't think of a better option."

"Marrying me is a better option."

It definitely would be, but only if he truly wanted me, which didn't seem to be the case.

"No, it's not. I don't want it. I don't think it'll work."

Alessio stepped forward and grabbed my arm.

"You're out of your mind, Luna. I'm not taking you back to Sicily again. You're staying here, even if I have to lock this door!"

My heart twisted in my chest because he seemed nervous. More than I expected him to be.

It was then that the furrow in his brow deepened, and I noticed the dark circles under his beautiful blue eyes. One of his curls accidentally escaped the gel's grip, falling on his forehead; almost like a reminder of the man I once knew and so wanted to resurface to rescue the new Alessio from his darkness.

BOUND BY BETRAYAL 143

Maybe I should accept the cold marriage proposal, if only to try to save him. But I wasn't the heroine, not even of my own story, let alone of someone else's.

I reached out and touched his smooth face, making him close his eyes.

"It'll be better. I agree with what you said. Something is wrong between us. It's not meant to be."

"That's not what I meant, Luna..."

If only he would call me *dolce angelo* again...

"But you did. It's probably a truer thought than those you're trying to believe. If we marry and you still can barely look at me, as you are now, I'll suffer much more."

With that, he turned to me, and I saw immense sadness in his expression. In a way, I also blamed myself for his suffering. How could I become his wife under those circumstances?

"Accept it, Alessio. I'll be fine. And so will you."

I wouldn't be, but life would go on. At some point, I would find myself again in my faith, in the work at the convent, and I could ask to start my vows.

I could find a purpose, something to occupy me.

The days would be long, the nights even longer. I would come to know things I hadn't known before, and the memories would be painful at first.

With time, they would become bittersweet. Until they transformed into delicate mists in my mind, of which I would remember with a smile.

That's what I hoped.

"We'll talk about this again, Luna. You won't convince me like this."

Without saying another word, Alessio simply turned his back on me and left the room, slamming the door as if he couldn't look at me any longer.

As soon as he left, I threw myself back on the bed, grabbing a pillow and surrendering to the melancholy of not knowing whether it was better to go or stay.

Which of the two would I regret more...

CHAPTER TWENTY-SIX

Luna

Alessio tried and tried and tried. In his defense, he didn't give up so easily. It was two weeks of arguments between us.

In none of them, however, did he come closer to kiss me. In none of them did he say he wanted to be with me because he was in love with me. Not once did he touch me.

I understood. In fact, I could see all the emotions he so desperately wanted to hide reflected in his eyes. The death of Massimo, in the way it happened, seemed to flip a switch in Alessio, and he became a completely different person.

When his father died, a part of Alessio died too.

I loved him. That had become a certainty I could never deny. Whether it was because I was an inexperienced girl, and he was the first man I had an intimate relationship with, or because he had truly captivated me, it made no difference. My feelings were evident.

Because I loved him, I would learn to deal with those new nuances. I would love each one of them and accept him that way, as long as he loved me back. I would try to save him; I would try to fix things, because that's what love was made of, right?

But how could I endure the way he could barely look at me? How could I think that before we woke up together, he might be watching me sleep and thinking that I was the sister of the man who caused the greatest tragedy of his life?

If we married and had children, how would those kids see their parents' relationship? As two strangers, two enemies, or as two people who had truly fallen in love?

It was very foolish of me to want a happy and healthy marriage within the mafia, and even as an innocent girl raised in seclusion, I held that hope. Things changed when I met Alessio and saw another side of the story: the possibility that a person, even living amidst violence, could have a good side. I began to believe my future wouldn't be as bleak as I thought.

But how much of the old Alessio would be spared? He wouldn't be the husband I wanted. I had no expectations about it, but after getting to know him better, it would be impossible to accept less than what he had offered me before.

When he finally accepted that I would be returned to the convent, I simply packed my bags and prepared for the return. The last thing I heard him say was:

"Go, but don't ask me to say goodbye. I won't accept that. I won't look back, and you don't either. It was *your* choice."

My heart, which was already shattered, finished breaking into countless pieces, but I held my head high and accepted that, indeed, the decision had been mine. He had given me a choice, but not one I wanted.

The trip was arranged, and days later, in the morning, I descended with my things, aided by a soldier from the Preterotti family. Sienna and Deanna woke up early to give me a hug, and each swore that they would always be there for whatever I needed.

I cried, thinking how I would love to have those women in my family. I wanted them to be my sisters-in-law, like older sisters, but that wouldn't happen.

When I reached the car, the soldier helped me put my suitcase in the trunk and got behind the wheel. I settled into the back seat and waited.

BOUND BY BETRAYAL

147

I stared out the window, feeling the tears prick my eyes from Alessio's absence.

He had said there would be no goodbyes, so what was I waiting for? In the last few days, he hadn't stopped by the house, and I had the impression he might be running away from me. I didn't even see him at night entering his room, even during the sleepless nights I spent trying to listen for him and provoke a meeting, making it seem accidental.

He hadn't spent those days in that house.

I wouldn't even say goodbye.

I had talked to the sisters days before, coordinating my return, especially with the Abbess, who was like a mother to me. I confided to her that I had given up my innocence, but that I wanted to start my vows and become a novice. I didn't know if she would accept me, but her response was warm enough for me to believe that this would be my destiny.

I was ready. Only my heart wasn't.

"Aren't we leaving?" I asked, realizing we were still parked.

"We will soon, miss," was his reply.

Were we waiting for something? I could ask, but I stayed silent, pulling out the rosary from my bag and holding it between my fingers, closing my eyes, taking a deep breath, and preparing to start the first prayer.

"Padre Nostro, che sei nei cieli.
Sia santificato il tuo nome.
Venga il tuo regno,
Sia fatta la tua volontà,
Come in cielo, così in terra.
Dacci oggi il nostro pane quotidiano,
E rimetti a noi i nostri debiti,
Come noi li rimettiamo ai nostri debitori.
E non ci indurre in tentazione,

Ma liberaci dal male.

Amen."

I recited the entire Our Father in Italian and began the first Hail Mary. I was still in the middle of the words, whispered very softly, almost just to myself, when the car door opened and closed.

My heart raced as I smelled that familiar scent.

I almost lost my breath when the voice I loved so much spoke: "We can leave now."

I finished the prayer and made the sign of the cross, trying to remain calm and serene. I opened my eyes, and there he was.

No longer with his hair slicked back. The curls were once again falling into his eyes, rebellious, and he wore the same clothes as before. I searched his eyes for something of *my* Alessio, hoping it could be a last flicker of hope, but it still wasn't there. In appearance, he might have returned to being the same man as before, but something inside his heart had been destroyed.

"What are you doing here? You said you weren't going to say goodbye..." I blurted out, even though I believed it might be better to stay silent.

"And I won't. But I can't let you go to Sicily alone with your brother out there. I'll accompany you on the trip. I'll leave you safely at the place you *want* to return to." He still seemed reluctant, but he didn't say anything more, just crossed his arms and turned his gaze to the window.

Like a child denied something, when he just needed to say the right words.

That trip would be much longer than I thought.

We talked very little during the car ride and even less on the plane. We didn't sit close to each other, and Alessio spent almost all his time in the cockpit. Despite that, one night, when I woke from a restless sleep, I felt him cover me, just as he had on all the previous trips.

BOUND BY BETRAYAL

149

I felt his warm, gentle fingers brush a strand of hair from my face.

I sensed his eyes on me, even without opening mine. It was like a magnetism. Something I could never overcome.

When I heard his footsteps moving away, I let the tears fall.

It was so much that we were losing. I was fully convinced that we could have something great, something meaningful. But it would be as God willed.

I would need to devote myself to Him again and believe that His choices for me would be the best.

We landed at Comiso airport, which was about eighty kilometers from the convent, but it was still the closest. The car ride would be long, and I could feel Alessio restless, shifting in his seat.

I didn't know what to say to break that almost painful silence. I didn't want to touch him because I couldn't bear it if he pulled away. I didn't want to cry. I didn't want to say anything wrong.

But there was one thing. One thing I only found the courage to do when the car stopped for me to get out.

Alessio wasn't looking at me. One of his hands was clenched into a fist, and his whole body seemed tense.

It would be better to leave things as they were... But I couldn't resist.

"Can I make one last request?"

He looked surprised by my words, having been silent for so long, but turned to me, and I almost felt myself melt into the leather seat of the rented car at the way his eyes were also misty.

"Whatever you want, *dolce angelo*. Ask for whatever you want."

Oh, no. He wasn't going to call me that just when we were facing the gates of the convent.

Not when it was too late. I had already committed myself to the people I loved. They were already expecting my return.

I swallowed hard and spoke a single sentence while reaching for the car door handle:

"Remember me."

In a rush, I jumped out, not even bothering to close the door. I simply ran away like a madwoman, not thinking about the bags or anything else. The last thing I could allow was to be swept away by that moment.

It was only because it was a farewell. Our emotions were running high. So much so that when I heard his name being called, I quickened my steps, fearing he would come after me.

From that moment on, I could no longer look at Alessio Preterotti. I had chosen another path in my life. I would live within the walls of that convent, serve God, and protect myself from the world outside.

If I left there, I would be a renegade to the mafia because I wouldn't be able to secure a respectable marriage. Or I would have to marry the man I loved, but being a renegade to him as well, one way or another. My feelings would not be reciprocated.

As soon as I entered, the first face I saw was Tizziana's. I threw myself into her arms and then into the Abbess's, and I cried like I hadn't cried until that moment.

I cried for everything I left behind.

CHAPTER TWENTY-SEVEN

Alessio

ONE YEAR LATER

The blood dripped onto the floor in a steady rhythm, almost like the second hand of a clock.

Tick.

Tick.

Tick.

A drop trickled down my back, traveling the length of my spine, getting lost in the fabric of my pants. I had already thrown my ruined shirt onto a chair because it was damaged. With nothing covering my chest, I rested one hand against the wall, trying to compose myself.

I was in excellent shape. At twenty-eight, in the peak of my physical form, the issue wasn't the effort I was exerting, but how much my emotions were affected by this kind of thing. Especially with the number of nights I spent as a hunter.

My brother had promoted me to his consigliere since our father died, and I took the position seriously. I wanted to do everything differently than I did with our father and worked hard to make him proud of me. During the day, I was his advisor, his right hand. We worked together on the family business and solved all problems with as much diplomacy as possible.

At night, I went hunting.

Enrico hadn't given up on finding Mattia and getting justice. I knew my brother well enough to know he wouldn't forget, let alone stop worrying. But with the birth of his first child, I didn't want to leave this task to him. It was a job I could begin to handle in the shadows.

This was the fourth man I had tortured that week. They all belonged to the group—or perhaps cult—that Mattia was gradually forming to carry out a coup against the Cosa Nostra. I knew powerful people were involved, but until that moment, I had only managed to catch small fish.

It was a ladder to climb. Each day a rung. I wasn't willing to give up, but I was in a hurry. Every additional day that son of a bitch was free was another day I feared for my family.

Deanna and Sienna had recently given birth. They both had small babies, and I loved my nephews. Dominic and Enrico were powerful heads who loved their wives, and those babies—two boys—were their heirs. It was a great vulnerability, and I needed to protect them.

This was my motivation.

Killing Mattia was the same as keeping my legacy alive and the people I loved safe.

"Sir, he's dead," was the warning I received. I was still turned away, leaning against the wall, after having punched the bastard tied to the chair until he slumped forward, blood dripping onto the floor.

I was furious when he threatened my sister-in-law and my sister. I should have been a bit colder, but things hit me a little deeper when it came to my family.

"Shit," I growled in anger, knowing I had lost my temper. That I had gone too far. I had been dirty, violent, and I wasn't proud of it.

He hadn't given much information, but in the midst of a session of pain, when we coldly pulled some of his nails off, he spoke a name.

It was always like that. One name led to another, which led to another... and thus a story was built. A path.

Where it would lead me was what I needed to find out.

"Take care of the body," were my only instructions, but to be honest, they weren't even necessary. The soldiers working with us knew the job very well. They were discreet and loyal.

I didn't have the courage to put my filthy shirt back on, so I went home like that. With my eyes fixed on the windshield of the car, knowing I would have to wash the bloodstains from the seats myself, because they would transfer from my clothes. There were companies that could do that for me, ones that had been working for people in the mafia for a long time, but I didn't want to draw attention.

My search was violent, but I wanted the destruction to reach Mattia slowly. I wanted to surprise him. Any word about Alessio's Preterotti car being covered in blood could alert someone who would then alert another person, and thus it would reach the ears of those I didn't want it to.

I entered the condo in Los Angeles where I was living, heading for the last house on the street. It was a duplex, not nearly as large as my family's house, where Enrico lived with Sienna and the baby. They invited me to move in with them as soon as Luna left, but I didn't want to.

I wanted a new place, one where her memory didn't exist. A small place, a modern house that wouldn't remind me of that enormous one in Scotland, where we stayed for two months.

To be honest, I didn't want to remember anything at all related to that girl.

But her memories haunted me every damn day.

And how could it be different when I was in an incessant search for a man who had the same last name as her? How could I not think about how it would have been if she had accepted to marry me? How we would be by now?

At times, I thought it was better that she had left because I couldn't be by her side while hunting her brother to kill him with all possible cruelty. How could I sleep in the same bed as a woman whose father and brother had done so much harm to my family?

She wasn't to blame. Neither was I. But we were victims of fate.

I stepped into the shower as soon as I arrived, still thinking about her.

I dressed, thinking about her.

I went down to the kitchen... the same way.

I ate some cold leftover pizza because I didn't even want to bother to heat it up. I wanted to throw myself into my leather chair, staring into nothing, wondering if it was worth it to drink a whole damn bottle of whiskey, but I remained standing, pacing around the house.

It wasn't as if she had lived here with me, so why did I feel like the house was completely empty when it had never been full?

It was just me and my loneliness. It had always been that way, for almost a year, since I moved in. On those days, however, when I came back from such dark moments, it was as if I felt even more sunk in the worst parts of myself.

It might be right in theory, but when my head flooded with thoughts of Luna, I could only repeat to myself that it had been a mistake.

I knew what she was expecting from me. I knew she wanted me to tell her that our marriage would mean more than just an obligation, but my heart, filled with pain, couldn't do it. Not even when I saw her cry.

I brought one hand to my forehead, free of untamed curls because I had cut my hair. I never let it grow back to the length it had been before because it made me look like a boy. I needed to convey respect and credibility. I had gotten used to the new look, but sometimes I still missed who I used to see in the mirror.

BOUND BY BETRAYAL

Not just for the curls, of course.

I realized, while thinking, that there was still a red stain on my fingers. That alone was enough to make me feel dirty. Maybe it would be a good idea to take another shower and then lie down.

The intercom rang, however, which surprised me.

I rubbed my temples again, massaging my head. I hardly ever had headaches like this before. It was light, carefree. After everything, it was as if my shoulders felt the weight of the entire world.

I went to the camera to see who it was. It could be Enrico with Sienna, with my few-month-old nephew; that's why I took the trouble to check.

The long brown hair didn't escape my notice. Nor did the long skirt that covered almost her entire leg, in a heavy gray tone—something no girl would wear.

When she lifted her face to the camera, I had no doubts.

It was Luna.

She was holding onto the gate but didn't seem very steady; as if she was about to collapse.

I ran over, even still believing I could be hallucinating.

But it wasn't. The moment I opened the gate, looking at her from afar, there was no doubt. It was real.

"Luna?"

She tried to take a step forward but needed to hold herself up again. As I approached, I saw she was panting, sweaty, as if she had run a marathon. She was pale too, which caught my attention.

"Alessio... Alessio!" She threw herself into my arms, clutching my shirt. I held her, starting to feel her desperation too. "They stole our son from me!"

"Our son? What are you talking about?"

But Luna didn't have a chance to respond because she fell unconscious in my arms, giving me no information about that madness.

A son?

Could it be...?

But what the hell was happening?

CHAPTER TWENTY-EIGHT

Alessio

It felt almost like the result of a spell. I was thinking of her, and then she appeared. Not in the way I would have liked, of course, because all she did was collapse into my arms after telling me something that could have completely stunned me if my priority at that moment hadn't been to help her.

I picked her up, feeling her skin burn, and carried her inside, laying her down on the sofa. I placed my hand on her forehead, feeling the fever radiating. I knelt beside her, breathing deeply and trying to get used to the idea that it was really Luna. That she had appeared in my house completely randomly, claiming we had a child.

I stood there for a moment, unsure how to act to help her, still grappling with my own feelings about this unexpected return, but I got up and started to walk away, ready to grab some alcohol and a cotton ball, hoping to bring her back to consciousness. Before I could take a step, a small hand grasped my fist, and I looked over my shoulder to see her open her eyes, although they looked heavy and almost delirious.

"Alessio... no... don't leave me alone. Please. I can't take it anymore."

"I'm just going to the bathroom to get something for you. I'll be back in a second."

"Please. Please..."

Her head fell again, and I sighed, thinking I was doing everything wrong.

She deserved more than what I was giving her.

It was Luna.

My *Luna*. My *dolce angelo*.

Somehow, she had returned to me. Even sick, with a fever. In fact, it was me she had sought out in that state.

Of course, the story about a child should have been a fever dream, but it didn't matter. Didn't I want to know whether it was right or wrong to have taken her back and left her behind? Wasn't it a regret that was eating me alive?

Finally, I would have my chance to turn the situation around, even if it was no longer an option for us to be together.

I picked her up again and took her to my room. Being a single man who didn't get many visitors, I didn't have a guest room. The other two were a closet and a sort of office, so there wasn't another bed where I could comfortably accommodate her. Mine would be the only option, but I wouldn't have to spend the night there if I needed to host Luna.

As soon as I laid her on the bed, I didn't comply with her request and went to the bathroom, not only to grab the alcohol but also to get a bottle of Tylenol, hoping to bring down her fever. I didn't have a thermometer, but I didn't need one to know she was sick.

I opened the mini-fridge, grabbed a bottle of water, and took it to the bedside. I used the alcohol and cotton to wake her up, which worked. Then I helped her drink the liquid and take the medicine. She seemed a bit more stable and less likely to succumb again because she stayed sitting up.

"How did you know my address?" was the first question I asked, because even though it wasn't what I wanted to know most, it felt safer.

BOUND BY BETRAYAL

159

"Sienna sent me a gift a few months ago. She left a note with that information, in case I needed it, saying that both she and you would always be there to help me."

Sienna was one of the sweetest people I knew—besides Luna, of course. Even after everything she had been through, she was always worried about others, and I saw the way she looked at me, with compassion, always trying to figure me out to offer help. It didn't surprise me that she wanted to care for Luna even from a distance.

Noticing that the girl was a bit more coherent, I sat on the edge of the bed near her legs, watching her closely.

"And do you need help?" I asked calmly, analyzing, trying to understand what was happening.

"Not just me, Alessio," there was a latent desperation in her voice, which became even more evident as she continued: "I've told you: our baby has been stolen from me! Our four-month-old son!"

That story again. It didn't seem like a delusion anymore. It seemed serious. And if I knew Luna well, she was sensible enough not to joke about such things.

But... a baby?

"Y-you were... pregnant?" I hardly ever stuttered over anything, but it was impossible not to fumble over my words a little.

"Yes. I was. I only found out later, but... I was." A tear slid down her face, and I had to control myself not to wipe it away with my finger, preventing it from falling into her mouth, which was very pale.

I got up from where I was sitting, allowing my feet to come alive and start moving back and forth. Much slower than my thoughts, which were racing at a thousand miles an hour.

"A baby?" the dumbest question I could ask in any situation, because obviously a pregnant woman had a baby.

But a baby *mine*?

"Yes, Alessio, for God's sake... listen to me. We had a baby. I was pregnant when I returned to Sicily. I just waited for him to get all his vaccinations and be cleared to travel. I was going to tell you, but..." She needed to pause, seeming to choke on her own tears. "My God, Alessio... they took him from me. How could I let this happen? We were leaving the airport... it all happened so fast, it was night... a commercial flight... My God, my God..." She brought both hands to her mouth, and her shoulders shook.

I moved closer to her, reaching out to touch her, but I was unable to do so. Not because I didn't want to, but because I had no control over my movements. I had no control over absolutely anything at that moment.

What I could comprehend from what she was saying: I was a father. We had created a baby. But that baby had been taken from its mother.

"Luna, for God's sake..." With all the care, I placed my hands on her shoulders. "Look at me."

She did what I asked.

"Am I understanding this wrong? We are parents of a baby who was kidnapped the moment you landed in Los Angeles? Is that it?"

I thought she was going to have another breakdown, start talking non-stop, but she simply nodded, looking sadder than anyone should.

"This has something to do with my brother, I'm sure..."

"We'll talk about that soon. First, I want you to tell me exactly how it happened."

I also wanted to know how her pregnancy had been, how she had taken care of the baby, if she had been protected, if they had been well-kept...

There were many things to uncover, but I needed to focus on what was most urgent: knowing what to do to find the stolen baby.

BOUND BY BETRAYAL   161

"Didn't anyone come with you? You came alone with a four-month-old baby on some random flight? Being a daughter of the Cosa Nostra? That's crazy. Those nuns knew very well it would be dangerous!" I raised my voice, truly finding everything absurd. I had left Luna in that damn convent against my will, believing she would be kept safe from all the violence, and that even though it was a life of seclusion and deprivation, at least she would be secure.

"Don't speak like that about the sisters!" she protested, crossing her arms. Even though it had only been a year, there was something different about her face. A maturity she had probably gained during her pregnancy.

She looked even more beautiful.

"I want to talk to Sienna. I think she'll understand me better."

"You can talk to me now and tell my sister-in-law later," I replied emphatically.

"No. I'm exhausted." With that, she got up from the bed, starting to head for the door. Her arms fell limply at her sides, looking like lifeless limbs, and she had no strength in her legs. How had she made it to my house? I couldn't say.

Before she could reach the door, I grabbed her and turned her towards me.

"Hey, hey, hey... where do you think you're going?"

"To the hotel. I got a cheap one. I haven't even been there yet. I..."

That girl really must be delirious. Before she decided to take more steps and hurt herself on my stairs, I picked her up again and carried her back to bed.

"Alessio!" she shouted.

"You must be crazy if you think I'm letting you leave here in that state." I gently laid her back down on the mattress. "Why do you have a fever, by the way?"

"Do I?" I nodded. "I haven't slept in a few days since I scheduled the trip. And then with all this... I think I'm a little out of control."

She thought so? I was already sure that *I* was a bit out of control.

"You're going to help me, right?" she added in a pleading, lamenting voice.

"Help? It's my baby too, isn't it?"

My God... it was surreal that I was saying that, but apparently there was a little baby of mine lost somewhere, in the hands of someone whose intentions I didn't know. Probably Mattia, but what did he want with all of this?

What did he want by taking his own nephew?

Luna and I exchanged glances while these thoughts hammered in my head. It felt like we were in sync, and it was as if I could read what was going on in her mind.

This was the moment I should assure her that we would figure everything out, that the baby would return to her arms and, consequently, to mine.

But I was completely lost.

I had a child.

I had a child...

CHAPTER TWENTY-NINE

Luna

A shower, a borrowed shirt from Alessio, and I let myself drift off to sleep, with my hair wet, as the medicine took effect.

When I arrived at the convent, the day he returned me there, I also had a fever like that. And then later, when I discovered the pregnancy. It was an emotional response, so I didn't worry too much.

The next morning, I woke up feeling a little better, just with a sore body. Nothing unbearable.

Nothing was unbearable, in fact, when it came to needing to get up to find my son. To get my little boy back.

Just thinking about it made me grab the nightstand next to the bed, hit by a wave of dizziness. It wasn't the fever, it was nothing but desperation.

And I hadn't even stopped to think about the fact that I was in Alessio's house. After a year... we were finally reunited.

I hadn't even left that room, and I was brought to him unconscious. It was a bit disconcerting to not know my way around a house because I didn't know it, but I found my way easily, not only because it wasn't a large place but because I heard the sound of a baby crying.

I ran like a madwoman, flying down the stairs, my heart racing in my chest.

Was it my baby?

Was it... was it him?

164 AMARA HOLT

I reached the living room, breathless, and the first thing I saw was Sienna's long hair cascading down her back, in that very peculiar shade of red. I must have made a lot of noise when I arrived, because both she and Enrico turned to look at me, and I saw the little baby in her arms.

With tufts of red hair, he clearly wasn't my little one, although they were probably about the same age. Cousins born around the same time.

I wanted to run back to the bedroom and hide in there, but that wasn't the attitude I needed to have. I also forced myself not to cry because my baby needed me whole.

"Luna!" Handing the baby over to Enrico, the redhead came over to me, wrapping her arms around my shoulders with a tenderness that left me almost speechless. "Darling, are you okay? I'm so sorry for what happened..."

So Alessio had already told her about our baby. I glanced at him over Sienna's shoulders, and he was sitting on the couch, with his arms resting on his knees and his large hands covering his face.

She stepped back, looking at me with compassion. She surely understood me because she was a mother too.

I looked at her baby in Enrico's arms, who held him like a crystal piece, and I was moved to see the contrast between the dark man, dressed all in black with that huge coat and broad shoulders, holding such a small bundle.

He greeted me with a respectful nod, and the first thing that came to my mind was that I was only wearing a shirt, with no shorts, nothing. I felt much more exposed than I ever had, because no man besides his brother had seen me this way, with my legs so bare. Still, Alessio was so much larger than me that the fabric barely reached the tops of my thighs.

Alessio stood up and came over to me, gently holding my arm, helping me to sit down. I didn't need that; it was an exaggeration,

BOUND BY BETRAYAL 165

but when he placed his hand on my forehead to check my fever, the touch was so comforting that I closed my eyes and took a deep breath.

"I think we all need to talk," Enrico said. "I've already called Dominic. He and Deanna will take the first flight here."

"And the baby?"

"They'll bring him too. Is that okay with you, Luna? I was worried about bringing Andreas, but he's still very little..."

I smiled as I looked at the baby, who was half-awake, half-asleep, with heavy little eyes. He had the same blue eyes as my little boy. Just that his hair was different.

"I'm glad you brought him," I replied, trying to calm myself. Of course, it was painful to see another baby and feel the pain of not having mine in my arms, but I had to believe I would have him back as soon as possible.

"Luna, we're with Enrico and Sienna here. I think it's time for you to start talking," Alessio stated after a few moments of silence, and I felt all eyes on me.

I looked at each of them, feeling tired again. That weight that hurt my shoulders didn't ease. It seemed to worsen with each hour without news.

When I was brought back to the abbey, I had the feeling that, inside, protected, I would never have to face the reality of the Cosa Nostra again. The sisters always told me that Lorenzo was trying to contact me, saying I could come home if I wanted, but that wasn't an option. Not when I knew I could find Alessio and that Mattia was still out there.

At that moment, the mafia became a hope for me again. Especially if Dominic was on our side too; I would have three of the most powerful men I knew at my disposal, in search of my baby.

What price would I pay for that? Being close to the man I loved but couldn't have? Yes. But it would be worth it.

"I returned to the convent, certain that I would live a life of servitude. When I discovered the pregnancy, I knew I couldn't be a novice anymore." I swallowed hard, remembering how distressing it was to wait for Conccetta, the sister who went to the pharmacy for me and bought a pregnancy test in secret. I had no doubts after days of nausea and my period being late. Still, when I saw the positive sign on the stick, I broke down in Tizziana's arms, crying. "The sisters were understanding, and the abbess found a family that took me in."

"What? How so?" Alessio raised his voice. "They didn't keep you there?"

"They couldn't. It's not allowed to keep pregnant girls. They did more than they should have, even. I should have been returned to my family."

"No way. They should have sent you to me. I'm the baby's father!"

I sighed as I heard him speak that way, so determined about our child.

"It wouldn't have been wise to take such a long trip in the early stages of the pregnancy. And then, as time passed, I had some complications." Alessio's eyes widened with concern. "I was well cared for. But now I'm not so sure they were good people."

"What do you mean?" Enrico asked after returning his baby to the stroller.

"I don't want to accuse anyone without proof, but how would anyone else know about my trip if I didn't tell anyone besides Tizziana? And I trust my sister."

Alessio and Enrico exchanged glances, as only two people used to communicating without words can.

"Do you think these people might be connected to your brother?" Enrico asked in his calm way, though he always seemed to be on high alert.

There was no doubt it had to do with Mattia, apparently. None of them were betting on any other possibility.

BOUND BY BETRAYAL   **167**

"The Luna of before would have said no, trusting everyone too much. But yes. Maybe, yes. They were very poor people, with a humble condition, and the sisters began to support them so they would stay with me. For enough money, I believe they could have given the information, not knowing how much harm they would be doing to me."

"How was the child's kidnapping, Luna? I'm sorry to ask; I imagine it's painful, but I think it might be important," Sienna interjected, still with that look of sympathy on her beautiful face.

I tried to detach myself from the scene, speaking as if I were recounting someone else's story.

"It was at the airport. I was a bit tangled up with the suitcase and the baby, and an elderly man tried to help me. He was over seventy, with white hair. I know I was naïve, but I never imagined he could be someone suspicious. He was just a kind man at an airport." I was starting to lose control, but I took a deep breath, trying to concentrate and keep myself steady. I felt someone's hand over mine and saw it was Sienna, giving me strength. So I continued: "But we were near the bathroom. He grabbed my baby and pushed me inside, making me fall and hit the wall. When I recovered, he was already gone."

"What did you do?" Sienna asked.

"I started screaming in despair. A security guard came to help me, and he was going to take me to the airport's Federal Police, but I began to panic. If they found out who I was... I don't know... my father always warned us never to involve the police, that the Cosa Nostra could handle anything without the law's help."

"If the Cosa Nostra can't, we will solve it. You're with us now, Luna. We're going to find our son and bring him back to you."

I glanced at Alessio while he spoke. I didn't know if he felt as confident about what he was saying, but I believed his words.

I believed it so much that my eyes filled with tears as my heart filled with hope.

CHAPTER THIRTY

Alessio

Sienna and Enrico stayed as long as they could, having a very small child and their commitments. As far as I knew, Dominic would arrive that night, and we would meet again the following morning.

Great. I needed all the reinforcements I could get. Not because I didn't believe I could handle the situation alone. The problem was how to do it while controlling my emotions.

I had spent the entire night awake, tossing in bed and trying to understand how this could be happening. I knew Luna and I had been as careful as possible with condoms, but I couldn't remember if we had used them every time we made love. Accidents could happen, and I didn't doubt for a moment the story she had told us. The despair she had shown when she arrived at my house was more than proof that everything was real.

I had a child. With the woman who still haunted my thoughts. I had tried to forget her for a year, but not for a single day had she left my mind.

And she was back. Sitting in a lounge chair by my pool, wearing one of her heavy outfits—a long skirt that reached her feet and a white blouse with all the buttons done up to the neck.

Her suitcase had been left at the airport in the middle of the chaos, but I had asked one of my men to go pick it up after I contacted them to see if it was possible to retrieve it.

I walked over to her and sat down beside her in another chair, far enough away not to make her uncomfortable with my presence. Even though we had talked that morning, with my brother and sister-in-law present, there were still many things we both needed to discuss in a somewhat more private manner.

"What's his name?" It was something I desperately wanted to know.

The name of my son.

Wasn't it absurd that my little boy was four months old, and I didn't know what to call him?

"Vittorio. I named him just before leaving Sicily."

It could have been any name, but the moment she answered, I nearly lost my breath.

That was my boy's name. Vittorio Preterotti.

"It's beautiful."

"Yes, it suits him. I wish I had a photo to show you, but... I didn't have a phone... I couldn't take any."

I shook my head, lowering my eyes, because she looked like she was about to cry again, and it was painful. Seeing her suffer for any reason would be unbearable, but thinking that she had gone through everything without my help made me feel like a piece of shit.

"How are you?" I asked, and she was surprised by the shift in the conversation. She prepared to respond, even opening her mouth, but I decided to interrupt her. "I want the truth, Luna. I want to know not just how you're feeling now, but how this past year has been. I need you to tell me without holding back."

"Do you want to martyr yourself?"

"Maybe yes. Maybe I deserve it since you suffered alone."

"It was my choice to return to the convent."

"I know, but it was my fault. Because I didn't tell you what I should have."

Luna seemed to lose her breath, looking at me with those beautiful brown eyes wide open.

"And please, don't say it now. Not at this moment," she pleaded.

"No. I'll only speak when you tell me you're ready to hear it."

I didn't have the right to put that shit in her head and just expect her to accept me. I was lost in such tormenting darkness, so violent, that it was hard to see anything ahead of me.

I still felt that way. It wouldn't change overnight. But her presence and the idea that there was a child, who was blood of my blood, lost and needing me, made everything gain a new perspective.

I needed to confess that I still hadn't grasped the magnitude of the situation. I still felt a bit dazed, a bit directionless, not quite knowing what to think about the idea of being a father. But when we had the child back, things would be different.

"Were you coming back to Los Angeles to tell me?" That was another thing I needed to know. The truth had been hidden from me for too long, but I could never blame her.

"Yes. I thought it would be better if we resolved this face to face. I could have called you from the convent, but I didn't know your number." Luna let out a bitter laugh. "It sounds like a pretty lame excuse in the twenty-first century, but it's the truth."

"If you had it, would you have told me?"

"Of course. I just asked that no one involve my family."

"Not even Lorenzo? He has been helping us a lot in the search for Mattia."

"I imagine so. Lorenzo is a good man." No one was completely good in the mafia, but I let that comment slide. "But I thought it would be an easier way for Mattia to end up finding out. I know they're not connected, but walls have ears."

That left me a bit intrigued. If I hadn't been so focused on the detail of our baby and everything else, I might have analyzed what Luna had said a little better.

Was there someone connected to Lorenzo passing information to Mattia? An employee, a soldier? Someone he thought he could trust? Because there was a good chance of that, considering that bastard was always one step ahead.

"Tomorrow, when Dominic arrives, we need to investigate that family you said took care of you. If they're connected in any way to the kidnapping..."

"Alessio, I don't believe they could have done it with bad intentions."

"We'll find that out too."

Luna swallowed hard and adjusted herself in the chair, leaning forward. She wrapped her arms around her body, hugging herself, and I noticed she was cold. I immediately took off my jacket, getting up and draping it over her shoulders.

As I leaned down to do this, our faces were very close, and our eyes locked for a few moments.

She reached out, touching the tip of my hair with her finger, very lightly, almost imperceptibly.

"Your curls... you cut them..." she whispered softly, in that sweet voice that had haunted my dreams.

"Yes. They didn't suit me anymore," I replied, not moving. I remained very close to her, inhaling her scent as my body began its involuntary responses to a woman I had long desired.

"Yeah... you're different."

I wanted to ask "different how," but I wouldn't be a hypocrite. I knew the answer; I just didn't want to hear Luna say it. I didn't want that woman to confirm what wasn't new to me.

I sat back down in the chair, and we both turned our gazes to the sky. We sat in silence for a long time, and it only seemed to increase the distance between us.

"Do you still think we're cursed?" Luna broke the silence with her question, causing me to lean forward and rest my elbows on my thighs, intertwining my fingers.

"That's not what I meant, Luna."

"I don't know what other sense it could have had. And maybe I agree. Now more than ever."

"What I think is that we are the products of a violent organization and that neither of us is to blame for who we are."

"Yes, you're right..." she said in a nostalgic tone, looking at the sky again, her arms wrapped around her body. "Our baby isn't either."

"He's even less to blame. But he will come back to us. And then we'll decide what will happen with us. It will be a conversation to determine our fate."

She shook her head but looked lost.

I couldn't look away because she seemed more beautiful than ever. Ethereal, mature, melancholic. Strong, too. I still hadn't heard the whole story of how that past year had been, but I already knew Luna had survived it and was there, standing, facing the whole world for the baby.

A baby who was also mine but for whom I had done absolutely nothing.

"Oh... I'm sorry, I forgot to say," she suddenly broke the silence again after minutes of quiet. "His name is Vittorio Massimo."

Then that little piece of information became my undoing.

She had named our son after my father. The name of the father I lost in such an absurd way, whose death separated us.

It was then that I felt a tear slide down my face. One that brought a few others until I had to hide my face with my hands.

It had been a long time since I cried. There was so much inside me, rooted in my chest, that needed to come out.

That was the moment.

Luna had returned to fill a heart that had been completely empty.

"Thank you. Thank you so much," was all I could say.

And it still wouldn't be enough.

But I hoped to be able to thank her with actions and not just words.

CHAPTER THIRTY-ONE

Luna

We gathered at Enrico's house. Not only because it was bigger, more spacious, and had an office where we could hold the meeting with everyone involved—but also because we thought it was better since Sienna had a small baby and Dominic and Deanna were staying there.

I felt envious among two women who had their babies in their arms, chatting about motherhood. Of course, they didn't notice that I wanted to join in, and I could have, but I would never be able to talk about anything related to my baby without breaking down.

It wasn't that I didn't have hope. Especially when faced with all those men ready to kill and die on their mission; even more so when I saw Giovanni on the screen—since he was almost an untouchable name within the Cosa Nostra, because since he got married and became a father, he rarely got involved in things like this, especially when it didn't pertain to his own work. If he was there, it was out of total consideration for the Preterottis. I needed to value that help to the utmost.

"So Luna has a suspicion..." Dominic began.

He was sitting in one of the armchairs around a table that was, in fact, used for small meetings. "Lounge" would be the more accurate term. With a glass of whiskey, he looked comfortable, almost dominating the place.

As the armchairs were spaced apart, after speaking, the man pulled his wife's chair closer, with her already seated—which made her flash a mischievous smile in his direction—and Dominic wrapped his arm around her, pulling her to him.

Even from afar, it was clear how much those two were in love. More than that, there was a huge sexual tension between them. It was palpable in their gazes.

"Yes. She gave me the names of the people, and look what I discovered..." Alessio started. "The couple is in Los Angeles."

My heart stopped in my chest, and my lips parted in a surprised expression as I brought my hand to my chest.

"Here? Attonio and Ginevra are here? They... They would never have the money for this. They could never..."

"Of course not. Unless they're being funded by someone, right? And what would they be doing here if they didn't have a very clear mission?" Alessio spoke through clenched teeth, visibly irritated, but more than that, looking very firm and professional.

"How did you find this out, *fratello*?" Deanna asked, adjusting her beautiful baby. He was undeniably the spitting image of his father.

All the princes of the Cosa Nostra—or kings, in the case of Giovanni, Dominic, and Enrico—had male heirs. Kiara was pregnant again, with a girl. The only one among the boys who would grow up as friends and cousins.

"It wasn't difficult. I have a contact in Sicily. I have contacts in many places, in fact. The ones there asked some questions here, questions there, and I think D. Ginevra let something slip to a neighbor. From what we gathered, it was reported as a trip they won in a raffle, like a vacation. I don't believe it. Do you?"

I looked around at everyone, and no one was nodding affirmatively. Everyone shook their heads.

BOUND BY BETRAYAL

"What are the plans?" Giovanni commented, and we looked at him, who stood out on the big screen. "With Kiara in her seventh month of pregnancy, I won't be able to go, but I will send a trusted man to help you."

"Thank you, Giovanni. For now, what I have in mind is to pay a visit wherever these people are. I believe they know something."

"Do you think my baby could still be with them?" I asked, straightening up and almost jumping from my chair in a burst of faith I hadn't felt in a long time.

"*Our* baby," he corrected, emphasizing the pronoun in a way that made me gasp again.

Before answering my question, he fixed his gaze on me, with such intensity that if I had been standing, I might have stumbled.

"There's a chance, Luna. Alessio is right. But we can't have hopes like that," Enrico interjected as he noticed the tension that had formed.

"Please be careful," Sienna said, worried.

"We are the elite of the Cosa Nostra, *cognata*," Dominic replied, calling Sienna his sister-in-law in Italian, with one of those charmingly wicked smiles of his. He then took another sip of his drink. "We'll come back unscathed and return to you."

At least, that was what I hoped. I glanced at Alessio, trying to think if he would come back to *me*.

It wasn't what I should be imagining, because we weren't together. There was no reason for me to believe we would ever be like Dominic and Deanna, for example, who hardly seemed able to keep their hands off each other.

We stayed gathered for a few more hours, having lunch while discussing other matters, and then we prepared to leave.

When we were almost out the door, Sienna turned to me and Alessio, concerned:

"Don't you want to stay here, Luna? We have plenty of space; it might be more comfortable and..."

"Luna is coming back with me," Alessio interrupted, full of determination.

Sienna smiled.

"I think the decision is hers, dear."

Alessio looked at me, with an embarrassed expression and nodded.

"I'm sorry... I didn't..."

"It's okay. Thank you, Sienna, but I'm already settled in with Alessio."

Not to mention that I wouldn't be able to be surrounded by two babies almost the same age as Vittorio without feeling miserable. But of course, I wouldn't share that with her.

Accepting my decision, Sienna said goodbye to us, and I got into the car with Alessio while another vehicle followed us for our safety.

The distance wasn't great, so we arrived quickly. He opened the door, signaled to the soldier who had followed us, who would probably stay nearby, and gave me space to enter. I took the lead, walking slowly through the entrance of the house and heading straight for my room.

I took a shower and put on one of my nightgowns, which were the only ones I had. Still with wet hair, I began rummaging through my things. I improvised an altar on the bedside table, moving the lamp and placing everything I needed on the flat surface, including a wooden cross—a gift from the Abbess—propped against the wall as if it were hanging, so I could look at it whenever I was there.

I grabbed a fluffy, soft towel, folded it several times, and placed it on the floor where I could kneel.

I held my rosary in my hand, touching the beads with my fingers, beginning the first prayer.

BOUND BY BETRAYAL

I heard the door open slightly, but I managed to stay focused, even knowing exactly who it was. After all, there was no other option.

When I reached the second Hail Mary, I needed to finish it and turn to him because I couldn't continue without losing my focus.

"You *really* still have faith. Even after everything," he commented when he noticed I was looking at him in silence.

"I try. It's not the same as before, I confess. And I condemn myself for that."

Alessio approached step by step, very serious.

"You don't need to kneel like that to pray. Remember what I told you that time. You don't need to kneel for *anyone*, Luna."

"It's not just anyone. It's God."

"God doesn't want you to hurt yourself. God wants only love."

I nodded, watching him lift my chin. He extended his hand to me right after, and I accepted it only because I didn't have the strength to react. To argue.

I stood up and swore he would let go of my hand, but he didn't. He lowered his eyes to our joined hands as he moved his to intertwine our fingers.

The tension was so thick it could be cut with a knife.

"Do you ever think about how it could have been?" he whispered. "Between us..."

I took a deep breath because it was an unexpected interaction. What did he want to do with me?

"I think about it. But it was a better decision."

"It wasn't, Luna. Definitely not. Now more than ever, I'm sure of that."

"Don't blame my choice for what happened to our baby," I said, almost angrily.

"I would never do that. But keep in mind that I would never have allowed you to have a child alone. I would never have taken you if I had known about the pregnancy."

"I probably wouldn't have gone either."

That seemed to be a sufficient answer for him.

I saw him lower his eyes to my mouth, even bringing his hand to my arm and tightening his grip slightly, which I interpreted as a reaction of desire.

But I turned my face away. I wasn't in a position to be kissed by him. I couldn't allow it until we resolved all our pending issues.

He could insist, he could even be more aggressive, but he stepped back, taking a deep breath, clenching his jaw, and reluctantly taking steps away.

When I was left alone, with him closing the door, I looked at my small altar and ended up sitting on the bed, trying to return to praying my rosary that way, but without the concentration I had before because my mind was already filled with other thoughts that didn't align with my religion and my faith.

CHAPTER THIRTY-TWO

Alessio

Giovanni kept his promise and sent a contact to join us on the mission to "talk" with the Gallo couple—Attonio and Ginevra.

I knew the guy's reputation. His name was Ilya Kravtsov, a mercenary who had deserted from the Solsnetskaya, the most powerful organization in the Russian mafia, though no one knew why. He had been a prisoner of the Cosa Nostra for some time, but somehow had become a trusted man among us, doing jobs for various families. His specialty was getting his hands dirty when necessary, and many called him Zver—the term for Beast in Russian.

That was the vibe of the man we had as an ally at that moment. When he showed up, I was surprised by his appearance. He stood about two meters tall and was two meters wide, with a huge beard and long blond hair. He instilled fear in anyone who looked at him, especially with his grim expression.

I didn't know what kind of instructions he had received, but I got the impression he was ready to take the lead and act as a shield for us. He hadn't said anything about it, but that was what I concluded from how fearless he seemed, ready for anything, with a massive weapon in hand, giving instructions and taking control of the situation.

"Who the hell died and made this guy the leader? Did anyone ask you anything?" Dominic walked beside me, also armed, whispering indignantly.

"Jealous, Ungaretti? Want to be the leader of everything?" I replied, trying to provoke him.

"Shut the hell up, *yebat'*!" Ilya growled, throwing in a "fuck" at the end of the sentence, and obviously, Dominic was pissed but said nothing.

If Dominic Ungaretti took orders from someone, that meant something.

We had three days of searching, trying to find the address where the two had been taken. I was hopeful that we would find the baby with them, considering the entire route that had been taken. It couldn't be a coincidence that two people had left Sicily for Los Angeles in that way.

It would be much easier to leave a couple who had some connection to the baby taking care of him because it would make the child calmer. They probably knew Vittorio and how to handle the boy.

Or I hoped so.

At the same time, I had a feeling something might have happened because there had been a purchase made in installments on a credit card in Attonio's name, which was picked up by the people I had investigating.

The speed with which we found something surprised me and made me very suspicious that we wouldn't get that far. If they had made that kind of mistake, they were probably no longer being assisted by someone bigger and more powerful, with better knowledge of escape strategies and experience hiding.

Still, there could be a chance. And I wasn't willing to lose any.

The address we reached was quite isolated from the rest of the city—perfect for hiding a kidnapped baby. The house was small, and we were led to it by tracking the purchase, which had been for return tickets to Italy, paid in several installments. It had been made from a laptop with an IP address that led us to that location.

I couldn't be wrong.

Ilya continued to take the lead, and I saw him as a wall, especially carrying that T4 Rifle—with a silencer—in one arm while he pushed a tree branch aside with the other, because we decided to invade from the back.

He didn't want to talk. He sent Enrico and another one of our soldiers to the front of the house, and we continued until he reached the door and simply kicked it down.

We passed through the ruined wood, and he signaled for me to start searching the area. Hearing the noise, my brother and the soldier entered as well, covering the entire house with little effort. Everyone armed, although Ilya seemed ready for war.

I was the first to find the two. What guided me was the trail of blood. The woman's body floated in a pool of it, while the man, still alive and semi-conscious, had visibly tried to crawl out of the room but was thwarted by our arrival, which forced him to retreat.

He was also injured, but I didn't know where his injury came from. I approached, grabbing him by the collar of his shirt and lifting him off the ground with a hatred that had become part of me since my father's death.

"There are people here!" I shouted, almost gutturally, announcing to all the others who were with me.

I threw the bastard into a chair, sitting him down and pulling out pieces of rope I had brought with me inside my jacket to tie his arms behind him.

" *Per favore*! My wife has just been killed. We did nothing... it's a mistake. A mistake!" he whined, visibly cowardly.

" *Per favore* is bullshit." With the back of my hand, I raised my arm and brought it down on the man's face without a second thought. It could indeed be a mistake, but the scene that greeted us left little room for doubt.

I grabbed him before he could fall to the ground, bringing him back to his previous position and tying his ankles as well.

"Is this Attonio Gallo?"

"Yes, it's me... It's me..." he didn't even have the courage to lie.

"Then you're the right person. We came to talk to you..." I explained with a wicked smile on my face, and then my partners in this mission surrounded him.

Of course, he first looked at Ilya, who resembled a Viking warrior armed to the teeth and even stopped to light a cigarette.

"So we have some fun for tonight, *kompan'ony*?" he called us companions, but besides his intrusive instructions, he had hardly spoken to us. Still, he seemed very, very excited about the little job.

As if he had nothing to lose.

"I imagine you have something to tell us," Dominic also said. The man had no idea how fucked he was with the most dangerous and violent men of the Cosa Nostra around him.

"I have nothing! Absolutely nothing..."

With all the patience in the world, Enrico approached him, crouching down and bringing his hand close to the wound. It was in his abdomen and was bleeding enough that he wouldn't survive if we left him tied up there. He wouldn't last until the next morning.

"Death can be a very lonely and painful thing, Attonio," Enrico spoke as if he were offering a prayer. In such a calm way that anyone would believe he was an elevated spirit guiding a lost soul to the light. "You will bleed for hours, suffering and crying, because you will feel a cold that will slowly penetrate your insides. Weakness will make your body more vulnerable, and the position we leave you in won't be comfortable at all. Moreover, depending on how you behave, the pain can be even greater. It will be torturous hours... You *will* die, but it's in our hands to decide *how*.

BOUND BY BETRAYAL

The man trembled, and his eyes filled with tears. From the way Enrico spoke, anyone would be terrified.

"I'm good at causing pain, friend. I saw some rats outside the house... I can be quite creative with that," Ilya said conversationally, taking a drag from his cigarette.

"No, for God's sake! No...! I'll talk... what do you want to know?"

We exchanged glances, forming a silent chain among men willing to do anything to get what they wanted.

And what we wanted was my baby back.

It took a bit more violence, threats, but Attonio told us what he knew.

He had been hired by someone whose name he didn't know to deliver Luna's location. Attonio knew everything, but he didn't tell his wife the nature of what they were doing. Until she died, the woman thought she was helping Luna and not colluding in the kidnapping of our baby.

All he could pass on was that someone from inside the convent was involved.

One of the people Luna trusted blindly.

After delivering the mercy shot myself to the bastard's forehead, we lingered for a moment, watching him alongside his wife's body. There were no regrets in my mind, no matter how much I always sought them. Not when the guy was truly guilty and had no remorse in selling out, with the price being to rip a baby from his mother.

"It was boring as hell working with you guys. I expected more excitement," Ilya said, his voice sounding like thunder, lowering his massive weapon from his shoulders and holding it with one hand as he marched out of the room. "Sort out your shit. I'll wait in the car."

I heard a door slam, along with other sounds of things falling to the ground. Probably the pieces of wood from the door he had kicked in.

"Can you believe that guy?" Dominic pointed with his thumb over his shoulder in the direction Ilya had gone. "Who does he think he is? Beyoncé, putting on a show and leaving just like that?"

I could have laughed, but I felt someone's hand on my shoulder. Turning, I saw the soldier we brought with something in his hand.

"Sir, I found this on the bed in another room. I believe it belongs to your son."

I turned my eyes to what he was holding almost in slow motion, afraid to see what it was.

It was a blanket. Blue, covered in cute little animals. One that I took in my hands, forcing me to drop the gun to the floor, because I couldn't even imagine keeping that innocent and pure piece between the same fingers that had held the instrument I used to take a life.

I stood frozen for a moment, staring at what had been handed to me, not thinking that Luna must have had many other things of Vittorio's like that at home, but I never considered asking.

I brought the blanket to my nose, inhaling the baby scent; the smell of my son.

It was the closest I had been to him since discovering his existence.

It was the most tangible and palpable evidence that he existed, somewhere in the world.

Or more precisely in Sicily, from what Attonio had said.

But it didn't matter. He could be in hell... I would find him.

CHAPTER THIRTY-THREE

Luna

I jumped up from the sofa where I had been sitting the moment I heard the sound of cars approaching.

They had arrived.

"Luna, wait!" Deanna tried to stop me, but I barely heard her. I just ran out, passing through the door and reaching the outside of the house.

It was early morning, cold, but I went out barefoot, holding up my skirts, until I reached Alessio's car, stopping beside it, waiting for him to jump out.

He was wearing a black shirt under a leather jacket of the same color, so it was hard to see if there were any blood stains.

"What happened there? Vittorio? Any news? Do you know anything about him?" I started asking eagerly, letting the words spill out nonstop, almost as if I couldn't breathe in between them.

"We need to talk, Luna. Let's go inside."

He was about to pass me, but I didn't let him. I stepped in front of him, blocking the way, even though I had no intention of winning a standoff if Alessio decided to push through. I was no match for him.

"No, Alessio. Speak now. I'm dying here!" I raised my voice and punched his chest when he remained silent.

Looking at me with a resigned expression, he fumbled in his jacket, in an inner pocket, pulling out a piece of cloth. In the darkness of Enrico's yard, it took me a moment to realize what it was, but it was Vittorio's blanket.

"We haven't found him yet, but we have leads. We have leads, Luna! We're going to get to him."

I knew it was good news. I also knew that when the men left a few hours earlier, the chances of them returning with my baby were very slim. If Mattia was indeed behind the kidnapping, he wouldn't be foolish enough to let us discover the location where the child was being kept.

I couldn't respond to Alessio because, despite the hope, it would still be another night away from my baby. Another sleepless night, thinking about him and wishing to hold him in my arms.

Vittorio hadn't nursed at my breast when he was taken from me. Unfortunately, I had never produced milk, attributed to the stress of my pregnancy and his birth. We had a wet nurse in Sicily arranged by the nuns, and in Los Angeles, I hoped to find one. Both Sienna and Deanna were breastfeeding and offered to help when he came home.

But I didn't even know what they were doing with him in my absence.

But I didn't want to think about that.

Clutching the blanket, I leaned forward, feeling my stomach churn with despair. It still held his scent. The scent that tormented me with longing.

I lost track of everything for a moment, but I felt Alessio's arms around me in an embrace, and I simply leaned into him, resting my head on his firm chest, which would be my refuge at that moment.

"Let's go inside, *dolce angelo*. Please..."

I eventually nodded and let him guide me. Then the women welcomed me and settled me among them, almost creating a barrier.

We waited a bit to talk until I composed myself, but when I looked around, I realized we were only among ourselves. The man

BOUND BY BETRAYAL

189

sent by Giovanni wasn't there. I decided not to ask because it wouldn't make much difference.

"You were right, Luna. The Gallos did have our son. Until the day before. When they made the mistake of using the card, they were killed."

The day before.

Twenty-four hours of distance between recovering my son and continuing without him.

"Was it really Mattia?" Sienna asked, trying to understand better than I did.

"He didn't mention a name," Enrico replied to her, sitting on the arm of the sofa to be close to his wife. "But the chances are high. Almost impossible for it not to be."

"The Gallos really betrayed me..." I whispered, staring into nothing, still in shock.

But this kind of thing shouldn't leave me so surprised. I shouldn't give my trust so easily to others. Just as I shouldn't have given my heart to Alessio so quickly.

"It seems Ginevra was innocent," Alessio replied. "She believed she was helping you. He didn't. He knew everything."

"That's a lie. Of course, the woman knew too..." Dominic said, but was silenced by a slap from Deanna. "But what the hell did I do?"

"It's to learn not to be a *stronzo*!" In any other situation, I would find it funny for anyone to call Dominic an "idiot" and get away with it. "You don't need to say that. Maybe the woman really was innocent."

He didn't say anything more, just muttered something in Italian and crossed his arms.

"Either way, he gave clues that the boy is in Sicily."

"In Sicily?" I repeated what Enrico had said almost shouting. "They took my baby so far away? My God..."

"We're going there, Luna. It's our next destination."

I stood up from the sofa, starting to pace back and forth, feeling like I might collapse if I stayed sitting there.

Alessio also stood up.

"Luna... you need to calm down."

He tried to hold me, his hands on my arms, but I shook him off.

"No! I can't calm down!" I raised my voice again. "I want to die every time I remember the scene of my baby being taken from me. I want to disappear every time I think he's not with me and that if I had stayed where I was, he wouldn't have been taken." I was distraught. I could no longer control my own words. "I said we are cursed, and I think we really are, Alessio. At least everything we touch turns into something bad. I should have stayed in the convent from the beginning; why did you take me out of there? Why?"

I punched his chest again, not even knowing what I was doing. He didn't stop me. He let me hit him on the shirt, pushing him and venting all my anger.

When I was done, I just stepped back and moved away, embarrassed by my outburst but still clutching the blanket. I threw myself onto the bed in the room that had been assigned to me at the Preterotti house, holding it tight, turning onto my side and curling up in a fetal position.

No tears were enough. Not while I wasn't with my baby. When Vittorio returned, I had made a promise to myself and to God that I would never again lament anything. That I would consider life something wonderful and be grateful for every day. Until he arrived, I would feel half of myself.

I cried so much that I ended up falling asleep. When I woke up, it was already dawn, and the first thing I saw was Alessio sitting in an armchair near the bed, sleeping awkwardly.

I got up, still feeling tired, as if I hadn't slept at all. Sleep, despite that, had revitalized me and made me dream, so as soon as I opened my eyes, regret hit me for how I had treated him the night before.

I wanted to talk, to apologize, because I believed that only in peace could we move forward together on our mission.

I also wanted to wake him and ask him to go lie down in a bed. He was too tall to remain in that position, and I feared he would hurt himself, especially his neck.

I put my hand on his shoulder, but he grabbed my fist and pulled me onto his lap.

I thought it was a reaction to being disturbed while sleeping, but he opened his huge blue eyes, focusing on mine, very serious.

I was breathless from the sudden movement and the closeness, so I tried to get up, but he held me tight and even stood up, carrying me in his arms, which made me squeal in surprise and hug his shoulders.

"Listen to what I'm going to say now, Luna Cipriano. I was wrong. I was overwhelmed with pain, distressed, and I still am. But a year has passed, and I understand that you were the best thing that ever happened to me, regardless of what your brother did or didn't do."

"Alessio..." I tried to say something, but I was interrupted.

"I promised I wouldn't say everything I have to say until you told me you were ready to hear it, but here it is. You are not a curse to me. You are the opposite of that."

Those were words I had waited a long time to hear. Would it be too late? Would it be a mistake to still wish to hear them? A misunderstanding to feel myself melting in his arms, longing for that passionate way I had missed so much?

I nodded slowly, agreeing, and Alessio carefully set me back on the floor.

"The guys and I are going to Sicily."

"Then I'm going too." Alessio was about to say something, but I raised a finger, not allowing him to continue. "If you leave me here, you'll have to handcuff me to the bed because I will catch a flight on my own and go after you."

I thought he would argue, but he smiled. It wasn't yet the smile of the man I had met and fallen in love with, but it was the closest we had come since we reunited.

"I like this stubborn side of you, *dolce angelo*. It will drive me crazy, but I like it."

"Great, because when it comes to my son, there won't be another Luna. This will be me."

"May your God help me then to resist you and keep my control."

That was all he said before leaving the room, closing the door, and leaving me alone, thinking about all the things he had said and what was yet to come.

CHAPTER THIRTY-FOUR

Alessio

As was to be expected, not only *we* went to Sicily. Deanna and Sienna also decided to come. With the babies. As if it were a family outing.

With Ilya tailing us, it was almost an excursion. Not to mention the two hired nannies who traveled with us to help the girls with the babies. And, hopefully, to help with Vittorio too.

Sitting in one of the airplane seats, I observed the group, and aside from the Russian, the unity of all the people I loved in life made me a bit emotional. My brothers, my sisters-in-law, my nephews—and... her. Luna.

We could be a family by that point. Our women could be at home, safe, taking care of our babies, but I was a coward and hadn't told Luna everything I should have. That she *deserved* to hear.

But it wasn't time to lament. At some point, we would have our baby back, and I could redeem myself with his mother. As long as Vittorio wasn't found, none of us would be able to think about anything else.

We landed and headed straight to the house where we would stay, provided by one of our contacts. We stowed our things, took advantage of the early hour, left the babies with the nannies, and set off for the convent for a quick visit.

The moment we passed through the gates, Ilya, who again took the lead of the group—without weapons this time—made the sign of the cross with a very solemn expression, surprising all of us enough that we looked at him in astonishment.

"What's wrong? I'm Catholic! Why the surprise?" he replied with a thick accent.

"Isn't the predominant religion in Russia the Orthodox Church?" Deanna asked, always cheeky.

"Russia is behind me. My mother was Norwegian, a fervent Catholic, and... Well... There was someone else who taught me to be more religious. I am a God-fearing man, that's what matters."

There was something incompatible in the words of a guy who was a killing machine but feared divine punishment. Ilya was a contradiction, apparently.

Ignoring the man's comments, we proceeded through the convent grounds, accompanied by a middle-aged nun, very kind but seeming more afraid of us than anything else. She obviously knew who we were.

We entered and headed to the Abbess's office. It wasn't a new place for us, as Dominic and I had already been there, and neither was it for Luna.

So much so that when the woman entered, the girl ran to her, throwing herself into her arms, even making a small reverence by touching the ground with her knees in submission.

"Blessing, Abbess."

"God bless you, my daughter. I am so sorry for what happened." I knew that this woman was one of the people Luna loved most in life, but I kept a close eye on her because, unlike the girl, I didn't give my trust so easily.

"My baby, ma'am... My little baby..." The nun took Luna in her arms once more, in a maternal way, and I swallowed hard, trying to maintain my composure. It wasn't easy to see the woman I loved like that. It wasn't easy to think of my son, whom I didn't even know, lost and unprotected.

BOUND BY BETRAYAL

"Unfortunately, I don't have good news to share, child."

Luna pulled away from the woman, scared.

"Tizziana? She...?"

"No, dear. Your sister is fine. She should be coming down soon, actually, because we called for her. The problem is that Mr. Preterotti, Alessio, contacted us, and we conducted small investigations here inside the abbey. We found suspicious things with... well... Conccetta. And she disappeared two days ago. Took her things one early morning, left, and hasn't returned."

Luna seemed surprised at that name, bringing a hand to her mouth.

"Conccetta was my best friend here. She was a novice..." Luna explained, still very shocked. "Ma'am... it can't be a mistake?"

"We were going to talk to her, but she didn't give us a chance. I'm sorry to say, daughter, but we suspect she entered the convent specifically to spy on you." The Abbess turned to us to explain: "Conccetta arrived here two years after Luna. The two became close immediately, even though the novice was a bit older. She hadn't made her permanent vows yet because I still felt she was insecure. Now I understand."

"Any idea where she might have gone?" Enrico asked.

"No, sir. But I think we can find out. We just need a few days."

"We don't have a few days, ma'am. With all due respect. It's a baby that's missing!" I said, with a bit more rudeness than necessary.

"We know that, son, but we can't do more than this. We have some records of each girl who arrives. Conccetta had no family, but we can try to find out some things because she received calls and visits. But we have no resources."

"We can provide them," Dominic replied immediately, but the woman smiled.

"Thank you, Mr. Ungaretti, but we cannot accept the *type* of resources you would provide."

Ilya chuckled, and we all looked at him.

"What's up? I just thought it was curious."

"Why?" Luna asked, confused, just like we all were.

"Because they kept a mafia princess in here, funded by one of the most powerful families in the Cosa Nostra, but they can't accept resources to look for a missing baby."

Apparently, Ilya's conclusion was enough for another type of help to be negotiated. After all, he served for more than just being a reinforcement in our defense and attack. He was a negotiator.

Our conversation was interrupted by Tizziana's arrival, who hugged her sister almost fiercely, and the two cried tears of joy at their reunion. She participated in the conversation we had next, providing some insights about Conccetta, of whom she was also a good friend.

When we returned to the house where we were staying, we paid attention to the babies, who had been left not only with the nannies but surrounded by security, and we gathered for lunch.

The first idea that came up might have seemed absurd at first, but it came from Deanna...

"If we have a few days of downtime here, I think we should have some kind of training. At least Luna and I, since Enrico and Sienna have been training all along."

"You with a gun?" Dominic exclaimed, his eyes wide. "Only if I were completely crazy or suicidal."

"I'm serious, Dom. We have security and you guys all the time, but I think it's important for us to know how to defend ourselves."

"I agree with Deanna," Enrico said.

"I also agree with the blonde," Ilya chimed in, earning a glare from Dominic that could kill.

"Show some respect for my wife. 'Blonde' is bullshit."

BOUND BY BETRAYAL

"Okay, okay. I agree with Mrs. Ungaretti," Ilya said with a visible mocking tone. "Anyway, I can help. I've been responsible for training some people back at Solsnetskaya."

None of us, to be honest, trusted Ilya too much, but we exchanged glances, believing it could be a fair way to make the girls a little less defenseless.

That evening, we waited for the sun to set in the sky and headed to the large backyard of the house, with our weapons and some mats, starting our training.

Silencers were used, even though the house we were in had no neighbors and was as far away as possible in the Palermo region. It was exhausting hours because Ilya was relentless, even with the girls. The other men and I didn't feel it as much, but the three of them ended up sprawled on their mats after the Russian left—I had no idea where he was staying, but he didn't want to remain in the house with us—which led Dominic to carry a protesting Deanna up the stairs, as she swore her legs felt like jelly.

Sienna was the least tired because she was more accustomed to it, and Luna just threw herself into the shower, taking a hot bath and burying herself in her room.

Both my brother and my brother-in-law were sleeping with their wives and could snuggle them in their arms at night. I, on the other hand, found myself sitting in my armchair alone, a glass of whiskey in hand, the weak light from a lamp illuminating the room faintly.

I planned to stay like that until sleep came, if it ever did, but someone knocked softly on the door.

I saw Luna peering through the crack, her eyes red and wearing one of her modest nightgowns, with a blanket wrapped around her shoulders because it was really cold. Her little feet were bare, and her hair was wet.

"Can I come in?" she asked, with her sweet little manner, her voice low and timid.

It was my girl. My *dolce angelo*.

Dio, how I wanted her back. I would do anything for that.

"Of course you can," my voice came out low too, whispered, almost hoarse.

Without waiting any longer, Luna entered and closed the door. I swore she would sit on the bed, which was right in front of my armchair, but she came to me and positioned herself, settling into my lap, sitting sideways on my legs.

"Luna? What...?"

"Don't ask. Don't say anything. I just want to be like this with you because I need to sleep. Can I sleep in your lap, Alessio, please?"

The surprise was so great that it took me a moment to get used to the idea, even though it was the most wonderful possible.

"Of course. Of course you can."

As soon as I said that, she nestled against my chest, and I held her after placing the glass on the side table.

I kept looking at her, nestled in my arms, still because I didn't know what it meant. I couldn't touch her, I couldn't do more than what she asked, which was simply to be a refuge for her sleep.

Luna didn't take long to fall asleep. I knew she had been having sleepless nights, but she found some sort of rest in my lap.

And that wasn't the only night. After that night, she began to do it regularly, until the first news from the convent arrived...

CHAPTER THIRTY-FIVE

Luna

According to the Abbess, the information was discovered in record time. As far as I knew, Ilya's help had been crucial.

For a desperate mother? It felt like an eternity had passed.

In just over a week, we had a possible location.

From what we were able to gather, Conccetta hadn't left the country, not even Sicily. The contact who always spoke with her was discovered as well, and as we suspected, he was one of Mattia's men. A man I already knew, who had worked for our family since my father's time.

Apparently, the man was Conccetta's lover.

He was the one financing her and had made some purchases of baby items at a store near La Kalsa.

With all this investigation done by Ilya, we had an address, a house. Reliable sources said they had seen a woman holding a baby inside and that there were two men guarding the location, in addition to the lover making regular visits.

At night, those two guards were more alert. During the day, only one of them patrolled the house.

The plan was for the guys to strike in the morning, taking advantage of how far the house was, so we would have the upper hand.

That night, I didn't sleep in Alessio's lap because he was making plans in the office with the men. Or rather... I didn't sleep at all.

Tossing and turning in bed, I heard someone come in and thought it was him, but I found Deanna and Sienna instead. Neither of them was in pajamas, but wearing black pants and tops of the same color. They were carrying something that looked like another change of clothes. This was casually thrown over me.

"Come on, Luna. Let's take advantage of the fact that they are all gathered. Get dressed!" Deanna said in a commanding tone.

"Take advantage of what?"

"We're going to get your baby back."

I didn't understand anything at all, but I started putting on the pants she handed me, which was probably hers, since we had similar body types.

"What are you talking about, Dee? I don't understand..."

"Ilya is waiting for us in the car, behind the house. We'll sneak out without them noticing. We have the address, we have everything. If we don't act, it might be too late," Sienna explained.

"But... us?"

"Why do you think I asked for us to be trained?"

"We weren't trained that much."

I continued getting dressed despite this because, honestly, I didn't even know why I was contesting so much. I would go get my baby even in hell, unarmed. The circumstances didn't matter.

"Enough. And we'll have Ilya."

I didn't know if I trusted the man enough to take him on a mission like this, but it was the option we had.

Without asking many more questions, I tied my hair back in a ponytail as we cautiously left my room. If any of the men caught us, we would be lost.

Still, we managed to get outside as discreetly as possible and got into the car. Deanna next to Ilya, and Sienna and I in the back.

"There are weapons in the trunk. The same ones you learned to use," he informed us with his thick accent.

BOUND BY BETRAYAL

He was such a big man that I barely knew how he fit behind the wheel.

"We're ready," Deanna replied, and he smiled at her, almost gleefully.

"You really are crazy, blonde. But let's go."

I had no idea if the journey was long or short, but just like the last few days during the investigation that had led us there, it felt like it lasted much longer. It was like being on a long trip, filled with immense anxiety to reach the final destination.

I felt Sienna's hand over mine, and then I looked at her. Her gaze was determined, but there was a touch of compassion.

What was the strength of these two women? Both had babies at home, yet they were doing everything they could so I could have mine back too.

I loved them. No matter what happened between me and Alessio. Deanna and Sienna would always be like sisters to me.

As soon as we arrived, Ilya armed us. He handed each of us a pistol and took something massive on his shoulder, which he checked carefully.

"This one I call Catja."

"A woman's name for a gun?" Sienna asked.

"And aren't you dangerous like one?"

No more arguments. If that was what he thought...

I felt strange holding a revolver. In fact, I could say the same about wearing pants. It was comfortable. Much more so than the long skirts I used to wear. For walking, no doubt. It hugged my body in a way that didn't leave any excess fabric.

And yes, I had never worn pants in my life. In the convent, it wasn't allowed, and even when I returned to Texas to be with my family, I didn't wear any because I wasn't used to it.

I followed the girls with quick steps, but not running. Any noise could be fatal. I didn't know if I was ready to shoot someone, but it was to save my child. If Vittório was really in that house with those people, and I needed to fire a shot to get him out and bring him back, nothing or no one would stand in my way.

Ilya was in front of us, giving the coordinates. He was also the one who stretched out an arm and stopped us when he noticed there were more people at the door of the house than our informant had told us.

"Back up. Stay in the car. I'll try to handle this," he said quietly, although his voice was so deep and thick it was hard to believe it wouldn't be heard.

"Alone?" I asked, my eyes wide.

"Better than putting the princesses at risk. Ungaretti and the Preterottis would cook me in a roasting pot."

"No way you're going in there alone. We came here to act."

With that, Deanna stepped forward, dodging Ilya's blocking arm and advancing toward the house with her weapon aimed.

I heard the sound of the first shot, muffled, just a weak pop echoing in the night silence. The second made me really tense.

" *Sumasshedshiy!* Crazy! Crazy, crazy!" he grumbled and also moved from his position, ready to cover Deanna's back.

Sienna and I exchanged glances and followed them. Before I knew it, I realized that Ilya and our friend had taken down about four people.

Someone came, surprising us, grabbing me from behind, but Ilya spun around, grabbing the man by the collar and pulling him away from me. He used his massive weapon to hit him. While he dealt with one, Sienna shot at another.

I was completely lost. Still holding the gun, I couldn't imagine pulling the trigger. And I had the impression that the girls knew this because they were both taking care to protect me.

I was still dazed when I was completely hit by the sound that followed. A baby's cry.

BOUND BY BETRAYAL

It could be any child, but it was *mine*. I was completely sure.

"Vittório!" I whimpered, swearing I would have a heart attack right there, because my heart was racing like it never had before.

"Let's go get him. I'll go with you..." Deanna said, moving closer to me and casting a glance at Sienna and Ilya, who had joined to cover the second floor.

We climbed the stairs, and I could swear Deanna looked more like a CIA special agent, holding her gun and very focused on her mission.

There were few rooms upstairs, and three of them had their doors open. The only closed one was the one we stopped in front of, and I could hear the crying louder.

I began to get more and more nervous, and Deanna wasted no time. She shot the doorknob, destroying it with enviable aim, and opened the door for us to enter.

The first thing I saw was Conccetta, standing in front of a crib. She was a tall woman, and I imagined her intention was to hide what was inside, although I had no doubt about what it was, given the constant crying.

My baby was there.

Just a short distance away.

With a few steps, I would reach him.

For the first time since this entire madness began, I raised the gun with full determination, aiming it at Conccetta.

"Get out of the way. Get the hell away from my child!" I shouted, frantic, letting out words I wasn't used to saying.

"If I let you take him, he'll kill me."

"He, who?" Deanna said, almost in a growl.

Conccetta turned to me with a frightened expression. Her brow was furrowed, and I didn't need much more explanation to understand.

Mattia.

Not that I had doubted for a moment, but his name flashed in my brain as I tried to comprehend how we had reached that point.

"Just get out of the way, Conccetta."

"I won't move. I'm not dying because of you, you mafia little bitch. You should have given it up to a Cosa Nostra son of a bitch? After your father and brother fought so hard for our revolution to mean something? This little bastard here doesn't deserve the life of a king he'll get and..."

I didn't even think.

But if I had thought, I would have done the same.

The shot hit her leg. Right in the thigh. And it wasn't a miss. I couldn't risk shooting higher and having the bullet diverted to somehow hit the crib. By the way I hit her, Vittório would be safe. Besides, I had the feeling that the woman I swore was my friend knew things that could be important to us. It was better to leave her alive.

When Conccetta collapsed onto the slate floor, screaming in pain, and was subdued by Deanna, the path was clear for me to go to my baby.

I let the gun drop to the ground without even thinking about how reckless that was, allowing my feet to move toward the wooden piece of furniture that held the most precious little thing in my entire life.

I closed my eyes as I stopped in front of the baby, absorbing the sound of his cries and preparing to take him. I didn't know if I would have the strength at that moment, but I leaned down and took him in my arms, cradling him against my chest.

Vittório stopped crying immediately.

Did he remember me? Or had he forgotten me in those endless days that separated us?

It didn't matter. What I knew was that they would never take him away from me again.

Never again.

CHAPTER THIRTY-SIX

Alessio

Someone knocked on the office door of Enrico's house, and we all straightened up to see who it was.

It was the housekeeper, looking flustered and paler than a sheet of paper.

"They've arrived!" was all she managed to say between gasps, placing a hand on her chest.

"Who arrived?" Dominic was the first to stand up, in a sudden movement, looking worried.

"The girls, sir. And they... they brought the baby."

The three men exchanged glances, startled.

"What baby are you talking about?" I asked, a knot in my throat. It couldn't be that...

"Yours, boy. Your little son..." The woman began to get emotional, and I froze for a second.

How? How was that possible?

I felt a hand on my shoulder and saw Enrico beside me, literally pushing me out of the office. Dominic shot past us like an arrow, seething with rage, and that movement, along with my brother's support, finally made me act.

We rushed down the stairs as if we were ready to save someone from death, and when we reached the living room, there they were.

206 AMARA HOLT

Luna had a bundle in her arms. Small, motionless, but there were tufts of brown hair peeking out from the cloth covering it. The shape of a little head left no room for doubt. It was a baby.

Her tear-filled eyes left no doubts either.

"What the hell have you crazy women done?" Dominic said again, furious.

I remained frozen in place, watching Luna and the baby. Unable to move, I couldn't take my eyes off them.

"We did your job. We're here, intact, with the child. You're welcome!" my sister replied with her usual feisty attitude.

"How did you do this?" Enrico also chimed in, much calmer than Dom.

While we were asking, Ilya appeared in the doorway, walking casually and pocketing a lighter.

"I even helped a bit, but the princesses handled it. I left a little gift for you in a nice spot. There's a man there taking care of her, and I think it won't be hard to get some information from the woman. I imagine that..."

He was going to continue, but Dominic approached and punched him.

"What authority do you have to come into our house and put our women in danger?" he growled. He wasn't that much shorter than Ilya, and Dominic was a big guy. Still, the Russian was a presence to be respected.

Ilya, still turned to the side, flashed a mischievous smile, as if the punch hadn't even tickled him, although I could swear it had hurt. He was probably just resistant to pain.

"I'll let that punch slide because I imagine I deserve it. But you won't hit me again, Ungaretti. The mission was accomplished, and I brought the three home safely. We still have a valuable witness in our possession. Accept that you weren't the hero this time, and everything will be fine."

After dropping that bomb, he simply left the house, casting a glance at the three women, slamming the door behind him and disappearing from our sight.

A grave silence fell among us, as I had the impression that no one really knew what to say. Sienna was the first to do something, as she moved and went to Enrico, nestling into his arms. My brother might have fought with his wife, but he simply hugged her tightly, kissing the top of her head.

"Are you okay?" he whispered to her, protectively wrapping an arm around her shoulders.

"Yes, I'm fine. I'm okay."

Looking at us, he pulled Sienna out of the living room, and I knew his intention was to give us privacy.

Dominic seemed to have the same idea but in a slightly different way.

"Crazy woman! Completely crazy!" He approached her with fury, but as soon as he stood in front of her, he seemed to melt and placed both hands on her face, kissing her. "You're going to kill me one day, *leonessa*. That's for sure. But you're a wonderful crazy." Then he crouched down and hoisted her over his shoulder, carrying her up the stairs like a caveman. "I'll find a way to punish you properly."

I didn't want to know what they planned to do, but my sister's laughter, who probably knew her husband very well, calmed me down, assuring me that he wouldn't hurt her for her audacity and insubordination.

And there we were: I and Luna, standing face to face. She with my baby in her arms, who seemed to be sleeping peacefully, completely unaware of what was happening around him. The blessing of innocence...

She hadn't looked me in the eye until that moment. She kept her head down, not even paying attention to the other couples or to Dominic's fight with Ilya. Something was wrong, which made me move closer to her.

"He... he's okay?"

Luna nodded.

"And you?"

She nodded again.

I took another step forward, extending my hand and lifting her face to look at her.

"What's wrong? Are you hurt?"

"No, but I hurt someone else," she confessed. "I shot Conccetta."

"It was for Vittório."

"It was. And I would do it again. But I can't get the sound of the shot out of my head, nor her face when she was hit." Luna sighed but lifted her head, swallowing hard. She seemed to be making a great effort to compose herself, though she clearly wasn't okay. "Well... anyway... he's with us again. This is your son, Alessio."

I pretended not to notice her trembling arms as she handed me the baby, and I certainly didn't want her to realize how disoriented I felt receiving him in my arms.

He was so tiny. So helpless. The most beautiful thing I had ever seen in my life. And I was passionate about my nephews, convinced they were the most wonderful children, but my son was...

My son was perfect.

His little heart-shaped mouth was slightly open, taking in air, and his tiny belly rose and fell with peaceful breaths. There was a dimple on his chin, and his nose was sculpted, perfectly shaped. He had perfect eyelashes and adorable cheeks.

Cradling him in one arm, I used my other hand to hold his, looking at his tiny fingernails, counting them, and admiring his chubby little arm.

"He has your eyes," Luna said, interrupting the moment.

BOUND BY BETRAYAL

It was the most incredible interruption at the perfect moment when I was really starting to wonder what his little eyes would look like.

"He..." I started to speak, but a devastating emotion washed over me. It wasn't a feeling that crept in gently, settling in my heart softly.

It was a hurricane of devastating proportions. A wave ready to knock me down.

It had been almost a month since Luna had returned to my life with the news that we had a son. From the beginning, the information hit me hard, and I was shaken, but nothing compared to the sensation of holding my baby in my arms. To see that he was real.

"He's beautiful, Luna. He's an angel." I raised my eyes to her, and I knew they were filled with tears. "An angel coming from another angel..."

She didn't say anything, just crossed her arms against her chest, somewhat hugging herself and shaking her head, also emotional.

We were both crying. That was undoubtedly the most intense moment of my entire life.

I don't even know how we found the strength to go up the stairs, to take Vittório to the little room where the other babies were. We had already set up a crib there for him to have a place to stay since our hope of bringing him home had never faded.

And there he was.

"I think I should give him a bath, but he's sleeping so peacefully," Luna commented after I placed him in the crib, with her help, because I had no experience handling such a small baby.

"He smells like soap."

"Yes, but it was *she* who bathed him," Luna spat, visibly irritated. That woman would always be a reason for hatred for the pure angel I knew.

I imagined Luna would never forget that experience.

210 AMARA HOLT

Thinking about that, I glanced at her, noticing for the first time the kind of clothes she was wearing.

I had never seen her in pants, let alone such form-fitting ones. Of course, the piece didn't belong to her, but it fit her like a glove, just like the tight blouse that made her waist look so thin against her hips. Dressed all in black, with her hair in a ponytail, she truly looked like a warrior.

My warrior angel.

"You can go if you want. I can't separate from him tonight," she said softly, after all, we were in a room with three babies who seemed to be sleeping peacefully. If one started to cry, it would be a symphony.

That almost made me smile.

Our family was growing. And however twisted it was, it was ours. Those three innocent little ones there, cousins, were the future of the Cosa Nostra. Heirs of powerful families.

"I'm not going anywhere. I'm staying with you and him," I replied, resolutely. It would take a crane to pull me away from that child and that woman. "In the meantime, you can tell me how you got to him, okay?"

I pulled two poufs so we could sit close to the crib, and Luna hesitated a bit, but nodded, smiling, and settled beside me.

We spent the whole night talking and looking at our son.

I didn't know of any moments better than those.

CHAPTER THIRTY-SEVEN

Luna

I woke up feeling disoriented, lying in an armchair, unsure how I had ended up there. I barely remembered what had happened before, though images of me with my head on Alessio's shoulder, sleepy and exhausted, flickered in my mind, hazy but seeming very real.

I blinked my sleepy eyes as I heard a soft baby sound. That served as extra motivation to jump from the armchair and run toward the sound.

Vittório was no longer in the crib but in front of the window, in his father's arms, who was rocking him back and forth. A delightful giggle made me stop.

The scene could easily make me crumble.

Noticing my approach, Alessio turned his body, and the first thing I saw was my boy's wide-open, very blue eyes looking at me. He broke into a huge smile upon seeing me, bringing his chubby hand to his mouth and drooling all over it.

He remembered me. He hadn't forgotten me during the time we were apart.

"Look, Mommy's awake," Alessio said in an adorable tone, shaking Vittório's other hand, the one that wasn't in his mouth, as if giving me a little wave. Then he informed me, "Sienna came by a few minutes ago. She fed him. She was afraid you wouldn't like it, but since you had talked about her being a wet nurse before..."

"No, it's fine." How could it not be fine? She was Vittório's aunt and had only thought of my baby's well-being. Did I want to breastfeed him? With all my strength. But I knew he would be in good hands.

I moved closer to the two, still emotional from the scene. Alessio handed me the baby, and I cradled him against my shoulder, hugging him tightly and beginning to cry.

I should have been tired of tears, but these were different. No longer from agony. They were from happiness.

I let Alessio pull me into him, resting my head on his chest, and we stayed like that, close to each other, the three of us, as a family.

I couldn't cling to that idea, but it was impossible, considering how significant the moment was.

But I couldn't delude myself. It also wasn't very possible, given that the mastermind behind the crime was still at large, and he was my own brother.

So when we gathered again in the dining room of Enrico's house, that was what I had in mind. I had never needed to live like this, and I suspected that the people around me had a different way of dealing with violence, fear, and tension, but I wasn't like that.

Shooting an unarmed woman was something very frightening. So much so that I swore I would think about it all day until we spoke with her, but I was surprised when I got downstairs and found a table set, full of food, with everyone gathered.

I shot a glance at Alessio, and he also seemed a bit lost.

"It's a welcome breakfast for Vittório," Sienna explained, bringing her little Andreas to us, placing the two cousins together to interact. "Look, son, the new family member for you to play with..."

Soon Deanna also came in, with the beautiful Nicollo, and the three of them together were the epitome of cuteness. They seemed so normal that I felt a spark of hope ignite in my heart.

BOUND BY BETRAYAL 213

I looked around at the men already seated at the table, so handsome, so strong, so connected, and at us: three women whose struggles united us, but who had become soul sisters.

Yes, anyone looking at us would see a family. Not a horde of mobsters, princes, and princesses of the Cosa Nostra. They would never think that Deanna had been kidnapped to marry Dominic; that Sienna had to fake her death to survive; or that I was the sister of the man who killed the Preterotti's father. Our baggage was dark, but the feelings we had for each other helped us overcome any obstacle.

"Why don't we sit down? I'm hungry!" Deanna exclaimed, excited.

"I... I wanted to change clothes..." Suddenly I remembered that I hadn't changed since I went to get Vittório, and that made me shudder.

"Of course, of course. Let me lend you something..." Deanna handed the baby to Dominic, quickly taking mine and leaving him with Alessio.

She intertwined her arm with mine, and we headed up the stairs. She was in charge, and I didn't offer any objections at first.

When we arrived at the room she shared with Dominic, the first thing she did was pick up a few things from the floor that looked more like handcuffs, restraints, chains... I couldn't quite tell.

"Sorry. Last night was... lively, you know?"

No, I didn't know. Did they use those things... in intimacy? In sex?

Well, it wasn't my business, but the surprise was great, as was my body's reaction to imagining...

I shook my head, trying to push those thoughts away, focusing on what was important: changing clothes.

"I can wear one of my clothes..." I said as she rummaged through her suitcase.

"No way. You can't possibly have not noticed how Alessio was staring at you in those pants. He looked like he had never seen a butt in his life."

I raised my eyebrows, surprised.

"Really? You think?"

"If I think? Honey, I know the look of a man filled with desire. Not that I want to notice these things because he's my brother, but Alessio is crazy about you."

I smiled shyly, tucking a strand of hair behind my ear.

"He's always been crazy about *many* women, right? Maybe he's just interested in that," I tried, eager to hear the opposite.

Holding two pieces of clothing in her hand, Deanna positioned herself in front of me.

"So you don't know, huh?"

"Don't know what?"

She chuckled.

"Alessio hasn't dated any woman since you two met."

"What?" it was an instinctive reaction.

"It's true."

"No, but he could be doing it off the record, right? Without you all knowing."

"He could, if we didn't talk a lot about these things. If he hadn't confessed to me recently. Unless he did it days before he met you again, which I doubt, the information remains true."

I was speechless, more so than before, and Deanna literally threw the pieces of clothing into my arms, forcing me to extend them automatically to catch them.

"Can I give you a piece of advice? One I would give to a sister, if mine were still alive?" I nodded, a bit dazed, absorbing everything she had told me. "I know things between you two have been complicated, but it's clear you love each other."

"He never said that."

"And he has to say it first, no doubt. But some men are caught by little details: sex, jealousy... Mafia men are very possessive."

"I don't even know how to do that."

"You don't need to. Just threatening will be enough."

"In bed... I'm not very experienced either."

"They are. Usually. Just mark your territory. Let him do whatever he wants with you and then take the sweet from his mouth. Leaving him wanting more is quite an aphrodisiac. The forbidden also works wonders."

With that, Deanna winked at me and stepped away, leaving me alone in the room.

My God, my head had turned into complete chaos.

So much so that when I returned to the dining room, freshly bathed and wearing Deanna's clothes, I focused on Alessio's gaze toward me, and I could swear he could strip each piece of clothing off me with just his eyes. The way he licked his lower lip and took a deep breath gave me the confidence I needed.

If I wanted him back, I needed to be clever and much less reserved.

This could be an interesting challenge.

CHAPTER THIRTY-EIGHT

Alessio

There was a very poorly done bandage on the woman's leg. Ilya was definitely not a good nurse, and I had the impression it wasn't his intention either. She was tied to a chair in a way that must have been painful, sweating, with her hair stuck to her forehead, pale.

She wouldn't live much longer without medical help. Surely the leg couldn't be saved.

I didn't like torturing women, not even when they were clearly the spawn of the devil, having served as instruments for the kidnapping of an innocent child.

Not even when they looked at the woman I loved with disdain and hatred. I could swear that if the roles were reversed and Conccetta was free, with Luna captured, it would undoubtedly be unprecedented violence.

The guys and I had decided to stop trying to convince the women of anything. If each of them was stubborn on their own, together they seemed like an organized crime syndicate, ready to agree on everything, always against us.

They went to the shed where Ilya had taken Conccetta. Deanna and Sienna had already participated in something of that nature before, and I knew they could handle it, but Luna...? I worried about her every second. Especially when we arrived.

BOUND BY BETRAYAL

I took her hand in mine, intertwining our fingers and guiding her, because I could feel the tension in every one of her muscles. She was again wearing borrowed clothes from Deanna: jeans and a T-shirt, probably because she didn't feel comfortable wearing something from the convent. This made me wonder how much of the true and sweet Luna was being lost in all this.

Some transformations are irreversible.

"Can I talk to one of you?" Ilya asked, and I nodded. We stepped away from the others, and he lit a cigarette. The place was closed, but he didn't seem to care much about that. "I found out some things about the girl there. She has a teenage brother. He's studying at an expensive school, a boarding school. Probably the money she was taking from Mattia was for that."

"Did you use him? Did you mention him?"

"No, I wanted to wait for you to tell me the best way to proceed."

That was enough for me. I asked Ilya some information about the boy before we returned to the others, and my strange companion moved ahead.

"The pretty one here is tired, you know? We had a long talk during the night... She only told me a little about all the hatred she has for the Cosa Nostra. It's ugly. I swear I'm not the biggest fan of this secret organization crap either, and I have my reasons, but I don't go around kidnapping babies," Ilya said, using all his sarcasm to talk to us. He sat in a chair, leaning the front of his body against the backrest, throwing the cigarette on the ground and extinguishing it with his boot. Very threatening.

"What's the reason for all that hatred? Is there one?" Dominic asked, taking off his jacket, kind of preparing for what was to come.

"Daddy was killed. A traitor. Tortured like she was."

Conccetta literally growled, with much of her strength drained.

"You animals!" was all she could say before moaning in pain.

"To me, an animal is someone who kidnaps a baby and takes him from his mother," Deanna said, equally irritated.

I approached the woman, keeping in mind that she was the reason my son had been taken from his mother; that Vittorio had been kept away from us for so long. I couldn't feel sorry for her, not at all.

"You can kill me, torture me, I won't say anything," she asserted in a thin voice. "If you don't do it, Mattia will. He wanted to use the baby in a blackmail scheme and won't be able to now. What do you think he will do to me for failing?"

"His opinions are not my problem, but I want to know what *you* think about talking about Mario, your brother?" People looked at me, not understanding anything.

Conccetta's eyes widened.

"You can't... He... He is safe. Very safe."

"Luna was safe too, and yet we got to her."

"He's just a boy! Innocent! He has nothing to do with this!" she raised her voice, desperate.

I looked at Ilya, who was smiling, playing with his beard.

"My son is too."

"I would never harm the baby!"

I opened a dark smile, crossing my arms.

"I can't say the same about your brother."

It was a lie. We wouldn't hurt the boy, but she didn't need to know that.

"No! You're bluffing!" Conccetta squirmed in the chair, and I saw a grimace of pain when she couldn't move much due to the restraints.

"I'm not." With a grunt, Ilya stood up. "I don't feel sorry for anyone. The choice is yours, little nun. I'll get to the kid in a few hours and send excellent panoramic photos and 4D videos so you can be filled with remorse." According to what he told me, the boy wasn't too far away; in Palermo itself. In fact, it wouldn't take long for him to reach him.

Since Conccetta didn't respond, he shrugged his massive shoulders and prepared to leave.

"No, wait!" that scream took a lot from her, because she was completely breathless afterward. "Mattia is trying to partner with David Damiano. He's the current leader of a group that has been gaining a lot of power..." She let out a groan and didn't finish the sentence.

"I know who David Damiano is. He frequents my club," Dominic commented. "I didn't know he was against the Cosa Nostra."

"He's not, but he has a lot of power in several states," Enrico explained. "He controls the entry and exit of methamphetamine in various locations, but he can't get into ours because the Cosa Nostra has its own suppliers."

"Maybe that could change. If we have him on our side, he could deliver Mattia," Dominic suggested, and there was an agreement among the three men, who nodded in agreement.

The conversation was taking a very specific direction, so we stopped planning in front of Conccetta. She had a few more things to say under threats, but we left her with Ilya until we decided what to do with her.

Still not continuing the discussion, we got into our cars and headed home, where the babysitter and our men awaited with the babies.

We granted ourselves a few moments with the children, but then we gathered again in the office, because there was much to discuss. It sucked that we had to talk about those things with our small children present, but the good thing was that they didn't understand anything yet.

But one day they would understand. And they would have to be part of it, one way or another.

"Can we trust David Damiano?" Sienna asked, worried. "If he agrees to a partnership with the Cosa Nostra, can we believe he won't betray us at the first opportunity?"

"In the mafia, this kind of alliance is made all the time," Dominic explained. "It's impossible to trust anyone. Just like the Ungarettis and the Preterottis, for example. The chances of betrayal would be the same."

"In our case, there was a marriage."

"We could offer one to him too," Enrico replied, but Dominic chuckled.

"Only if it's with Alessio. He's still single, after all."

"What do you mean?" That surprised me.

"Damiano has a huge crush on you. He's bisexual, but he's asked me several times if you were going to my club. I think he would love to be your voyeur." We all fell silent, thoughtful. "He tends to get quite chatty after a few drinks and when he's happy. What satisfies him is spying. More than doing," Dominic added.

"If that makes him talk, can't we let him see?" Luna spoke out of nowhere. I shot a glance at her, but she was focused on Deanna, who was smiling encouragingly. "If he's so interested in Alessio, he might feel gifted and more malleable."

The eyes then turned to me. Absolutely all of them. I had the impression that even the babies were watching me.

"I don't want to flaunt myself in front of any woman."

"What about with me?"

Oh, damn! No...

It couldn't be possible that Luna was considering that shit.

"No chance," I asserted without even thinking.

If I had thought...

Damn it.

BOUND BY BETRAYAL

If I thought of everything we could do during that little exhibition, I would accept without hesitation, with all the recklessness.

"Why not? It's my responsibility too. It's my brother. It was my child they used."

"No, Luna," I growled, already feeling my blood boil.

It wasn't like I had never been to Dominic's club. It wasn't like I didn't *enjoy* the things that happened there.

Even less: it wasn't like I was a saint. Far from it.

The problem was that Luna was too pure to even set foot in a den of lust and debauchery. I couldn't even imagine how it would be to restrain her in a bed, dominate her, and...

Damn it! I could imagine, yes.

"I think you two should talk alone and decide..." Sienna advised, and Luna and I stared at each other, as if we were opponents in a ring.

She was standing with her arms crossed, head held high. She barely resembled the innocent little thing that had seduced me without the slightest intention of doing so.

And there was still that damn outfit. Who would have thought I would get all excited seeing a woman in jeans and a cotton top?

Sienna handed Andreas to Enrico and came to take the stroller with Vittório so that Luna and I could really be alone.

I didn't even know if I wanted to have that conversation with her, but apparently it would be inevitable.

I just didn't know if I would be strong enough to fight to make her change her mind when I was already surrendered to the possibility.

But damn it!

CHAPTER THIRTY-NINE

Luna

I couldn't let him see how nervous I was. So, I crossed my arms over my chest, gripping my hands as tightly as I could because they were trembling.

What did I know about the kind of things that happened at Dominic's club? I had seen the evidence of the sex they had on the floor of his room that morning, but one thing was how far my imagination could go, and another, very different, was knowing the truth.

And no, my imagination wasn't very fertile in that regard. I knew what Alessio had taught me, which was already quite a lot, considering he was pretty experienced.

Despite that, I realized he had taken certain precautions with me because he thought I was too innocent. He wasn't wrong, but his reaction to the idea left me a bit disappointed.

"You must be crazy to suggest something like that," he started, running a hand through his hair and scratching his eyebrow with his thumb. His voice sounded deep, and I could swear he was very convinced of his statement, which again caused a pang in my chest.

"If you don't want to have sex with me, you should make that clear from the start," I provoked.

"What?" He frowned, confused.

"You're denying it quite emphatically."

"I'm denying the *kind* of sex you want to have."

BOUND BY BETRAYAL 223

"Why don't you want to?"

What the hell kind of straightforward woman had she become? It was disconcerting.

"No, damn it. I want to. I always want anything with you, Luna."

"It doesn't seem like it."

Pulling away from her a bit, I ran a hand through my hair, taking a deep breath, hoping to find patience to deal with the situation.

"Luna, the situation is a bit more complicated. You're innocent and..."

"I'm not anymore. I stopped being innocent a little over a year ago when you had sex with me. Since then, I've had a child who was kidnapped, and I've shot someone. There's nothing pure left in me."

"It's different."

"If it were with another woman, would you?"

"No!" he replied emphatically, which made me a bit more satisfied. "No, damn it. There hasn't been anyone after you. Absolutely no one."

Deanna had already told me that, but it was something completely different to hear it straight from Alessio's mouth.

So it was true. He had maintained his celibacy since I left. The Don Juan of the Cosa Nostra. The biggest jerk of all... had gone a year without sex, as if he were waiting for me, even though neither of us knew I would come back.

That could have unsettled me a little, but I held onto my determination.

"Then let it be with me."

It was meant to be a definitive statement, but it seemed to infuriate Alessio. He stopped pacing and strode toward me, gripping my arm just above the elbow with a firm hold.

"Do you have any idea what I'm going to have to do with you?" he asked through clenched teeth, and I lifted my chin to look at him.

"No, but will it give you pleasure?"

I saw him exhale sharply and his shoulders drop, almost as if he were conceding defeat.

"Just thinking about it, Luna... Just thinking about it, I'm struggling like crazy not to take you right here, right now."

I didn't expect that response, nor the intensity with which it was delivered. Nor the way his fingers dug deeper into my skin. I noticed how Alessio's jaw clenched and how he looked almost feral.

"Then accept it."

"We haven't had sex in a year. We haven't even kissed since you came back. How will I know if you're ready?"

"Because I'm saying I will be," I asserted with conviction, though it was just an attempt. "And as for the rest... It will work. It worked once before, didn't it?"

Alessio wrapped an arm around my waist and lifted me off the ground, pinning me against a wall. One of his hands came to rest beside my head on the concrete. With his leather jacket and black shirt, his stubbled jaw, he was the embodiment of an anti-hero from a romance novel. More handsome than should be possible. More than should be acceptable for the balance of the world.

"Are you going to accept being restrained, blindfolded? Will you let me touch you when you can't move, when you feel vulnerable?"

Oh my God... his voice, husky, whispered, and deep. A sound that truly came from his chest. And why did I feel so anxious about everything he was saying? Did that make me a pervert?

No... right? Deanna and Dominic did this, it was normal. The people who went to the club did too. It was a healthy taste, just peculiar.

Maybe I needed to pray a bit harder after I was done? But I already owed a rosary for the shot at Conccetta... what would be worse?

"That's the deal, isn't it?"

"People are going to see us."

"One person only, as far as I know."

"It doesn't matter. He'll want you. He'll want me. He might even masturbate while watching us." I knew he was trying to scare me. He probably would succeed, but I would try not to show it.

"I won't be thinking about that at the moment."

"Oh, but you won't..." Alessio chuckled mischievously. "You won't be thinking about anything other than my hands and my mouth touching you. My cock fucking you while you scream for more."

I was taken aback by the way he spoke, and I condemned myself for it. Of course he was provoking me.

"You can surprise me with your words, Alessio, but you won't convince me otherwise. I'm in. I know he has a crush on you, but I can find another man to accompany me on this mission."

I wriggled out of his arms and started walking toward the door, but I was grabbed and thrown onto the office table with an ease that left me dizzy. It was like being manipulated like a doll.

"Don't you dare," he shouted with immense violence. "You are mine. It will be you and me there. If you want to be fucked like never before, if you want to *play*..."— there was something wicked in the way he used the verb —"it will be with me. No one else." Leaning closer over me, bringing our lips together, he repeated: "No one."

Before I knew it, his mouth was pressed against mine, his hand gripping my thigh to keep it against his hip and bent. I needed a few seconds to get into the game because he didn't come gently. I was surprised by the frantic pace, by how he seemed to really want to claim me with that kiss. It felt like he was trying to prove a point.

And the point was: I belonged to him. Completely.

Was I ready to venture into a different kind of sex? I had no idea. But if it was with Alessio, I could feel a bit more secure that he would do everything possible—and impossible—to make me comfortable and make me feel pleasure.

"You're driving me crazy with those tight pants on your body... Completely crazy, *dolce angelo*."

It was the nickname that brought me back to reality. It was that peculiar way he called me that forced me to open my eyes and gently push him away. I didn't want him to feel rejected, but I needed air. If I wanted to do this right, to keep Alessio in my grasp, I needed to be strong.

He slowly pulled away, and I managed to stand up, positioning myself in front of him, adjusting my blouse and hair.

"So, do we have a deal?" I asked, slightly breathless, extending my hand to him to seal the pact.

He hesitated, looking into my eyes, appearing just as dazed.

Perfect. That was exactly what I wanted.

He would be at my feet very soon.

"We do. This *will* drive me crazy too, but yes, we do." Alessio squeezed my hand, and that was it.

From that moment on, the plan was in our hands.

CHAPTER FORTY

Alessio

It was my third glass of whiskey. I wanted to stay as lucid as possible for all this shit, but it was impossible to face what was coming completely sober.

We had arrived in New York the afternoon before and had very little time to prepare everything, but it had to work.

An idiot had sat down next to me at the table Dominic had reserved for me and Enrico. Sienna was with them, but the two got up to greet someone and moved away a bit. I tried everything not to be bothered by the capo who was glued to us, as if we were idols he wanted to suck up to, but annoyingly he poked me.

I could have been waiting in the room on the second floor, in the VIP area, the one I would occupy with Luna while Deanna prepared her. It wasn't just the sex that needed to be a huge display; she also needed to be dressed appropriately. No jeans or her modest, heavy clothes.

The idea of being in the room, ready to receive Luna, might be appealing, especially for the privacy, but damn it... I was nervous.

In all my sexual experiences—and I lost my virginity at fourteen—I had never felt this tense at the prospect of being with someone. I had never felt this anxious, either. So just looking at the room and thinking about all the things I could use with her, everything I could do...

It was overwhelming.

"Hey... It must be hard looking at your brother's woman, huh?" He paused, opening a grin full of mischief. "Sienna Esposito, who would have thought. What a fucking gorgeous girl. Never felt desire, huh? A wish to..."

Turning to him, happy to unleash all my stress, I grabbed him by the collar and looked at him with a pure hatred expression.

"It's Sienna Preterotti for you. Wife of the boss in Los Angeles. Your lady. Show some respect."

I finished my drink in one gulp and stood up, almost knocking over my chair. That night was starting off very, very badly.

I headed for the corridor leading to the rooms and the VIP area, climbing the stairs and using the key I'd been given to enter what would be my suite with Luna for the night.

Although I was ready for the most perverted kind of sex, it was a tasteful place. Dark, discreet tones, a huge comfortable bed with tall columns and an iron headboard, plenty of space for all sorts of restraints.

Not to mention the bars on the ceiling for the same purpose, along with the chest in the corner that held various items that could be used. All sterilized, clean, and ready for pleasure.

Just as I had said, it wasn't my first time there. Sex was my favorite sport, of all kinds. I loved making love, I enjoyed something rougher, and I adored games. Domination and submission were my favorites, without a doubt, and I could be very creative when I wanted to, especially in a space like that.

But it would be Luna in my hands. She wasn't just any woman.

She was the one I loved. The mother of my child.

And not that this made her any less of a woman or any less desirable. Of course, it ignited a different kind of respect, but nothing stronger than the lust I felt.

That, in fact, became even more evident the moment I heard the timid knock on the door.

BOUND BY BETRAYAL

"Come in." I should have taken a bit longer to respond to prepare myself. Leaving her waiting, however, wasn't a valid option. Especially if she was alone. Assholes like the one drooling over Sienna down there could be lurking everywhere, ready to pounce.

But I was definitely not prepared for what I saw when she walked in.

I had no idea if it was a dress borrowed from Deanna or if they had bought it, since my sister had taken her out in recent days, but that didn't matter at all. If I had gone crazy seeing her in a simple pair of jeans, that right there would give me a heart attack before I could even touch her.

The dress clung to her body, short and black. A strapless, lace-covered number that made it sexy on a sinful level. Every curve of her body seemed highlighted, explored to tease my instincts. The air felt like it was missing from my chest as I watched her.

"Sorry if I made you wait," she said. Despite her femme fatale appearance, she still sounded like the innocent girl I once knew. A little more mature, more confident, but this mix of layers only fueled my desire. "Deanna seemed excited to dress me up like this," Luna pointed to herself.

"She definitely outdid herself. But you're beautiful either way."

Luna smiled, her face flushing.

"The makeup and the dress help." She started to walk around nervously, taking in the room.

I wanted to tell her she didn't need any of that to look stunning, but the words got stuck in my throat as I watched her, feeling my most primal instincts stir.

I spun around, following her, and it was clear how tense she was.

"I think I should have a drink, right?" she asked, stopping in front of the sideboard.

"If you want, I can serve you." I didn't intend to let her get drunk, but a drink might help her relax. After all, this wasn't a conventional situation.

I stepped closer and caught her scent in waves, hitting my nostrils. It wasn't overly sweet, but had a subtle citrus note—something quite peculiar.

I poured a shot of whiskey without taking my eyes off her and did the same in a glass for myself. She took the initiative to lift her glass and toast, which surprised me.

"To our son. May he always be safe from now on."

"Salute!" I replied, and we both raised our glasses to our lips, taking a sip.

Luna coughed discreetly because the whiskey was indeed strong, and I had even added two ice cubes.

Things weren't happening the way they should. We seemed too shy with each other, and we couldn't afford that luxury.

"If you want to back out, Luna... It's still not too late."

"No, it's not. He's already out there. I know because Deanna told me. He's watching us."

I made an effort not to look at the glass. It was two-way, but we couldn't see what was happening outside. We could be watched without knowing who was doing it. According to Deanna, they would only open the VIP area for Damiano. No one else could see us. It would be like a courtesy for him, which would undoubtedly make him feel very VIP.

"Can he hear us?" Luna asked.

"No. He can only see us."

"Okay," she replied, very nervous. "I guess we need to do something then, right?"

God, she was nervous. It was my role to try to ease that.

BOUND BY BETRAYAL   231

I stepped forward and took the glass from her hand, placing it on the sideboard next to mine. If Damiano was already watching, we needed to start the show.

I held Luna by the arm, with a little more force than necessary.

"I'm going to do things with you and treat you a little more harshly, okay? It's part of the game. Part of what he's going to want to see in here. If I hurt you or if it goes too far, let me know."

She shivered.

"Okay."

Practically dragging her from where we were, I placed her facing the bars, where two chains with leather restraints hung.

"Look at this..." I ordered. "This is where I'm going to tie you up."

"Not on the bed?"

"Later, yes. For now, it will be here." I moved her hair from her shoulder, leaving her ear exposed so I could lean in and whisper, "I'm going to make you all wet, Luna, I promise. And then I'm going to fuck you on the bed, hard, with your arms tied too. It won't be gentle; it'll be... *different*. I'm going to make sure you never forget this night."

She squirmed, and I saw her rub one thigh against the other.

Great; she was getting into the mood.

I reached into my pocket and pulled out a black cloth I had saved for the occasion. It was a blindfold that I placed over her eyes and tied behind her head, covering them.

"Is this necessary?"

"Everything *is* necessary in here."

She didn't say anything else and let me guide her to the right spot where I wanted her to stay. I left her standing and unzipped her dress, pulling it down and letting it fall to the floor. I helped her out of it and hung it over the back of a chair.

Luna stood almost naked in front of me, and she wasn't wearing a bra, but her panties were small, black lace, riding high on the sides, accentuating her waist even more. I didn't take them off because it was sexy as hell to see her like that.

I tried to be careful with every step, lifting each of her wrists and calmly securing them to the leather restraints hanging from the bar. We could be there to put on a show for our audience, but I wasn't going to be completely rough with her.

At least not the first time.

Because I hoped there would be others... The way she was responding, we would certainly come to a consensus not only about our relationship but about repeating this experience.

Luna let out a little whimper the moment she found herself defenseless. It was delicious to hear, but it left me a bit concerned.

"Are you okay?"

She hesitated but soon nodded.

"Y-yes... I'm okay."

It could get even better.

Taking advantage of the distance between her arms, I grabbed her hair and arched her head back a bit roughly, diving into her mouth while she was in that position. The angle of the kiss was different because I was sideways to her, but Luna seemed to respond with surrender, sighing against my lips, accepting everything I was willing to give her.

When I let her go, she adjusted her body again, and the first thing I did was use my fingers to twist her nipples, knowing she was quite sensitive there.

The moment I did it with force, she moaned loudly and tried to lower her arms, but was prevented. I let out a chuckle because it was common for Luna to try to cover herself when the sensations were stronger than she believed she could endure.

"I like this chance to do whatever I want with you without being stopped."

BOUND BY BETRAYAL

I tugged on both nipples, stretching them, and Luna gasped, throwing her head back as she had before. I took that as an invitation and dove my mouth onto one while still stimulating the other with my hand.

"Alessio! Oh, my God..."

I nibbled, licked, and sucked, then moved to the other, repeating the process. With the hand that was touching her, I sought a spot between her thighs, finding Luna's slit completely wet.

If she was enjoying it... all I had to do was keep going and try to savor the moment.

CHAPTER FORTY-ONE

Luna

I had no idea what was happening to me. I could swear that since I suggested to the group that Alessio and I take that VIP room at the club for explicit sex, I wouldn't be able to relax and forget that someone was watching us.

At that point, it was completely the opposite. With him touching me and sucking on my breast as if he wanted to make me come just that way, I couldn't think of anything else. Just that mouth and those incredible fingers.

But I knew he was just getting started.

"Enjoying it, *dolce angelo*?"

"I shouldn't, but I am. It's... intense."

"It's going to get even more intense."

I couldn't say how he did what he did, but Alessio pushed back the iron bar where the chains holding me were secured, bringing me closer to something he was obviously going to use. I soon felt something cold touching my calf and another restraint closing around my ankle. The other received the same treatment.

There were two other iron bars, parallel, right behind me, and I was secured to them, having no idea what was to come.

With my eyes blindfolded, it was hard to understand what was happening, but soon I felt my panties being pulled aside and a hot, wet tongue hitting the spot on my body that was starting to ache. It was pulsating.

BOUND BY BETRAYAL 235

"So very, very wet, my naughty angel."

With an open hand, while he started to suck on me, he slapped my ass, probably to test that kind of thing. I shouldn't have liked it, but...

My God...

(I probably shouldn't even involve God in any of this)

It was so liberating just to let myself feel pleasure without holding back, without being afraid of being wrong. In that room, I was chained, but I felt freer than ever.

While he sucked my clit, he slid two fingers inside me, opening me up and exploring.

"I still remember how you liked it. I remember exactly how I could make you scream. I wonder if I can do it again."

It wasn't hard to find out. With a few movements and thrusts, he drew the first loud moan from me. With a bit more effort, I screamed his name.

"Delicious little kitten. I want to suck you completely."

I didn't know if the way he spoke to me drove me crazier or if it was his touches and his skilled mouth.

But just as I threatened to come, he pulled away and made a few movements that I could only hear.

"You're going to come, but with me inside you."

In seconds he was behind me, lifting my ass as high as it could go and penetrating me. I could feel the latex of the condom sliding over me with incredible ease because I was so wet. More than ever, in fact.

Alessio was big, but he fit perfectly inside me. It had been a long time since we'd touched that way, but he definitely still knew how to pleasure me. He hadn't forgotten any of my sensitive spots.

"Fuck, Luna. I want to fuck you so hard, so hard. You have no idea how excited I am right now, how much you're turning me on like this, surrendered, with that innocent way about you and all wet for me."

I moaned loudly because as soon as he finished speaking, he thrust again. And again. He slapped my ass once more and grunted in a very primal way.

"I'm not going to hold back, love. Is that okay?"

"It's... it's all o-kay..."

Barely finished responding, he came at me hard, pulling in and out, holding my hips and moving me back and forth.

With all that intensity, I prepared to come again and let go, him still hard and firm inside me.

I thought I would finish, that I would climax too, but he pulled out, releasing my ankles and arms, scooping me up and carrying me to the bed. As soon as he laid me down, he took off my blindfold.

"I want you looking at me," he whispered hoarsely, gripping my wrists tightly. "I want you to see who the man giving you pleasure is."

"I know who it is."

"That doesn't matter. Say my name, Luna..."

"Alessio. My fallen angel," I said softly, taking a deep breath, and he closed his eyes, bringing his mouth down on mine, biting my lower lip and tugging at it, sucking it and swirling his tongue around it.

After kissing my mouth, he slid down my neck, finding my collarbone, and as he did that, he also returned inside me.

When he penetrated me deep, thrusting hard again, I was ready for more. I was already longing for another orgasm, to be taken to that state of total ecstasy that only Alessio could provide.

"I love you, Luna. It doesn't matter if you don't believe it, or if you're not ready to hear it. I've saved myself for you because I didn't want anyone else. I can't imagine being with anyone but you."

I wanted to respond, but Alessio knelt on the bed, holding my legs and placing my feet on his chest. In that position, he penetrated even deeper, and I screamed, tilting my head to the side and gripping the sheets, as it was the only way I could stay anchored to reality.

Alessio didn't take long to reach his climax as well, and I ended up having another, from the force of his thrusts, the atmosphere, and from him being him.

I was once again in the arms of the man I loved. The circumstances didn't matter, nor the reason we were in that bed... The look we exchanged after the climax said so much more.

And we didn't even need words for that.

CHAPTER FORTY-TWO

Alessio

I wanted her to say something. Anything damn thing.

We finished making love, lingered in bed for a while, and I wanted to know if she was okay, but I couldn't bring myself to ask. I was afraid of the answer, afraid she would say I did something wrong or that I had gone too far.

Worse: I was terrified I would hear that she only did all those things as part of a mission. That it had nothing to do with desire or any feelings for me.

We got up sometime later, still silent, and dressed. It was impossible not to take in every detail of her in that dress, especially when she asked me to zip up the side because she couldn't reach it.

As soon as I did, she tried to pull away, but I held her.

"We need to talk," I stated, looking into her eyes, wanting so much more.

Not that I didn't desire her before, but after that night, if I couldn't touch her again, I would go insane.

"I thought things were settled from the start. We did what we had to do," she was struggling to stay composed. But I knew her. I could see in her eyes that she was crumbling inside, just like I was.

Or maybe that was what I *wanted* to see.

"It wasn't just an obligation. We both enjoyed it. You clearly enjoyed it, Luna."

"I did. You're good at what you do."

BOUND BY BETRAYAL 239

Holy shit! She was driving me insane. I wanted to grab her, shake her, and make her see that it wasn't just that. That there was so much more between us. That we loved each other.

I loved her. I had said that the night before. I wanted to hear her say it too. But she had probably buried that truth a year ago, and maybe the love she felt had died.

"As I said: now that I've experienced this, I can try. I imagine there are other men out there interested in a former almost-virgin who enjoys sex this perverted. It must be an interesting contradiction."

She tried to pull away again, but I still held her arm and guided her to the wall, pinning her there.

I didn't want jealousy or possessiveness to take over me at any moment, but it was an involuntary feeling. Something that made my blood boil inside my body, burn, and left me filled with incoherent thoughts.

"Don't you dare *think* about that. Any man who lays a hand on you will regret it..."

"Even if I wanted to?"

"And you would want to?" I leaned in and brought my nose to her neck, inhaling her scent. "Do you think anyone would know your body like I do? You screamed in pleasure, Luna. *I* caused that."

It was bullshit to have to say that kind of thing, but it was uncontrollable. I couldn't accept that if she were to give herself to someone else again, it would be with another man.

Of course anyone would want to possess her; they would want to devour her like a rabbit over its prey. She was precious in every sense. I had always been so lucky from the start, but things between us had gone so wrong that I was prevented from appreciating the gift fate had given me.

I wasn't going to neglect it anymore. Not for any reason.

"I've already said... you're good..."

240 AMARA HOLT

I was going to kill Deanna because I had a feeling she was the one giving my Luna advice on how to brush me off.

My own sister!

"I'm good, but I become better because I love you. I became a better man since you came into my life. When you left, I lost myself in darkness." I paused, sighing and raising my hand to her face, touching her with my knuckles. "Don't do this to us, Luna. Don't push me away again."

"I won't... but first we have to deal with my brother. We can't be together in a world where he exists."

"So when he's caught, you'll marry me."

"That wasn't a question, from what I can tell."

"It wasn't."

I leaned toward her and touched her lips gently. I wanted to kiss her again and lose myself in her mouth, but my phone rang. It was on the bedside table, and I cursed in anger for having to pull away from Luna like that, in the middle of a kiss.

I answered the phone angrily, stressed out.

"Are you coming here, or are you going to spend the whole night there?" Dominic asked in his usual disdainful tone.

I didn't respond; I just hung up on him and finished getting dressed, leaving the room with my hand intertwined with Luna's.

"The dress is beautiful, but I feel a bit exposed. I'm not used to it," she commented as we walked toward Dominic's office at the club.

Without thinking twice, I took off my jacket and draped it over her shoulders. Luna smiled at me and held it closed around her body, hiding the parts she didn't want revealed.

We arrived at the office and found everyone there—my brothers and my brothers-in-law. Luna lowered her head, completely embarrassed, and I imagined it must be difficult for her since they knew what we had done.

BOUND BY BETRAYAL

241

"We left Damiano with a couple who will satisfy him. He was very excited," Dominic said, but I could sense the respect in his tone. "We managed to talk a bit, and he's willing to negotiate."

"Only because of what he saw?" I asked, surprised.

"Not exactly. From what I understood, Mattia wasn't very honest with him, and the purposes were a bit different. Damiano had no interest in destroying the Cosa Nostra; he just listened to what Cipriano had to say."

"He can be quite persuasive when he wants to," Luna chimed in.

"I imagine so."

"Either way, is it safe to trust? I know we've asked this before, and it's already been brought up, but I'm scared. We have a lot at stake; you all know that," Sienna said, very serious.

"Fear should be our constant companion, *Scarlatta*. Fear for ourselves, for our children, and for our place in the Cosa Nostra. We need to be careful, and Dominic and I talked and came to the conclusion that while we're in this negotiation period with Damiano, while we're trying to find Mattia, you and the kids should go somewhere else. Not home. Maybe to Scotland, where Alessio and Luna stayed. It's safe and secluded enough."

Enrico spoke, and I nodded in agreement.

"Are you going to discard us? Knowing we did a much better job than you did to save Luna's baby?" Of course, Deanna was going to give her opinion, and she didn't seem satisfied at all.

"We're not discarding any of the three of you. Just trust us; you're our weak point. If you become vulnerable, we'll be vulnerable too. We can't afford that," Dominic was very emphatic, and we all fully agreed with him.

"Maybe we should back down this time. Our kids are at stake," Sienna said cautiously.

I looked at Luna and realized she was looking at me too.

"I agree," she replied, while we were still exchanging glances.

Deanna was the last to agree, but the babies undoubtedly played a role in calming her down and admitting it would be safer.

We returned to Dominic's house shortly after, and we would have some time to say our goodbyes and just rest.

The next morning, just before six, I woke up in the empty bed, which left me disappointed. Not that I expected things to change after those moments at Dominic's club, but I missed her body next to mine after touching her and having her in such an intense way.

I just threw on a shirt over the sweatpants I had slept in and headed to the kids' room, wanting to at least see my son.

None of the other babies were in the room, probably with their parents. Vittório was the only child in there, but I also found Luna. Standing, she held him against her chest, gently rocking him from side to side, soothing him.

Smiling, I stretched out my arms to take him, and she handed him to me in silence. The baby was awake, but his little eyes were heavy. Upon seeing me, I realized he recognized me. I didn't know if he understood I was his dad, but he seemed happy to see me.

"Hey, son. Good morning!" I greeted, excited to see an even bigger smile on his beautiful little face.

"He just finished nursing. It was Deanna who came this time..." Luna explained. "It hurts me. Not being able to breastfeed him anymore. They've been wonderful with that."

"I can imagine. But it's not your fault." I sat in the armchair, and she settled next to me, holding one of Vittório's diapers in her hand.

"It's not... We made it this far. He's fine. That's what matters, right?"

"Absolutely. You've been very strong."

Luna nodded, her gaze seemed a little lost, as if she were staring at the wall searching for answers, though it was clear she wouldn't find any.

BOUND BY BETRAYAL

"We're going to separate again..." she said out of nowhere, in a somewhat nostalgic tone. Almost as if she were talking to herself.

"For a short time."

"I hope so. Vittório is starting to get used to you."

I cradled my baby under his arms to get a better look at him, taking in his adorable face that could melt my heart.

I would do anything to protect him, and it was terrifying to think that he would, at some point, need to know who his father was, what kind of world he lived in. Who the people around him were—the people he would end up loving: uncles, friends, a future fiancée? What would my son's youth and maturity be like? Would he always be in danger, always running from something, like in that moment when we needed to be kept apart for safety?

I sighed, looking at him and thinking that if I could, I would do everything to shield him from all of this.

I reached out to take Luna's hand, which was resting on the arm of the chair, and she responded. Silently, our fingers intertwined, dancing with each other, capturing all our attention.

As the minutes passed, the baby began to fall asleep again, as he hadn't been fully awake since I arrived.

I didn't want to let him go because I knew it would be a long time before I had the same opportunity, at least in peace.

Okay, I wasn't at peace, because we feared Mattia's influence and the power he had to reach us. I also didn't know what our future as a family would be. Despite all of that, that moment was ours.

Luna, apparently thinking about something very similar, leaned toward me, held my face, and kissed me.

It didn't take much more for me to understand. We had little time to say goodbye, and we needed this.

I stood up, placed the sleeping Vittório in the crib, and took her hand, leading her to the bedroom, where we entered and closed the door, losing ourselves in a world that was just ours inside.

CHAPTER FORTY-THREE

Luna

I took a few steps forward, taking the lead and pushing my hair back from my back, exposing the buttons of my shirt to Alessio, showing them off.

"Can you open them for me?" I asked softly, whispering.

I condemned myself that morning for feeling discouraged when putting on the clothes I had worn for so long. Vanity was a sin I had always feared, something that had always scared me because I knew it was something that could easily affect me, especially when I had to attend Cosa Nostra events and saw women made up, adorned with jewels and luxury, wearing dresses that made my eyes shine.

Even though I dressed up like a proper mafia princess, because I had to be presentable to avoid embarrassing my family, I tried to maintain as much modesty as possible, because it was in my nature.

What I did the night before, however, contradicted my personality in many ways. Not just in how I dressed, but in everything else.

The problem was that I wanted more. I wanted to explore much more and find pleasure in many other ways.

"Are you sure?" he asked softly, and I could feel his breath hitting the back of my neck, which was free of hair, tossed forward.

"I don't know how it works during the day... can we still... well... do the same thing we did at night? In that rougher way?" I should have been blushing from head to toe, totally unaccustomed to that

BOUND BY BETRAYAL

kind of approach. I wasn't the type of woman to take initiative in anything.

Alessio chuckled.

"Yes, *dolce angelo*. Anytime, we can do whatever you want."

He began to slowly unbutton my shirt, taking it off completely. Still holding it in his hand, he ripped off my skirt, letting it fall to the floor, and took off my panties as well. Using the shirt, he twisted it into a strip and stretched it around my waist, keeping my arms at my sides.

He tied it behind my back and pulled me toward him roughly, pressing me against his chest, almost crushing my hands between us.

Knowing what I liked, he squeezed my breasts between his fingers, twisting my nipples, and I leaned my head on his shoulder, panting. As he did this, he used his teeth to bite my shoulders, as well as his tongue to kiss me, sucking my skin and tasting me.

Holding the shirt, he pulled me along, almost as if he were using a leash, leading me to the bed. He left me standing in front of him while he undressed. He also put on a condom, not giving us much time to think.

He sat me on his lap, but with my back to him. He fit me perfectly onto his member, making me slide slowly. It didn't take much to get me excited, especially since my body already knew the sensations. I already knew what he was capable of doing to me.

I was filled with anticipation. And when he pushed deep inside, in a position we hadn't tried yet, with my arms pinned to my body, while he still teased my nipples, I swore I was going to explode.

Alessio opened my legs, pulling my thighs apart, and I felt very exposed, my feet barely touching the ground. He moved me, forcing me to literally bounce on his lap, rising and falling.

Sitting on him.

Riding him.

It was incredibly erotic. So far from what I could have imagined I would do someday.

With his hands on my waist, he pushed me even more, up and down, while he also arched his hips. I could feel him so deep it was as if we were one.

With a quick motion, as if it took no effort, Alessio threw me onto the bed, face down. Kneeling on it, he grabbed the fabric of the shirt, twisting it, keeping my hands glued to my body. He took my hair with his other hand, wrapping a strand around my wrist, and then resumed thrusting.

I moaned loudly, liberating myself in every way, finding an orgasm that told me that every time we made love, Alessio would show me something new that would bind me more and more to him.

There was no way around it. I belonged to him.

It didn't take long for him to find his release as well, coming and pulsing inside me, united and moaning as if our voices wanted to merge too.

Alessio laid me on the bed, no longer with the shirt around me, and we lay on our sides, facing each other.

He extended his hand, caressing my face, with reverent eyes.

"Dolce angelo... I love you. I won't tire of saying it. Everything I didn't say when I should have, I promise to say forever."

I took a deep breath, thinking once again that it would be impossible and inevitable to escape Alessio. And I didn't even want to.

"I love you too." Alessio closed his eyes, seeming to absorb what I had said, almost as if it were something that granted him enormous relief. "Tell me it's only for a little while. That we'll see each other again soon..."

"It will be for a short time. You'll see. And when we're together again, we won't separate anymore. Never again."

BOUND BY BETRAYAL 247

He leaned in, and we were about to kiss when a whimper interrupted us. Laughing, we got up and prepared to get dressed.

Alessio turned his back to me to put on his shirt, and I noticed something I hadn't seen before. Something I could swear was recent, at least from the past year.

A tattoo. A phrase in cursive, small, subtle.

I instinctively reached for it, and his body immediately tensed.

"Ricordati di me" I read aloud. "Remember me" I repeated, translating the small text.

"That was the last thing you said to me when we parted. You asked me to always remember you, and I wouldn't need a tattoo for that, but I wanted to mark you on my skin somehow."

What could I say? How could I respond when a huge lump formed in my throat hearing that enormous proof of love?

"You..." I barely knew how to finish the sentence. I just wanted to reciprocate, although it probably wasn't necessary.

Alessio finished putting on his shirt and turned to me, taking my face in his hands.

"Losing you was unbearable. I knew from the moment I saw you walking into the abbey. I wanted to run and go after you, to kidnap you if necessary, but I knew I wasn't ready for that. If I brought you home, we would marry and be unhappy because my father's shadow would loom over us."

"And now, not anymore?"

"I will never forget, Luna. Don't ask me that, because it's not possible. But not having you is even worse. Because back then, I lost two important people in my life. I don't want that to happen again." He paused, kissing my forehead. "You'll go to Scotland with the girls, and when you come back, your brother will be dead by my hands. Will you be able to handle that?" I hesitated, shuddering slightly, but nodded. Then Alessio continued: "Then we can survive anything."

One day...

One day we would have our life together. One day we could start our family, and it wouldn't matter that we had the Cosa Nostra on our backs or all the ghosts of our past. We would create our own happiness and our happily ever after.

CHAPTER FORTY-FOUR

Alessio

The smell of cigars filled the place, just as the music reached my ears. Both in an uncomfortable way. Girls danced on the stage, but none of us were looking at them, except for our guest of the night. He was, after all, the only single one.

I was too. At least on paper. But I didn't feel available.

Luna had left as my wife. She would return that way as well. And when she did, I would make it official. We would marry, she would take my last name, and she would never have to be referred to that family again. I knew she loved her other siblings, that she would have a relationship with them, but the less we had to remember what had happened in our past, the better.

"So? Years and years to get a partnership with the Cosa Nostra... it took someone to start a real chaos for this to happen?" With the same hand holding the cigar, he pointed at us, at our meeting. There was a bit of disdain in his voice, which made my brother-in-law shift in his chair.

Dominic had a very low tolerance for that kind of thing. I feared he would explode and we wouldn't even be able to talk.

Enrico must have thought the same because he shot a glance at him, almost like a tamer trying to control a beast.

"There's an opportunity for everything, don't you think?" Dominic replied, and I had to give him credit for managing to stay composed, even if it meant taking a big gulp of his whiskey. "And we still don't know if we can trust this partnership. How are you going to prove to us that you're not working for Mattia?"

"Because I know where he is, and I'm willing to give you that information if we sign the contract."

We exchanged glances. This could get us excited, but it was equally dangerous. If he didn't care about betraying someone like that, why wouldn't he do the same to us?

Noticing our hesitation, he continued:

"Don't look at me that way. Mattia and I broke any agreement the moment we found out he took my sister as a fiancée, but he also raped three women who worked for me and killed one of my best men."

I remembered that. Before Mattia became the monster we knew, he had announced he was engaged to a girl, who we never knew who she was. A much younger girl, but we didn't pay much attention to it because the topic wasn't discussed further.

"Why is that?"

"With every frustration, he takes it out this way. Women are his favorites. He wasn't exactly kind to my sister either."

"I would have killed him immediately," Enrico replied. I imagined that because of his relationship with Sienna, he was even more compassionate toward women who had been sexually assaulted.

"That was my wish, but when I found out, it was roughly at the same time as Dominic's call. I thought it would be more interesting to have leverage. I want him dead, but I also want him to serve a purpose for me. For those on my side."

A calculating soul. *Very* calculating. We were talking about his sister, but that didn't seem to matter.

"I had plans to offer my sister to Alessio in marriage, but from what I see, he already has a fiancée..."

BOUND BY BETRAYAL 251

"My *fiancée*," I said firmly, and neither of the other two contradicted me.

Damiano gave me a sly smile.

"What a pity. But either way, I believe in marriage alliances. I wonder if any of Cipriano's boys wouldn't agree to marry Patrizia? She's a good girl, beautiful... young."

"That's not up to us to decide. We need to talk to them," Dominic asserted.

"I imagine there's a lot at stake. The safety of their sister, their nephew, and not to mention Lorenzo would benefit greatly from a good wife. He's too young and has had to assume a position he wasn't prepared for."

"Again: only they can decide. And it's not something that can be resolved with a phone call."

"No, it's not. But I think our contract can be signed tonight. I can provide the location of Mattia."

"And what would be the condition for marriage to Lorenzo?" I asked, suspicious.

"I can do more than that and set a trap for him. You still believe we're on the same side, that we have common interests. We can set a snare that will make him fall like a rat in a trap."

The three of us exchanged looks, a bit tense. Without hesitation, I discreetly reached for my holster. If necessary, I would grab my weapon because all of this felt very strange. All those bargains.

The last thing I expected was to receive a marriage proposal.

"We'll sign the contract as long as we confirm Mattia's location," Dominic replied, his shoulders tense. My brother seemed ready for anything, just like me.

Calmly, with a rehearsed smile on his face, Damiano set the cigar down in the ashtray and pulled out his phone. He opened a conversation on WhatsApp, saved under the name MC. The conversation consisted of audio messages, and he played one where a male voice alerted about a request for a meeting. He revealed he was in Los Angeles—too close for comfort—and needed to talk to Damiano.

I would never forget that voice.

"Don't you think some people die for a greater cause?"

His words echoed in my head, a nightmare I couldn't forget.

"It's him," I asserted with complete conviction.

"It could be, but we can't be sure he's still where he said he was, let alone that he isn't colluding with you to deceive us," Enrico said, keeping his voice very dark.

Damiano shifted in his chair. For the first time, I noticed he was starting to get nervous. That worried me.

"I need you," he said quietly, not looking at us.

"What's going on, Damiano? Why aren't you being honest with us? If we're going to be business partners, we need to be... *friends*," Dominic was even more alert. We all were, actually.

"Mattia has my sister. He took her as collateral. That's why I need us to sign this contract and for someone to agree to marry her and help me get her back. If we close this partnership, I can deceive him and ask him to take Patrizia, then I'll find a way to free her."

Mattia was doing to Damiano what we had done to his sister. I didn't take pride in that, but I treated the girl as best as I could, and we still fell in love. I planned to be the best husband possible for Luna, and I knew that wasn't the case with that lunatic. The girl was certainly not in good hands.

"So things are a bit different," my brother-in-law began. "We both have much to share in common interest. You want to give your sister in marriage because you imagine she's ruined."

"Yes. With a man like Mattia, I have no hope of Patrizia coming home as she was, in any sense. But if I can find a husband for her, she will probably have better chances. Especially if it's a husband within the Cosa Nostra."

BOUND BY BETRAYAL 253

Once again we exchanged glances. This meeting would stretch on longer; the decisions were more complex than they seemed. I didn't expect it to be easy, but I also didn't want to take too long to see my son and Luna. I knew the same was happening with Dominic and Enrico, but those choices also determined the future of our families.

Damiano agreed to stay under the guard of our men, in a hotel funded by us. He would be confined to a room, without access to a phone or the internet, until we spoke with Lorenzo Cipriano.

To our surprise, however, the guy immediately agreed to the marriage, which made us believe there was some story behind it, even more so when we said Patrizia Damiano was in danger.

He might have known her. But that didn't concern us.

With that response, we signed the contract and began to outline our plans.

We would have a chance against Mattia, who, according to Damiano, had few men left, his strength diminished since he started to go mad and act more violently. Still, we would have to kill him and give a warning to anyone who might still want to follow him.

The Cosa Nostra would prevail. It didn't matter what happened. We were stronger.

CHAPTER FORTY-FIVE

Alessio

It wasn't like I had a problem with traps. As long as they weren't set for me, I knew they could actually work. The biggest issue was that I always had the impression that many things had a huge potential to go wrong.

Not to mention that I still vividly remembered the night my father was killed. It sent chills down my spine and filled me with immense distrust, especially knowing that the same person who had fired that shot would be present and involved in this situation.

I always felt like Mattia was one step ahead in everything.

"Alessio," Enrico spoke to me while we were in the car. Both of us in the back seat, with two of our soldiers in the front. Dominic was driving ahead with three more men. Lorenzo Cipriano was also with us, a huge insistence I didn't even understand.

We tried to be discreet, but we couldn't arrive without all the possible security. We knew Mattia could be suspicious. Even though Damiano was somewhat of an accomplice to him, a man living on the edge, making enemies like someone leaves footprints in the sand, he could never fully trust anyone.

The fucking problem was his, of course. I didn't care. More than that, that night I hoped we would take care of the bastard.

"What's wrong?" I asked very seriously, without even looking at him. That bothered him.

BOUND BY BETRAYAL

255

"Look at me, *fratello*," it was hard not to respond to Enrico's request because he knew exactly the tone of voice to use, and behind all that facade of the Shadow Knight of the Cosa Nostra, Enrico was one of the most empathetic people I knew. Besides Sienna. The two were made for each other. "I know tonight is going to be hard for you."

"For you too."

"Yes, but I know your memories are a bit more vivid. He died in *your* arms."

"Rico... no. Don't say that. Not now."

"I'm sorry. That was... unfortunate of me," he said, lowering his head and taking a deep breath. "I just want to know if you can handle it all."

I let out a bitter laugh.

"You want to know if I can handle it? If I'm going to freak out?" I was a bit irritated by the way he doubted me. People always doubted, right? "I'm not an idiot. I can act under pressure too, just like you," I shouted, feeling completely immature with those reactions. But my stress wasn't just about the conversation. It was about everything.

"I never said you couldn't," my brother replied, looking at me with a very serious expression, his brow furrowed. "I never underestimated you, Alessio. You're my consigliere now, do you think I chose you for the position just because you're my brother? I put you as my most trusted man because you truly are the person I trust most in the entire world. I would give my life for you, and I know you would do the same for me."

My shoulders slumped, almost as if I were disappointed. In truth, I was, but not with him. Maybe with myself.

Oh, damn. I didn't know anything anymore.

"I really would," I affirmed with all my conviction, and Enrico placed his hand on my shoulder, squeezing it. It was probably the most affection he could show. And it was enough for me.

We entered the place where the meeting between Damiano and Mattia would take place, sneaking in like thieves. It was the three of us, armed, and our men would spread out outside, guarding the surroundings to prevent the bastard from escaping.

I confess I felt a chill down my spine when I saw Mattia approaching with his thugs. There were two surrounding him, and he was dragging a girl by the arm— a firm grip just above the elbow, almost dragging her. She wore a short white dress, almost virginal, and was clearly a prisoner.

Mattia held her against his body, using her as a shield, and kissed her cheek, which made her pretty face twist in disgust.

"Sorellina... are you okay?" Damiano asked. Of course, that was Patrizia, his sister. The girl he desperately wanted to save.

"She's great. Isn't she, darling? Once we get out of here, we're getting married. Isn't the dress I bought beautiful?" Mattia said, pulling her even closer.

The tension escalated even further.

It was clear that the girl didn't want to get married at all. In fact, it wasn't even certain if she would accept Lorenzo Cipriano, that bastard's brother, but it might be the only way to save her.

"Leave her alone, Mattia. We can negotiate without involving her."

"David, my dear David... Do you think I can trust you?"

"If you can't trust me, why should it be reciprocal?"

"And it will be. The beautiful Patrizia here will be my guarantee. Don't they say the strongest alliances in the mafia are made by marriage? If I become your brother-in-law, you'll need to be on my side."

Damiano was starting to get nervous. He looked at Patrizia, and she was clearly trying to hold it together, by force. But she was a young girl, and the prospect of marrying a monster undoubtedly frightened her.

BOUND BY BETRAYAL 257

I saw a tear escape her eyes, sliding down her face as she pressed her lips together in a look of utter disgust.

"What do you say, Damiano? I will no longer accept that our agreement is one of gentlemen. I brought a document. We'll have to sign it. Both of you."

"What will we sign, Mattia? A treaty? An agreement against the Cosa Nostra?"

"Something like that. A partnership in a new organization. A new way to do business within the United States. Controlled by us. No more Cosa Nostra handling the import of weapons, drugs, and alcohol into the country. It will be our way. With our tariffs, a fairer supply. Our rules. Our people in charge."

It was a somewhat unrealistic plan, and it was easy to see that Mattia was completely out of control. I could understand that there was an immense hatred against the Cosa Nostra, and it wasn't like I didn't understand it. I couldn't imagine what he might have gone through with his father and what Pietro had put in his head, but it made no sense.

The organization was centuries old. It was strong. People not only supported it but feared it. How did he want to take control of something so immense this way?

"Mattia, you no longer have the power you once did. When your father was alive, when you had Esposito by your side... things were different. I'm with you, *amico*, but we need to be cautious."

"I've been cautious for too long. I can't wait any longer. The bastards took my sister, recovered the baby. They were my guarantee. Now what I have is you. I know you have power, you can convince people."

"I don't know if I can. I think we can talk a little more and try to find a way to..."

It was like déjà vu. I saw Mattia's quick hand fly to his holster, grab a gun, and his fingers pulled the trigger.

BAM!

The shot exploded and echoed through the warehouse where we were, and it took me a moment to understand what he had hit until I saw Damiano collapse to the floor.

A bullet in the head was what remained for the man who had closed an alliance with us.

Patrizia's scream followed, and she began calling "David" with a heart-wrenching agony.

"Stop screaming, bitch. Look what I was forced to do! If you had helped me with your brother, if you had done your part..."

She tried to break free from his grip, but all she got was a slap to the face, which made her stumble. But Mattia didn't let go.

Blood quickly spread across the floor, and I focused on that, my brother at my side, but Enrico drew my attention to the hall just as Lorenzo appeared, gun pointed at Mattia.

"Lorenzo!" Patrizia exclaimed, surprised, her black hair all in her face after the slap she received. A trickle of blood ran from her lips.

"Enough, Mattia. Enough of this nonsense. Let Patrizia go. You're surrounded. You won't escape here alive."

The presence of his brother seemed to shock Mattia. He stood frozen for a few seconds, watching the man in front of him. The girl knew Lorenzo and seemed to trust him, in some way. It was like a glimmer of hope shining in her eyes.

"What the hell are you doing, kid? This is big boy business," he growled. Two men stood beside Lorenzo, also armed, protecting him; after all, he was the mafia boss in Texas.

A twenty-five-year-old young man, inexperienced, but at that moment he seemed willing to do anything.

"We are the damn Cosa Nostra, Mattia. Do you really think you can destroy us? You are nothing. All you've done is follow our father, who was another lunatic. It's such an absurd idea that everyone abandoned you."

BOUND BY BETRAYAL

"Fuck you! I can build an entire world on my own," he yelled, completely out of control.

He shoved the girl to the ground, leaving her exposed, raising the revolver and starting to shoot. However, he didn't aim at his brother. His shots, once so precise, seemed a bit delirious, missing their targets, which were Cipriano's soldiers.

He managed to hit a shoulder, not much more than that.

With all the chaos, we decided to act as well. I looked at Enrico, and with a nod, we agreed to leave our hiding spot and charge into the small war that was forming. Dominic did the same.

We were more exposed than ever, especially when more of Mattia's thugs also entered, just as our men did, storming the warehouse amidst the gunfire.

I don't know where it started, but when I realized and managed to look around, there were some flames starting to form. I couldn't tell if it was intentionally provoked or accidental. But the smell of gasoline didn't escape me. Amidst the unending gunfire and the bodies falling to the ground, a fire could ignite.

I saw Lorenzo rush toward Patrizia, grabbing her off the floor and taking her to safety, out of our sight. When he returned, he was the first to hit Mattia, making him drop the gun from his reach.

It was a shot to the arm. Probably calculated. Maybe he could have aimed for his chest if he wanted. I imagined that despite being younger and less trained, Pietro Cipriano wouldn't have trained his sons poorly.

"Son of a bitch!" Mattia screamed like a savage, over the sound of the shots. He was about to run at his brother, but I flew over him, knocking him down.

So there we were on the ground. Both armed. Both with hatred in our eyes.

He had killed my father.

He had kidnapped my baby.

Amidst the fire that had formed, it was just the two of us against each other.

That's how it would be. That's how it would end, one way or another.

CHAPTER FORTY-SIX

Alessio

He was injured, and I had some advantages, even though he seemed to feel no pain amid his uncontrolled rage. It was as if the emotion was numbing his body.

That made him very dangerous.

I raised my torso, swinging my arm and hitting his jaw hard. He retaliated, and I pointed my gun, ready to shoot at point-blank range, but one of his men came at us, ready to hit me with a shot.

To defend myself, I aimed the gun at him, pulled the trigger, and dropped him with a hole in his head. My distraction, however, was enough for Mattia to disarm me.

He landed another punch on me, but we managed to get up, both dodging and standing cautiously to avoid being caught off guard.

It was just the two of us in a one-on-one fight.

The flames began to rise higher, surrounding us. I couldn't look around to see if my brother and my brother-in-law were okay, and at that moment I needed to take care of myself. That was always the best advice anyone living amidst violence could share: take care of yourself before taking care of others.

It was my family at stake, but they knew how to protect themselves.

"I'll accept fighting Dominic or Enrico, but the little dog of the Preterotti? The cheeky kid who dared to fuck my sister?" he sneered.

262 AMARA HOLT

"Watch your mouth when you talk about Luna," I shouted, my body tense, facing him.

"A little whore. She's not fit to be a Cipriano. None of them are, actually. That's why my father only trusted me."

I charged at him again, throwing a fist and surprising him with another punch. He managed to defend the first, but I was quicker, hitting him in the stomach and then in the face.

He staggered, and I had a moment to look around. There was a gun within my reach, which I could grab with a little effort.

The fire continued to grow. Amidst the crackling flames, I heard Enrico's voice calling my name.

I just wanted him to get out of there. This fight was as much his as it was mine, but it was my right to finish Mattia Cipriano after everything he had done. Not just to my son, but to my wife.

Because Luna was that to me. I knew she feared her own brother, that her relationship with him wasn't good, and he had done what he did to her as a mother. He had ripped the baby from her arms; a newborn. It was the kind of cruelty that only the most insane people could commit.

I moved closer to the gun, but Mattia came at me as well. I didn't know if he had noticed the revolver, but the punch I received was almost enough to disorient me. Along with that, I felt another kind of pain.

A sharp stab at my waist. Like something tearing inside me.

I had been stabbed.

"You little shit. What do you think? That you can fight me? Even if you throw your best punches, I'm stronger. I was trained to be a warrior while you were busy eating half the Cosa Nostra with that pretty little face of yours."

I brought my hand to the spot where the pain was excruciating and felt the hilt of a dagger. Or a knife. I couldn't say for sure, but it didn't matter. The blood soaking my fingers was more relevant.

BOUND BY BETRAYAL

An amount that could surely lead me to death.

I didn't know if I had hit any organs, if a vital artery had been ruptured. I just felt dizzy.

I thought of my son. I thought of Luna.

I thought of everything I had done up to that point. I didn't want to die. There was so much to live for, so much to discover.

As I backed away, dragging myself on the ground, making an inhuman effort, my hand fumbled along the floor, and I found it.

My father's gun.

It was the one I had taken that day. He never gave it to me, never presented it to me as I knew Dominic had done. He hadn't given it to Enrico either because he didn't know he was going to die.

It had been taken that day, but he hadn't even had the chance to use it against the same man who threatened me.

So I would take my revenge. With it.

My hand was a bit shaky, but I held the grip firmly. Mattia approached, saying something I could no longer hear, not only because my attention was completely focused on staying awake amid the pain to kill him, but also because there was so much noise around.

But he looked at me with a smile on his face.

That would be his last expression before death came to meet him. Just like my father had died, I hit him in the middle of the forehead. Piercing his brain.

"It's not... p-personal..." I repeated the phrase he said after killing my father, watching him fall. "Or maybe... it is," I stammered, letting myself drop as well, growling in pain.

I knew I was going to lose consciousness. I knew I could die not only from the bleeding but also amidst the fire.

A kind of death I wouldn't wish even on my worst enemy.

Lie. I would love for Mattia to perish slowly, his flesh burning as if roasting at a barbecue. But I killed him first.

It was me or him. If I missed, with my hand faltering from pain, it would be dangerous. A bullet to the forehead had no room for error.

Better this way. I hoped he would suffer in hell.

My head tilted to the side, and I somewhat lost consciousness. I awakened to slaps on my face. It was Enrico.

"Fratello? Damn it... Damn it... Alessio!" My brother paused. I didn't open my eyes to see what was happening. "He was stabbed."

"Let's get him out of here. Now!" I recognized Dominic's voice, but didn't hear anything else.

I groaned in pain as I was moved, feeling light as they carried me. The heat was unbearable, and I couldn't tell what was blood and what was sweat, likely mingling on my skin.

And then darkness took me, and I saw nothing more. I heard nothing and felt nothing.

It was almost welcome.

I had lapses of consciousness, especially when I felt a lot of pain, forcing me awake. I heard familiar voices, and Luna's name was mentioned.

I wanted to know about her. About my son.

Had Mattia really died? Were they safe?

Damn, how was I going to protect them being so weakened?

The first time I managed to open my eyes, I saw Enrico close by, which made me call him with a whisper of a voice.

"Rico..." I hardly recognized my tone. It sounded like that of a seventy-year-old man, on the verge of death.

"I'm here, Alessio."

"What happened? I know what it was, but now... what's happening now?"

"I just donated blood for you."

That wasn't the information I needed, but my disorganized and dazed mind didn't lead me to the question I really wanted to ask.

BOUND BY BETRAYAL

"Take care of them..." I said in a breath. I wasn't going to last much longer awake, but that message was the most important. "Of my family."

I wasn't married to Luna, like Enrico was with Sienna. Maybe I had no right to call them family after everything that happened. Still... I wanted them to be.

"Luna is coming. Hold on. For her and for Vittorio."

Yes... I would do anything for them.

After this episode, it took me a while to return. I had very tormenting dreams, where I relived my father's death incessantly. In others, I saw Luna leaving again, entering that convent, but the walls rose like doors, as if she were being swallowed and could never get out.

In the worst of them, my son was torn from *my* arms, and I couldn't save him.

On calm nights, I just wandered through the darkness, trying to return.

Until the day her voice brought me back.

I knew the prayer.

Padre Nostro, che sei nei cieli,
Sia santificato il tuo nome.
Venga il tuo regno,
Sia fatta la tua volontà,
Come in cielo, così in terra.
Dacci oggi il nostro pane quotidiano,
E rimetti a noi i nostri debiti,
Come noi li rimettiamo ai nostri debitori.
E non ci indurre in tentazione,
Ma liberaci dal male.
Amen.

She prayed it fully, and then recited the Hail Mary. Always very softly, always making it sound almost like a melody. Always in Italian.

It was the rosary, for sure. She did it with such concentration, her hand clutching mine, and sometimes I knew she was crying. Pleading to God. Asking.

It was for her that I forced myself to open my eyes.

She was in the middle of one of her prayers, tireless, and I squeezed her hand, trying to draw her attention to the fact that I was awake.

"Alessio?" she almost jumped from the chair, looking at me with those innocent eyes, blinking. She looked so tired but still so beautiful... "Oh, Dio! Dio santo!"

I saw her get up, probably to call a doctor, but all I wanted was her. At least at that moment.

"St-stay. Wait."

She glanced back at me over her shoulder, looking a bit dazed.

"I need to call someone. They need to check your vital signs. To know how you are."

I knew the situation didn't call for it, but I tried to smile. I wanted to believe the worst had passed and that Mattia was defeated, even without confirmation. Regardless, I was alive against all odds. I needed to cherish this chance and try to be the Alessio I had always been.

"I'm weak, in pain. But a k-kiss can heal me. I'm the S-sleeping Beauty."

Luna laughed, a bit silly. Even blushing. That was how I liked her. She deserved to regain a bit of the innocent girl I had known, although none of us, obviously, would ever return to who we were in the past.

But I got my kiss. She leaned over the bed, cradling my face in her hands, touching my mouth with her warm, soft lips.

If I had the strength, I would have held her there with me, but I had to let her pull away.

BOUND BY BETRAYAL

A doctor and a nurse appeared, checking my vital signs. Luna went to inform Enrico while I answered questions and listened to information about my condition. My liver had been hit and needed reconstruction, and I had received two blood transfusions, all done by my brother, but overall my recovery was good.

I would need rest, but I would survive.

I would survive and could form my family.

Later, Luna stepped out of the room for a few moments and returned, and I had to hold back tears because she held my baby in her arms.

"Look at daddy, son. Daddy..." she spoke in that sweet voice we use for children, as she approached.

Vittorio seemed to have grown so much in the brief time we had been apart. My little boy looked chubbier, even more beautiful.

"Hey, son?" I felt stronger, so speaking wasn't such a huge effort. I also sounded a bit more coherent and with a more audible voice. "I wanted so much to hold you."

"You will. Just a little longer..."

"And then we'll be a family, right? You'll be my wife..." I let slip, looking at her, who didn't seem surprised.

"Is that a proposal? I hope so, because it's more than time."

"No, we're months late, so as soon as I'm well, I want you at an altar, receiving my last name."

"I like this urgency."

"And I like you..." I grasped her hand again, pulling it as much as I could. "I love you. I love *everything* about you."

"I love you too."

I didn't need to hear anything more. Except, at most, Vittorio's little laugh that almost seemed to understand what was happening.

I had just asked his mother to marry me. And I had the impression she had accepted.

"We're going to be happy, you know?" she said, out of nowhere, smiling a little nostalgically.

"Oh, really? And how are you so sure?" I asked playfully, holding my son's little hand, which had wrapped his fingers around mine.

"I feel it. I'm psychic, you know?" Luna replied with a playful smile.

She was joking, right?

"Are you serious?"

"I don't know; we'll never know. But we will be happy. My intuition tells me so."

"Then there's another thing I like about you: your intuition."

I sat up a little from the bed, trying to kiss her, but I groaned from the effort, and she came.

The kiss was still gentle, and I wanted more, but it was what we had.

And I also felt we would be happy. We would both strive for that every day.

CHAPTER FORTY-SEVEN

Luna

SIX MONTHS LATER

A mafia bride. That's what I was, but it wasn't how I felt.

If this had happened nearly two years ago, when my father promised me to a man I didn't even know – but whose reputation as a scoundrel was legendary – I would have been trembling, scared like a little bunny in the woods.

Standing before the mirror, admiring myself fully, I smiled at the beautiful dress designed by Kiara Caccini. It truly made me look like a princess, with its delicate sleeves and no neckline. Even though I no longer wore the same clothes I had before leaving the convent and had adopted jeans because they were Alessio's favorites, I still didn't feel very comfortable in low-cut or short outfits.

Except when we went to Dominic's club, which had only happened twice since Alessio made a full recovery.

I even blushed just thinking about it.

But erotic things aside, there was a delicate transparency in my bodice leading to a heart-shaped neckline. It was sexy enough but modest, as it was mostly covered. On top, a little chain with a cross.

The dress also had a huge skirt because it was a dream. It had stones and lace, a not-so-long train, and it was completely designed with my taste in mind. It was so me.

A knock on the door made me look to the side, seeing Lorenzo there. I no longer had my father, and that young man had become the head of the family. He would be the one to lead me to the altar.

I loved him. Lorenzo had always been the good brother, comforting and protecting me, while Mattia was... well... the monster he had always been. Still, I didn't have much to compare to, which made us two people who perhaps didn't even know each other well. We were siblings by blood legacy, but we had never been able to coexist, especially after becoming adults.

I didn't know who he was, who he had become, but I hoped he would do a good job as a chief and as a husband, since he married Patrizia shortly after she was rescued from Mattia's hands.

"You look beautiful," he stated gently.

He had always been a gentleman. Trained to be a prince, not a king. Although he was a second son, he had always been quiet, restrained, completely different from Giulio and Tizziana. Lorenzo and I were similar, while our two other brothers had similar temperaments.

Giulio was a pest as a child. But I didn't know him very well anymore, to be honest, especially since he also studied abroad. We only met on holidays. Maybe one day we would have the chance to spend some time together?

"Thank you," I replied to Lorenzo, picking up my bouquet from the dresser. "I'm ready; we can go."

I walked toward him, adjusting my skirt, but when I raised my head, he was standing in front of the door, blocking my way.

I raised my eyes, almost startled by the interruption.

"Luna... are you sure? You like him, right?" he asked, with his southern drawl. "Because if you don't, we can work something out. It's no problem if you have a child. I'll never force you to marry someone you don't want."

BOUND BY BETRAYAL

271

I smiled, indulgent, almost as if I were the older of the two. I reached out and touched his face, feeling it smooth. He was much bigger than me, so I had to stand on my tiptoes to give him a brotherly kiss.

"I love him. He loves me too. We will have a good marriage, better than most."

He sighed, looking satisfied.

"Yeah, not everyone has that luck."

I preferred not to ask anything, but that information would stay in my mind. Lorenzo wasn't happy. At least that was the message he wanted to convey to me. Maybe he wanted to vent, make a confession, something like that.

But before I could respond, he turned, opened the door, and put a smile on his face. Then he extended his arm for me to link with him.

"Shall we, beautiful girl? Let's go live your fairy tale."

I was still a little worried, of course, but I accepted, because it wasn't the moment for that.

He guided me to the entrance of the convent church, which was huge, with a high ceiling and doors that opened before us, heavy and almost making it seem as if we were in a medieval castle.

The options were that place and our little chapel in Scotland. The house was still ours, as Alessio had bought it, but we thought that a wedding of this magnitude, within the Cosa Nostra, should be done with all the pomp. Enrico and Sienna had already done something too discreet by the standards, so we needed to splurge. Especially since the case with my father and my older brother was still very recent, and the Ciprianos had lost some power after so many betrayals. The wedding would elevate our status once again.

Weddings made by marriage... well, we already knew how they ended.

The wedding march began to play, and everyone stood up. At the altar, Alessio was waiting for me, handsome, in a tailored suit, and the few curls that had already started to sprout were beginning to show. He was in that phase between short and long, but nothing about that man looked bad. And I asked him not to use gel. I wanted my fallen angel untamed as always.

Near him were our dear couples: Dominic and Deanna. Enrico and Sienna. Giovanni and Kiara. My brothers, Giulio and Tizziana, would also be our godparents. Cássia had settled, taking care of the children, and next to her was my sister-in-law, Patrizia, very serious, very melancholic.

I walked a little further and was surprised to see Ilya, alone, in a suit that made him look even bigger. He certainly didn't belong to that kind of clothing, and the definition of a wardrobe fit him immensely.

I reached the altar and was handed over to a smiling Alessio.

God... his smile was indeed a temptation. I had always heard about this, and no one was lying. It could melt any heart.

My brother kissed my forehead and sat down next to Patrizia, who hardly moved when he sat beside her. The coldness between the two was evident.

Sad, yet evident.

The priest was about to start speaking, but Alessio gestured to him, raising a finger, stopping him from beginning.

"Sorry, Father, just a minute..."

I was surprised by that, but my fiancé leaned in my direction, whispering in my ear.

"I have a surprise. A wedding gift."

"A gift? But..."

He started to open the cuff of his shirt, raising the sleeve of his jacket. There was a new tattoo there: *"Per sempre ricorderò"* – *"I will remember forever."*

BOUND BY BETRAYAL

I was left speechless, in the middle of my own wedding ceremony. But none of the people around us could understand what was happening. It was a little secret just for us, in the middle of the altar.

The priest cleared his throat, and I didn't even have time to respond. So we straightened up, and Alessio announced:

"You can continue."

With a giggle, we looked at each other, and I instinctively turned to the Mother Superior, who was near the priest, and she was looking at me with a sweetly reproachful expression.

But we managed to proceed with the wedding without any further interruptions.

After the priest's beautiful words, a special blessing from the Mother – requested by me – and the kiss of the newlyweds – which was a little longer and more intense than it should have been –, we went to the outdoor area, where a beautiful party had been prepared.

I ran to get my baby, who was the cutest thing, in a little suit mimicking his father's, complete with a carnation on the lapel and everything. Alessio was with me, and so we stayed, because we simply didn't want to separate.

We went from couple to couple, and I congratulated my dear Deanna and Sienna for being pregnant. At the same time. Soon I knew I would receive that blessing too. We would fill our families with heirs, who I hoped would gradually write different stories within the Cosa Nostra.

It would always be an organization marked by violence, but I hoped that times of peace were coming. At least we knew that none of our boys would suffer cruel training or be psychologically abused by their parents.

In the distance, Alessio and I spotted Ilya somewhat escaping the party. There was no longer a tie around his collar, and his shirt was more unbuttoned than etiquette allowed.

We looked at each other and went after him. It didn't matter what his past was, what his story was, that man had helped us save my baby. He would never be forgotten.

"Sneaking out?" Alessio asked, wrapping an arm around my waist.

His light eyes narrowed, and he scratched his blonde eyebrow with his thumb.

"It's just that this thing here itches." He held his lapel, showing he was talking about his suit.

"We appreciate the effort of wearing one, but you could come less dressed up," I said playfully.

"Are you kidding? You all look elegant. I wasn't going to be left behind. Just thank me, kid, for not stealing the bride. She looks stunning."

I smiled shyly, and Alessio took it in stride.

"Only if you were crazy."

"If she wants, there's still room on my bike..." he continued joking, but then let out a sigh. "Actually, I'm heading out, okay? I'm not good with goodbyes, but I can't say if we'll see each other again. I have a... job to do."

I raised an eyebrow.

"Dangerous?"

"A little. But I need to do it."

"Are you sure? Whatever they're paying you, we can pay more," Alessio asserted.

"Well..." Another scratch of the eyebrow, as if he seemed shy, uncomfortable. "It's kind of like I won't get paid for this. It's just that there's an old friend with problems. Serious problems. And you know how it is..." He opened a cynical smile and brought his hand to his pocket. "I can't see a damsel in distress."

BOUND BY BETRAYAL

Pulling out a pack, he took a cigarette from inside and lit it. We were in an open area, but even so, he blew the smoke to the other side.

"Take care. I hope you can help her," I said, walking up to him and giving him a kiss on the cheek.

That left him a little flustered, even causing him to blush.

My God, a man that size all flushed was something to consider. Almost cute.

Without saying anything more, he simply left, walking to get his bike and go wherever the wind took him, after the "friend" with problems.

Alessio and I, embracing, returned to our party, but before we reunited with our friends and family again, I held his wrist and pulled him to a corner.

He was going to say something, but I didn't let him. I put a finger to my lips, asking for silence, and he obeyed.

There was a part of the decoration where we put some papers and some markers for people to leave messages for us. It was a little romantic thing, nothing matching a mafia wedding, but we weren't a conventional couple. We loved each other, and I wanted everything I could have.

I grabbed one of those markers, opened it, and turned my wrist up, writing on it: *"per sempre tu"* – *"forever you."*

"It's not a tattoo, but know that you are always engraved in me too. And you always will be," I said, my voice emotional, and Alessio stepped forward, bringing both hands to my face, kissing me so passionately that it was hard to breathe.

Then he leaned his forehead against mine, still holding my cheeks, whispering:

"Forever, dolce angelo. Forever."

We would be forever. My intuition told me so. And I usually trusted it.

EPILOGUE

Alessio

TEN YEARS LATER

The world hadn't changed. Nor had the mafia. But we were different.

There was violence outside the walls of our homes, but our households were sacred. Our families were precious to us.

Not just those imposed upon us by blood, but the ones we chose to keep.

The table was enormous, surrounded by loved ones. We had been through so much, lost loved ones, and almost lost others. Our stories intertwined in unimaginable ways. Our alliances weren't just by marriage, but by bonds of friendship.

It didn't matter that Dominic was married to my sister, or that Giovanni had married Dominic's cousin. We would do anything for each other. For our children.

And we had many. Giovanni and Kiara had two boys and a girl. Dominic and Deanna couldn't stop procreating and had five children, all boys. Enrico and Sienna had two, a boy and a girl. Lorenzo and Patrizia had one.

Luna and I had two boys.

Then there were Giulio and Tizianna's children. We were a huge family. No one could complain about not having heirs. The Cosa

BOUND BY BETRAYAL

Nostra would be safe with our children, grandchildren, and all future generations.

Our gatherings couldn't be held just anywhere, so when we managed to take a vacation, we went to the house in Scotland. It was large enough to accommodate everyone and had a vast yard where the kids could play.

Not to mention it held a thousand wonderful memories for Luna and me. Some of them we loved to share with our children. Others we kept as our own secrets.

At that moment, only the adults were seated, as the children had just finished eating and were running around. I reached for Luna's hand, intertwining our fingers.

Dominic sat at one end of the table, and Giovanni at the other. Even though there was no hierarchy among the bosses, we both knew they were the ones in charge. Not because they imposed it, but because we respected them. All of the Cosa Nostra saw them as examples, as role models to follow.

My brother-in-law raised his wine glass, a smile on his face. Time had treated him well; he had matured into a family man. He hadn't lost his cynical side, of course, and that probably would never happen.

"Who would have thought, right? Who would have thought we'd be here after all this time?" Everyone looked at him with a nostalgic expression. All the couples, including Cássia and her husband—she had married a capo of Dominic; a trusted man who treated her as she deserved.

"No one can say we aren't persistent," Giovanni said, adding to Dom's thoughts.

"And we'll be here for a long time yet. We've sown our seeds," Enrico pointed at the children.

"So be it!" I raised my glass as well, looking at Luna who was smiling and doing the same.

Soon, we all had our drinks in hand, raising our glasses high in reverence to our future.

It didn't seem bad at all. Not bad at all.

THE END

Did you love *Bound by Betrayal*? Then you should read *Betrayal in Blood* by Amara Holt!

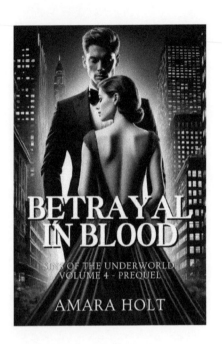

Betrayal in Blood

In the dangerous underworld of Chicago's **Cosa Nostra**, loyalty is everything—but for **Giovanni**, the ruthless mafia boss, **betrayal** is closer than he ever imagined. Raised in a world of **violence** and power, Giovanni inherited his father's empire along with its **dark secrets.** He is cold, calculating, and unstoppable—until a woman threatens to unravel his carefully controlled life.

Kiara was born to be the perfect **mafia princess**: obedient, dedicated, and destined to marry the feared Giovanni. But behind her innocent facade lies a **fierce determination.** Despite the terrifying age gap and his possessive nature, she believes she can turn their **arranged marriage** into something more than a cold transaction. However, her hopes are shattered when Giovanni

abandons her just before the wedding, leaving her future—and her heart—in ruins.

But in a world where power is everything, one **betrayal** changes everything. To protect herself from the violent fallout within the mafia, Kiara is forced to marry the man who once rejected her. Now, she's determined to make Giovanni **fight for her**—and for their future. Can she melt his **heart of ice**, or will their pasts destroy any chance at love?

Betrayal in Blood is a gripping **mafia romance** full of dangerous secrets, **steamy passion**, and high-stakes drama. Fans of **dark romance**, arranged marriage, and forbidden love stories won't be able to put this book down. Will Giovanni protect what's his, or will the mafia world tear them apart?

About the Author

Amara Holt is a storyteller whose novels immerse readers in a whirlwind of suspense, action, romance and adventure. With a keen eye for detail and a talent for crafting intricate plots, Amara captivates her audience with every twist and turn. Her compelling characters and atmospheric settings transport readers to thrilling worlds where danger lurks around every corner.

Milton Keynes UK
Ingram Content Group UK Ltd.
UKHW042034031224
452078UK00001B/126